MURDER À LA RICHELIEU

RICHELIEU

ANITA
BLACKMON

LOST CRIME CLASSICS

www.lostcrimeclassics.com

🦅 PEPIK BOOKS

This edition published 2015 by Pepik Books, Blake House, 18 Blake Street, York, YO1 8QH

Copyright © 2015 Pepik Books

Murder à la Richelieu by Anita Blackmon (1893-1943) was first published in 1937.

Published by Pepik Books (www.pepikbooks.com) as part of the *Lost Crime Classics* collection.

www.lostcrimeclassics.com

ISBN: 978-0-9932357-2-6

Printed and bound in the EU

MURDER À LA RICHELIEU

RICHELIEU

ANITA BLACKMON

LOST CRIME CLASSICS

www.lostcrimeclassics.com

1

I, Adelaide Adams, spinster, was knitting in the lobby of the Richelieu the morning it all started. Not that I realized anything was starting. I am not a timorous woman. I understand I have occasionally been referred to by certain flippant members of the younger generation as 'The Old Battle-Ax.' Be that as it may, had I suspected the orgy of bloodshed upon which we were about to embark, I should then and there, in spite of my bulk and an arthritic knee, have taken shrieking to my heels.

However, it would have been difficult on that bright April morning to have found a spot which appeared more peaceful than the lobby of our small residential hotel. The Richelieu is grandiloquent in name only. It caters to quiet, respectable people, mostly permanent guests, many of whom, like myself, have occupied the same room or rooms in the hotel for years.

With one exception the staff, like the clientele, is of long standing.

Both the elevator and Clarence, the man who operates it at night and also acts as porter, are old models of their kind. Laura, the elderly maid on the two upper floors, had been at the Richelieu longer than I, as had Pinkney Dodge, the night clerk.

Sophie Scott, the proprietor, is herself crowding sixty, although after she married a man fifteen years her junior she tried to ape Sweet Sixteen, an experiment which was distinctly not a success.

Because of its staid ways people about town prior to April of this year had been in the facetious habit of alluding to the Richelieu as "The Old Ladies' Home." Needless to say, that was before the man was discovered, hung by his own suspenders to the chandelier in one of our best suites, with his throat cut from ear to ear.

Nevertheless, as I have intimated, there was nothing on this particular morning to indicate the reign of terror into which we were about to be precipitated. Coming events are supposed to cast their shadows before, yet I had no presentiment about the green spectacle case which was to play such a fateful part in the murders, and not until it was forever too late did I recognize the tragic significance of Polly Lawson's pink jabot and the Anthony woman's false eyelashes.

It seems inevitable now, but, as I sat there purling three and knitting two on the afghan which I intended to present to the orphans' home of my church, there was nothing to warn me that it would serve instead as a shroud for a woman who was to die horribly at my feet. Nor at that time could any power on earth have convinced me that I should find myself late one terrible night, sans my dress and my false hair, dangling from the eaves of the Richelieu Hotel in pursuit of a triple slayer.

There is a parlour at the Richelieu, a depressing place on the second floor furnished in dreary black walnut and a bilious green carpet. The guests consistently prefer to sit in the lobby. It faces the only boulevard in our small Southern city, and, the entire front and one side being plate glass, it is uniformly light and cheerful.

The drugstore opens off to the left of the lobby as you emerge from the elevator, the Coffee Shop to the right. Two large divans, flanked by lounge chairs and a radio, face each other opposite the desk.

The staircase descends on the right of the elevator. On the other side is a telephone booth.

At the rear of the lobby a door opens into a long corridor which separates the kitchen on the inside of the building from the beauty shop on the outside. The corridor terminates at the employees' entry off the alley. Between the plate-glass windows at the front is a revolving door, the main entrance to the hotel. One may well say the lobby is the heart of the Richelieu. At least, to one who sits as I have sat day in and day out for years in my favourite chair by the radio, it is possible to keep one's finger on the pulse of everything that is going on.

To some people an interest in the behaviour of your fellow creatures is idle, if not morbid, curiosity. I have been called "that nosy old maid" because I am a close student of the human comedy. The fact remains, nonetheless, that very little happens in the Richelieu Hotel of which I do not sooner or later become aware, and I have a tenacious memory, especially for detail. Not much escapes my eyes and ears and nothing escapes my memory, though I may mislay it for a while.

Actually, it all began with my mislaying my green spectacle case. I seldom take the case out of my bedroom unless I am traveling, my glasses being the last thing I remove at night and the first I don of a morning. I had a distinct recollection of placing them as usual in the drawer of my bedside table the night before when I was ready to snap off my light. I remembered taking them out of the case that morning as soon as I washed my face. I thought I remembered replacing the case in its customary drawer. Nevertheless, there it was, lying between the cushions of the front divan in the lobby.

The shabby little man in the inconspicuous grey suit called it to my attention. "Isn't this yours, Miss Adams?" he inquired.

As he spoke he reached down, extracted the case from between the cushions and held it out.

"Yes, Mr Reid," I said in a startled voice, "it is."

I have few vanities left, but my memory is one of them, and I felt not only confused but irritated because I could not recall bringing the spectacle case downstairs. That is why it did not occur to me till later to wonder how a man who was a transient guest in the hotel, and a recent one at that, should not only have known my name but should also have recognized one of my personal possessions which rarely, if ever, makes a public appearance.

It was not unusual that I knew more about him than I would have expected him to know of me. While the permanent people in the house have little to do with those who drift in and out of the hotel for a day or a week, I generally glance over the register every morning while I am waiting for the Coffee Shop to open. In this way I was aware that the small insignificant man with weak blue eyes and nondescript brown hair had arrived six days before and signed himself, in a thin wavering hand, James Reid, New Orleans.

"I can't understand how the case came to be here," I began in a vexed voice. "I could have vowed that I ..."

I was interrupted at this moment by an exclamation from the Adair girl. "Mother! You've dropped your handbag again, and – for the fifth time, isn't it? – the contents are all over the place."

As I recall, there were only the four of us in the lobby at the time, not counting Letty Jones, who worked behind the desk in the day. Because it was a stimulating spring morning, everyone else had gone out to enjoy the air. I remember thinking to myself that it was a shame for a pretty young girl to be cooped up indoors on such a morning with two middle-aged women, one with stiff joints and the other, to all appearances, a semi-invalid.

Not that until then I had had anything to do with the Adairs.

They had been in the hotel a little over a month at the time, and the old guard, as we call ourselves, do not let down the bars overnight.

We put newcomers through a stiff inspection before, if ever, we admit them to our closed circle. Those of us who have lived at the Richelieu for years have learned by bitter experience not to make up to every Tom, Dick and Harriet who takes a room there for a few weeks or even months. I have known people to wax quite indignant about the snubs with which their overtures were met. I remember one young woman who said it was easier to enter the Kingdom of Heaven than to be admitted among the elect at the Richelieu Hotel.

In fairness I must record that the Adairs had shown no disposition to force themselves upon anyone. They had, if anything, avoided other people. Yet from the first they struck me as a forlorn pair. Although the girl, in the manner of modern youth, had adopted a defiant pose, I was convinced she was far less self-sufficient than she pretended to be. About her good looks there can be no question. She had bright brown hair, the true chestnut colour, and clear brown eyes and really beautiful skin, nor did she indulge to excess in make-up, a point I found distinctly in her favour.

She also had a firm chin and a pleasant, even voice. To one brought up, as I was, to believe a lady is above everything else a person of refinement, she was a welcome change after the painted, boisterous, slangy young females one encounters everywhere nowadays with their cigarettes and their rolled hose and their flippant, high-pitched ejaculations, to say nothing of their complete lack of veneration for their elders.

I had only that morning compared Kathleen Adair favourably with young Polly Lawson as she raced through the lobby on her way out to some appointment or other. For a young woman who on both her maternal and paternal side inherited blue blood, Polly in my opinion was fast putting herself beyond the pale. I could have shaken her. It was only ten o'clock, but she had already begun on her daily round of highballs. I did not wonder that her aunt, Mary Lawson, was looking her age since Polly came to live with her. I had made up my mind at the first opportunity to tell Mary a thing or two which I believed she should know about her niece, though it has not been my experience that one is better liked for doing one's duty in such cases.

At any rate, Polly had disposed me to look kindly on the Adair girl. If she smoked or drank, she did so in the privacy of her room.

Just as she did not cross her legs in public and ogle men young or old. I had myself seen her put several in their places when they tried to scrape her acquaintance. Nor could one overlook her devotion to her mother, who impressed me as a spineless woman, with her plaintive voice and her frail, ineffectual hands and her general attitude of being a little foggy about everything.

It seemed to me there was no excuse for any adult to be quite so helpless, but her daughter watched over her as if she were her lone chick. If she lost patience, it was not apparent. Even now, when for the fourth or fifth time that morning Mrs Adair had allowed her overloaded handbag to slide off her knees onto the tiled floor, the girl did not scold. She was laughing as she stooped to recover the scattered contents.

"Darling," she said, "I think I'll get a chain and fasten it to your wrist."

Mrs Adair's thin white hands fluttered weakly. "I do hope the mirror isn't broken. Oh dear, I don't believe I could bear it if we were to have seven more years of bad luck."

"The mirror's all right," said the girl quickly, rising to her feet.

She thrust something shiny into the pocket of her woolly brown skirt and glanced at me with a strange, almost desperate appeal in her eyes. I said nothing, but I thought again that the mother was a peculiarly feckless person not to see the glittering fragment of shattered glass beside her foot. She did not see it, however, for her small pale face lighted with relief.

"It's silly to be superstitious," she said with a faint smile, "only I never knew a broken mirror not to bring trouble, black trouble."

To my surprise the girl shivered. I expect old Laura, the maid on my floor, to grow pale if a black cat crosses her path. Clarence, the night-elevator man, is convinced if a bat gets into the house someone will die within twelve hours. I myself have a prejudice against laying a hat on a bed, and Kathleen Adair's anaemic little mother looked as though she might be a bundle of inhibitions and outmoded superstitions. The girl, on the other hand, belonged to a generation that scoffs at such things.

I must have been staring at her fixedly, for she flushed clear down inside her lacy knit blouse and gave me a hostile glance from her narrowed brown eyes. "A broken mirror means nothing," she said sharply, although her voice trembled.

I shrugged my shoulders. Again I thought the girl was far more vulnerable than she wanted to appear. It was certain she possessed the brains of the family. Her mother most likely had once been a pretty woman, but I did not believe she had ever had a great deal of practical sense. I do not care for clinging vines or for wilted blondes, however pathetic. Something of my sentiment must have been reflected in my face, for the Adair girl for the second time gave me a hostile look.

"Everybody can't be strong minded," she said hotly, "and not afraid of anything. Some people are born defenceless, but that doesn't make them less lovable."

She was all but scowling at me, and for a moment she reminded me of someone. It gave me a pang, though I could not to save me place the resemblance. Then she smiled ruefully and the teasing likeness was gone and with it the curious cramp in my heart.

"I'm sorry," she said. "I didn't mean to rant."

"Whatever became of the man who discovered your spectacle case, Miss Adams?" asked Mrs Adair in her soft blurred voice. "It was a spectacle case, wasn't it? And he did call you Miss Adams?" It had not occurred to me till then that the small insignificant man in grey had faded out of the picture as unobtrusively as he had melted into it. I could not recall exactly when he had joined us. I had no idea at what time he walked away.

"Yes," I said none too cordially, "I am Miss Adams, and it is a spectacle case, although it seems to have powers I didn't suspect. I mean, I never knew it could go up and down stairs of its own accord."

The girl smiled at me without a trace of her former antagonism.

"Maybe you are like Mother. She can lose her glasses without ever leaving her chair."

"I am not absent-minded," I said stiffly. "On the contrary, I happen to be a bit proud of never forgetting anything, at least not for long."

"Really?" murmured Kathleen Adair.

I eyed her sharply. I thought I detected a cynical note in her voice, but I could not see her face. She was fussing about her mother, collecting her shawl, her smelling salts, a magazine, and the other impedimenta with which she seemed always to surround herself.

"If you're to lie down before lunch, darling, we should be going upstairs, don't you think?" murmured the girl tenderly.

"Yes, yes, of course, dear."

Mrs Adair rose to her feet and, clinging to her daughter's arm, moved toward the elevator. Again I thought it a criminal waste for youth to be bound hand and foot to ailing age. It made no difference that in this instance the girl appeared to be passionately fond of her elderly charge or that the mother plainly adored the daughter.

I have seen too many young lives sacrificed on the altar of devotion not to pity the victims.

I believed this girl in particular deserved better than such a fate. I am subject to strong likes and dislikes, and I do not deny that Kathleen Adair had in some inexplicable manner begun to exercise a tug upon my heartstrings. I remember thinking, though I do not as a rule permit myself to luxuriate in self-pity, that it must be rather wonderful to have a daughter like her.

Unfortunately, at that moment the elevator creaked slowly down from the upper floor in response to Kathleen Adair's ring, and, as she assisted her mother inside, a small man with mousy brown hair materialized from the telephone booth back of the desk and stepped into the elevator with the Adairs. The door closed, shutting off my view, and the car ascended with whining cables, while I stared after it with a chill playing up and down my spine.

I did not understand, I almost doubted my eyes, yet I knew what I had seen. It was not to be effaced from my mind, then or ever.

That nice child, Kathleen Adair, had stepped between her mother and Mr James Reid as if he were some wild beast who might leap upon his prey and rend it limb from limb, and while he observed the girl in the vaguest way, her eyes blazed back at him as though she would, if she could, have slain him with a glance.

2

The coffee shop at the Richelieu opens for lunch at twelve o'clock noon. I am generally the first person inside. I do not care for food that has grown soggy on the steam table, and I do not have so many things with which to occupy my time that I need be late for my meals. I was slightly nettled on this occasion to discover a new waitress in charge of my favourite table opposite the lobby door.

If the employees in the hotel proper were not subject to frequent change, the same thing could not be said of the dining room during the past year. It was one of the grudges I had against Sophie Scott's new husband. He was responsible for doing away with the venerable men-waiters who had served the Coffee Shop for years. Cyril said it was more up to date to have attractive young girls. I thought it a fool idea at the time and I told Sophie so, but, like all women, when she lost her head she lost it completely, and so Cyril Fancher had his way.

I must have been frowning over my thoughts, for the girl who had come over to take my order gave me an apprehensive look.

She was a slight young thing with a soft mouth and timid eyes, pretty in an indecisive way and totally inexperienced as I could see at a glance. That was the trouble with Cyril Fancher's scheme – his attractive waitresses never lasted. About the time one was well enough broken in to know her job, she left, usually to get married or to have a try at Hollywood – or so I understood.

However, it was not the girl's fault that Sophie Scott was an idiot, so I smiled at her reassuringly. "And what's your name, child?" I asked.

She drew a quick breath. I think until then she had been afraid I'd swallow her alive.

"Annie," she said, "thank you, ma'am."

"That's a pleasant change after the Gwendolyns and Franchelles and Imogenes we've been having," I remarked dryly.

She flushed. "It was my mother's name." She hesitated and then went on, her chin quivering. "She died last year."

I reached over and patted her hand, rather awkwardly I'm afraid. "There, there," I said.

Sympathy was the worst thing I could have offered her. It seemed to break her all up. A tear slid down her cheek, and then another.

"I lost my father, too, the other day," she whispered.

I know what it is to be left alone in the world and I felt very sorry for the poor young creature, but it is not easy for me to put my gentler emotions into words. I can roar with the best of them but when I want to coo, my throat closes up. I think I was patting the girl's shoulder and making inarticulate sounds much like an old hen with the croup when Cyril Fancher strutted up to us, his thin fox like face dark with anger.

"What's going on here?" he demanded. "You were employed, young woman, to wait tables, not to weep on the guests' shoulders."

The girl gave him a terrified glance and then scuttled away toward the kitchen. "You needn't have scared her to death," I remarked tartly.

He looked me over as if he wished he dared say exactly what he was thinking of me. I shrugged my shoulders. There had never been any love lost between me and Sophie Scott's new husband, but he knew better than to go too far. I occupy one of the most expensive suites in the house, I pay my bills promptly on the first of every month and, because my family was once prominent, I lend a certain social éclat to the Richelieu which it would regret to lose.

"I was merely trying to prevent your being annoyed, Miss Adams," he said stiffly. "The first thing a well-trained waitress has to learn is not to use the guests for her 'True Confessions.' I assure you, it shan't happen again."

He moved rapidly away toward the kitchen, to give that poor child a curtain lecture, I felt sure, staring after his dapper back which was as stiff as a ramrod. He was fifteen years younger than Sophie, but he was not a young man. Somewhere in his middle forties, I should say, and not bad looking in a thin, dark, secretive fashion. That had been my objection to him when he first came.

He talked a great deal about where he had lived and what he had done and this and that. It was only when you were away from him that you realized how few grains of actual information you had gathered from the chaff of Cyril Fancher's conversation.

He said so little to which he could be pinned down. He was born and reared somewhere in the East. He had been engaged in some kind of business connected with selling stocks and bonds.

He had been married, and his wife had died some years ago. He had come South because of his health. It was not apparent precisely what ailed him, though he spoke of asthma and sinusitis. He set his cap to marry Sophie from the beginning, and there was nothing vague in his courtship. He went about it like a high-powered salesman in a whirlwind campaign.

In my opinion, nothing about the man, including his name, rang true. I warned Sophie that he was an artful dodger if ever I saw one, and of course she told him. I said among other things that he was marrying her for a soft berth in which to lie up the rest of his life. I even came out plainly and told Sophie that, while she was a good businesswoman, she was fat and grey and on to sixty. I believe I went so far as to say that no man would look at her except for her income.

Naturally Mr Cyril Fancher did not feel kindly in my direction, and Sophie herself had been cool to me since her marriage. I suppose every time she looked at me they rankled, the things I had said for her own good. She went to great pains to tell me at every opportunity how happy dear Cyril made her. She said she had never known what happiness was till he came into her life.

My only response was "Humph!" which did not improve matters.

I had known Sophie's first husband, the man who built the Richelieu, and I wouldn't have given a hair of Tom Scott's toupee for a thousand Cyril Fanchers. I felt positive that Tom turned over in his grave every time Sophie looked into Cyril's romantic dark eyes and murmured, "Dearest Lover."

The girl Annie came back from the kitchen with my lunch upon a tray. She was inept, and I could see that she was still close to tears, although she said nothing and neither did I. To do so was to bring down upon her head more vials of wrath from Cyril Fancher, and I had no desire to aggravate the child's troubles. Pretty young girls who earn their living as waitresses have enough problems of their own. It did not surprise me that they were constantly shifting from one place of employment to another, though it was generally out of the frying pan into the fire, so far as I could judge.

People were straggling into the dining room as I sat there. There were always fewer for lunch at the hotel than for dinner. Mary Lawson, looking careworn, nodded as she passed my table, but she did not stop for our usual chat. I pursed my lips. Mary had long been a favourite of mine, a widow, still comely, in her late thirties and, as I had every reason to believe, comfortably well to do.

I thought I knew why Mary was going to obvious trouble to avoid me. She did not want to discuss her young niece with me or with anyone else. She had ordered her lunch before Polly came bounding in, a little breathless and talking very fast to cover up the fact that her tongue was a trifle thick and her eyes slightly blood-shot, pulling out her chair with a hand which I could see was far from steady.

"So sorry," she cried. "Meant to be here on the dot. Don't know where time goes."

Mary sighed, and I saw her glance quickly at Howard Warren and then as quickly away. Howard stared straight before him.

If he was aware of Polly's entrance, he gave no sign, nor did she acknowledge his presence, although there had been a time after Polly first came to live at the Richelieu when she and Howard had hardly been able to step without each other.

They were, in fact, never apart except during banking and sleeping hours. From his mother Howard had inherited a hand-some block of stock in our First National Bank. As soon as he fin-ished Harvard, with honours I should add, he began to work at the First National. He is a clean-cut, well-bred young chap, blond, and highly dependable. At twenty-five he was well on his way to becoming one of the pillars of the community.

I for one did not blame Howard for having, during the past three months, broken off with Polly Lawson, nor, I am sure, did Mary, though naturally she was bitterly disappointed. Without being exactly a prig, Howard was the last man who would allow himself to become seriously involved with a girl who, practically overnight, had begun to drink too much and smoke too much and otherwise behave in the most reckless manner.

"It was such a gorgeous morning for golf," Polly rattled on to Mary, "and Steve's so fascinating."

There was an odd silence as if everyone in the dining room was listening for the next word.

"Steve?" echoed Mary in a tight voice.

"Stephen Lansing," said Polly loudly, for Howard's benefit, I dare say.

"But, Polly..." protested Mary, turning quite white.

Polly giggled. "Don't look so shocked, darling."

Mary was shocked. So was I for that matter, and I saw Howard's hand clench on the edge of his table.

"I didn't know you had met Mr-er-Lansing," said Mary slowly, almost painfully.

Again Polly laughed, a trill of mocking laughter that for some reason hurt my ears. "We haven't been properly introduced," she said flippantly. "I'm afraid Mr-er-Lansing picked me up in the lobby. He's clever about that sort of thing."

"So I've heard," said Mary, looking a little ill.

So we had all heard and seen with our own eyes. In spite of her recent outrageous behaviour, I had expected better of Polly. After all, she comes of the best stock. Instead of being ashamed, however, she was boasting about something that I for one felt unable to forgive, and a glance at Howard's set face informed me that I was not alone in my reaction.

Mr Stephen Lansing had at that time been among us off and on for something over three weeks, and from the day he entered the Richelieu he had stirred up one hornet's nest after another. He was a traveling salesman for a well-known line of cosmetics in Chicago. He travelled in his own car, a flamboyant scarlet model that glittered with chromium gadgets and burst on the vision like a blast of trumpets.

It had twelve cylinders and all the latest streamlined effects. Mr Stephen Lansing was himself streamlined, being very tall and extremely broad shouldered and almost fantastically narrow as to waist and hips. He had blue-black hair and very white teeth which he showed at every opportunity in an impudent smile. His lazy, insolent grey eyes possessed what in my day was called plenty of come hither, the something people now refer to as sex appeal, I believe.

At any rate, Mr Stephen Lansing was undoubtedly what is known as a ladies' man. He had only to walk through the lobby to make every woman there stare after him, a fact which was no secret to the gentleman. He knew perfectly well that he unsettled the feminine pulse. It seemed to be his chief stock in trade. What time he was not rushing off to various small towns in the vicinity to demonstrate cosmetics, he made his headquarters at the Richelieu and occupied himself by making a fool of every female who gave him an opening.

His specialty apparently was to pick up a woman on one pretext or another, rush her madly for a day or so, and then drop her slap-bang while he dashed on to his next conquest. We of the old guard had derived considerable diversion from observing the course of Mr Lansing's hectic flirtations, to call them by no worse name. I need not say that none of us had ever spoken to the man.

At that time I never expected to. If anyone had told me then that I should eventually be discovered in the pitch-blackness of the Richelieu basement, clinging about Mr Stephen Lansing's neck with both arms... However, that comes later.

So long as the gentleman confined his activities to outsiders none of us was disposed to resent the matter. In a hotel there are always a few women who are no better than they should be. Our group simply looks through them when we meet. We may discuss their affairs among ourselves; we seldom even pass the time of day with the person in question.

It is possible for a woman of dubious reputation to live at the Richelieu year in and year out without receiving more than a blank stare from permanent guests like myself. As a rule, however, such people become discouraged much sooner than that. We of the closed circle present too unified a front for them. I have seen more than a few quail and take to flight under our silent treatment.

None of us had cared a great deal when Stephen Lansing took Lottie Mosby for a whirl. She was a silly little piece. It was not her first indiscretion, and everyone knew that her husband was a boor when he was drinking, which he had been doing steadily for some time. Nor had anybody objected to Stephen Lansing's brief affair with Maude Crain. She was a thin intense brunette who fancied herself the hotel siren. We had all been glad to see her get her comeuppance for once.

But Polly Lawson was something else again. Polly belonged to the inner court. She was, by way of Mary, one of us. For Polly Lawson to allow herself to be picked up by the flashy young man who was at that moment the Sheik of the Richelieu was treason in high places, and none of us could afford to overlook it.

I did not wonder that Mary looked ill. I felt slightly ill myself. I had had a bit of a weakness for Polly, with her flyaway red hair and her sweet, wilful mouth and her green-flecked, gay blue eyes.

I had known she was a little minx, but I had believed there was no harm in her outside of youth and high spirits. Now I was being forced to revise my opinion, and it stung. Howard Warren looked stung also as he rose from the table, leaving his dessert untouched.

He had been quite desperately in love with Polly. I suspected he still was, but he was the type to cut off his right hand if it offended him. He did not once glance in her direction as he strode toward the door, but her shrill mocking laughter pursued him, for I saw him wince. I could have shaken the girl, and I suppose I looked it when I stared at her, because her lips curled and she laughed again, but not before I'd seen her eyes – and they were not mocking; they were full of tears.

It was a stifled exclamation from the next table that distracted my attention. I turned and raised my eyebrows. Lottie Mosby always lunched alone, her husband being employed as a clerk in a large sporting goods house downtown. I had never liked either of the Mosby's. They were common; no other word will express it.

Of the two, although she was a cheap young flibbertigibbet who went in for sex novels and loud dresses and coarse perfumes, I preferred the wife. At least she did not befuddle what brains she had with liquor. Just now I even felt a little sorry for her. Her small over-rouged face was puckered up as if she were about to cry. Following her glance I perceived that Mr Stephen Lansing was ushering Hilda Anthony into the Coffee Shop.

I have said that women of questionable reputation seldom stayed long at the Richelieu. The Anthony creature was the exception to prove the rule. I understand she once said that it was like running the gauntlet to walk through the lobby of the hotel in front of 'The Knitting Brigade,' by which she meant me and my closest friends I have no doubt. Nevertheless, she stayed. Seemingly social snubs ran off her the way an umbrella sheds water.

She had come to town originally for a divorce, attracted by our new state law which requires only a three months' residence to procure a legal separation. She came from New York where she had been a successful gold digger. She made no secret of the three husbands she had already separated from large alimonies. With all her faults she was appallingly frank. She did not deny that she was thirty, that she blondined her hair, and that her gorgeous figure had been her fortune.

She was a thorough adventuress, as we all recognized from the first and as she made no effort to conceal. I myself heard her say once right out in the lobby that she was out to feather her nest and she did not in the least care how she did it. The only mystery about Hilda Anthony was why, having secured the divorce she came for, she remained in town.

There were no gilded playboys in our little conservative city whom she could pluck. After the fine birds she had bagged, the men she met at the Richelieu were small change. Nor did she make any effort to inveigle them, which was still more surprising, it seemed to me. She was like a buccaneer who had suddenly paused with one foot in mid-air for no adequate reason. One or two of the more charitably disposed had suggested that perhaps she had seen the error of her ways and reformed, but there was no hint of ashes and sackcloth about Hilda Anthony, nor did I think that particular leopard would ever change its spots.

She did look startlingly like a leopard as Stephen Lansing pulled out her chair for her that day, or a lithe, beautiful tigress with a tawny coat and malicious yellow eyes. "You're too sweet," she drawled, gazing up at him through her long artificial black eyelashes.

"It's sweet to be sweet to you," he murmured caressingly.

It occurred to me they were well matched, those two. I remember thinking he was a little like a beast of prey himself. I shuddered when I thought of frivolous little Polly Lawson in his clutches, and it gave me a feeling of warm satisfaction to recall that I had seen him on three separate occasions attempt to insinuate himself upon Kathleen Adair, only to have her look through him as though he were so much air.

I glanced into the mirror at the side of my table. The Adairs always sat behind me, but I could see them reflected in the glass.

The mother was toying with a dish of lemon pudding. She never ate with any appetite. Like young Howard Warren, the girl had left her dessert untouched. She was looking at Stephen Lansing from under her lashes, and her eyes were wistful, as if the man attracted her against her will, as if she could not keep from watching him.

When he leaned nearer and smiled into Hilda Anthony's yellow eyes Kathleen caught her breath, and for a moment her face puckered as Lottie Mosby's had done.

I can't remember when I have ever felt more irritated. I glared across the room at the man. I am afraid I looked bloodthirsty. The Adair child was too nice to lose her heart to a cheap philanderer, I thought peevishly. To my astounded sense of outrage the young man caught my eye, lifted his glass, and with an impudent smile toasted me silently before he emptied the glass.

"Why-why the insolent young whippersnapper!" I exclaimed weakly.

Across the room Stephen Lansing winked at me.

3

My most intimate friends in the hotel are three widows, acquaintances of long standing. We have a bridge foursome which meets nearly every afternoon, that being one of the few interesting ways in which four elderly and unattached females can kill time. Although I do not approve of gambling we play for a quarter on the corner, merely to add point to the game, as I have explained to the members of my church circle.

I recall that on this day it was Grace Jernigan's turn to have us in her room. In fact, as I came out of the Coffee Shop after lunch she was complaining to Pinkney Dodge, the night clerk, because her card table had not been returned since it was borrowed for a lotto party in the parlour.

"I didn't present it to the hotel, you know," snapped Grace.

"Yes, Mrs Jernigan," sighed Pinkney.

"You'll see to it at once?"

"Yes, Mrs Jernigan," said Pinkney again.

He caught my eye and made a faint grimace. I suppose in twenty years anyone might grow a little tired of being hounded by the demands of peevish guests off duty and on, though somehow one never thought of Pinkney as having any emotions of his own. He was just somebody who was behind the desk at night to take your calls over the switchboard or hand you your key. I had never known him to obtrude his personality upon the guests, granting he had one - which seemed unlikely. His nickname Pinky was a natural outgrowth from Pinkney, but it suited his weak eyes and pinkish hair. In many ways Pinkney resembled a white rabbit more than anything else, even to the feeble twitching of his long upper lip.

"How's your mother, Pinky?" I inquired as usual.

"The same, thank you, Miss Adelaide," he said as he always did.

I shrugged my shoulders. I have heard it said that the way to live forever is to get an incurable disease and take good care of it.

For twenty years, that I know of, Pinkney Dodge's mother had been in a sanatorium out on the edge of town, not expected to last the year out. He did not tell me, because he never discussed his personal affairs, but I heard somewhere that Pinkney had just graduated from law school when his father died.

If so, he had never practiced. I suppose he had to find a paying job in a hurry with a dying mother on his bands. It is quite likely that he believed it would be for only a short time. Nevertheless, he was still at the Richelieu, occupying a tiny back bedroom jammed up against the roof with meals free and enough of a salary to pay the sanatorium bills but not much more.

I had stopped at the desk to see if there was any mail in my box when Polly Lawson came dashing out of the elevator, almost upsetting old Judge Beecher, who glared at her.

"Sorry," said Polly, making for the door.

"Where are you going, Polly?" demanded Mary Lawson, who was standing across the lobby drumming on the back of a chair with her fingertips.

"Out," was Polly's succinct rejoinder.

I saw Mary glance at Mr Stephen Lansing's white and scarlet roadster, which was nonchalantly resting against the 'Don't Park Here' sign before the hotel entrance, and then look quickly at me. I shrugged my shoulders, and, two spots of hectic colour in her cheeks, Mary called out to Polly in a sharper voice than she generally employed.

"You've forgotten your jabot," said Mary.

Polly giggled. "You mean the pink jigger for my neck?"

"Your dress looks unfinished without it," said Mary severely. "You can't go out half done, Polly."

"I'll have to," declared Polly with a derisive grin. "The pink jingaboo just ain't, Aunt Mary. I looked all over for it."

"Nonsense!" said Mary. "I saw it on your chifforobe just before lunch."

" 'Tain't there now, ducky," cried Polly and whirled through the revolving door like a dervish.

"These young things are so thoughtless," murmured Mary to me as we went up on the elevator.

I compressed my lips, and she flushed.

"Perhaps I was mistaken," she said defensively. "It's possible the jabot went to the cleaners or-or something."

I still said nothing, and Mary laughed, rather wearily, I thought.

"After all," she said, "one's neckwear doesn't have wings."

Mary has a two-room suite like mine on the fourth floor, except hers is on the front while I have the corner at the end of the back corridor. Old Laura, loaded down with carpet sweeper, dust mop, and scrub bucket, was just coming out of Mary's bedroom when we came along. We both had to stop while the old maid got herself and her paraphernalia out of the way. That was how each of us came to spy at the same moment something frilly and pink lying on the foot of one of the twin beds in Mary's bedroom.

"No," I murmured dryly, "one's neckwear doesn't have wings."

Mary's lips trembled, and I put out my hand and took hers.

"Why don't you send the child away for a while?" I asked. "Give her a chance to find her feet again in a new environment. A summer camp for girls or a cruise, say."

Mary's fingers were cold in my grasp and she looked at me with such despair, I started and dropped my handbag.

"On what?" she demanded.

I stared at her. "You can't be financially embarrassed, Mary!" I exclaimed incredulously.

She released my hand as if it burned her. "No. No, of course not!" she stammered, but her eyes refused to meet mine.

"If I can help..." I began, only Mary with a queer choked sound had gone into her room and closed the door behind her.

I was puzzled and disturbed. So, apparently, was old Laura, whom I came upon halfway down the hall muttering to herself and shaking her kinky grizzled head from side to side.

"I ain't no thief. I ain't never stole nothing," she was mumbling. "What would old thing like me want wid trick eyelashes?"

"What on earth are you quarrelling about, Laura?" I demanded.

She pouted her thick pale lips. "That fancy woman in 409 claim I stole something of her'n."

Privately, I had the same opinion of Hilda Anthony, but one has to maintain one's dignity. "Are you referring to Mrs Anthony?" I inquired sternly.

"I ain't seen no eyelashes. I ain't seen no little red tin box. I ain't had nothing to do with it," muttered Laura, rolling her eyes till they were all whites in her wrinkled face. "I ain't no thief!"

"I can guarantee that," I said soothingly. "If the lady has accused you of taking something of hers, she's mistaken. Probably she's mislaid it."

"Is that so?" demanded a metallic voice.

I had not till that moment realized that we were standing practically outside Room 409 and that the door was slightly ajar. Sweeping it wide open, the Anthony woman confronted us, her yellow eyes blazing, looking more like a tawny tigress than ever in a cloth of gold negligee wrapped tightly about her body. Not until then had I fully understood the meaning of the word voluptuous.

"You may think it's your privilege to poke your nose into everybody else's business in this house," Hilda Anthony informed me, "only I warn you, keep out of mine."

"My dear woman ..." I began with, I'll confess, considerable heat.

"Don't bother to dear woman me," she snapped. "Just stay out of my affairs, all of them."

"In my opinion neither you nor your affairs would bear investigation," I snapped.

"Is that so?" she repeated and whipped the train of the negligee about her like a cat lashing its tail. "Well, let me tell you, you..."

What had all the earmarks of a nasty scene was at that minute averted by a faint wail behind me. "You mustn't quarrel! Oh dear, please don't."

I turned sharply. Kathleen Adair's mother was standing on the threshold of her room next door.

"Mother can't bear for people to be mean to each other," explained Kathleen Adair in a breathless voice.

She came out into the hall, as if she meant if necessary to step between me and the Anthony woman.

"I ain't stole no red tin box," contributed Laura abruptly, swishing her mop about and glaring at us.

The Adair girl stooped swiftly and came up with something.

"Could this possibly be what you are looking for?" she asked and held out a small shiny scarlet box, labelled in gold with the name of a famous beautician on Park Avenue in New York.

The Anthony woman opened it, looked inside. "Nothing's missing," she said in an odd voice.

"If you are in the habit of strewing your belongings all over the place, you should be careful about accusing people of theft," I said.

She gave me a baleful look. "Is that so? Well, I'm not careless, see? Not of anything that costs money. And artificial eyelashes do, plenty, this far from Broadway. The only place I ever strewed that box was in the top drawer of my dressing table. So what do you think of that?"

Having no desire to argue with her ilk, I walked on, my nose appreciably elevated, but I glanced back as I entered my suite and saw that Hilda Anthony was still regarding the tin box with a baffled frown between her thinly plucked eyebrows.

Our game starts promptly at two and ends on the stroke of five, no matter who is losing. It has been my experience that with stakes up, if only a quarter, one has to have ironclad rules. Nothing so sharpens the disposition as anything which touches on the pocketbook - or so I have observed. I have learned things I would never have dreamed about human nature at the bridge table.

Ella Trotter is my best friend and I myself am not a good loser, but nobody has ever bid to suit Ella or led to please her. She would win every hand in every rubber if she could. She might give you the quarter after the game is over, but during it she would as soon claw your eyes out as donate you a trick. There have been times during a session at bridge when relations between Ella and me have been strained to the breaking point. However, she is a good sort at heart.

I had no more than walked into my sitting room that day when Ella telephoned me. "My sister-in-law's coming by late this after-noon. She has a stocking-mending machine. Bring down any you have with runs, Adelaide. I'll get her to fix them."

"Thanks, Ella," I said.

"Don't mention it."

After she hung up I went through my laundry bag and collected a couple of pairs of hose which needed mending. Nothing now-adays, I reflected, has the wearing quality it used to have. That reminded me of my knitted bag. I have had it since I was twenty-ish. I distinctly remember that I made it the winter Father's asthma was so bad and I was shut up in the house with him for months. It helped to while away the long tedious days to have something to do with my hands.

The bag is now out of date. Beside the smart envelope purses of today, it looks huge and clumsy with its dark green roses on a sap-phire background and its heavy green glass handles. Nevertheless, though I seldom carry it any more, I have a sentimental attachment for the old relic, and on one of the capacious sides the stitches had broken.

"I'll ask Ella's sister-in-law if she can do something about that," I said, laying the handbag on my bedside table.

Someone knocked at the door and called out, "Miss Adams! Could I see you a minute?" I frowned. It was Lottie Mosby. My face must have worn a forbidding expression, for she glanced at me in a feverishly apologetic way when I let her in.

"I hate to bother you," she cried, the words tumbling over themselves in her haste. "I know you don't like me. But..." She drew a long breath. "If I had anyone else to go to! But I haven't."

"You have a husband," I reminded her.

As I have said, I had nothing in common with either of the Mosbys, although of the two I preferred the wife, scatter-brained as she was.

"Yes," she said, her pretty, common little face going bleak, "I have a husband. That's why..." She paused abruptly.

"Yes?" I asked.

Again she drew a long breath. "Dan's the last person on earth I could go to in a jam."

I raised my eyebrows. "In that case, it might be a good idea to stay out of jams."

"But if you're in, you can't stay out. You just get in deeper and deeper," she cried and added wildly, "It's a vicious circle!"

"You read too many trashy novels," I snapped.

She sighed. "I didn't think you'd help me. I know, to a lady like you, I must seem impossible."

She turned toward the door, her narrow shoulders sagging. In spite of her cheap rouge and her skimpy skirt, she suddenly seemed to me more like a scared, hopeless child than anything.

"What did you want me to do?" I asked stiffly.

She shook her head. "You wouldn't."

"Come, come," I said gruffly. "Out with it."

She looked back over her shoulder, and I was surprised to see how haggard she had grown since she moved into the hotel the year before. She couldn't have been twenty-five and she had looked younger than that then. Now she had dark arcs under her eyes and a pinched look about her mouth.

"Would you lend me ten dollars?" she whispered.

I regarded her over my spectacles. "To throw away, as you've thrown the rest away, betting with the bookies."

"You know everything, don't you?" she asked sullenly.

"When a woman guest in this hotel keeps the porter busy running down the street to the bookmakers, everybody knows it, sooner or later."

"I guess so," she murmured drearily.

"Look here," I said, "a place like this is the worst spot on earth for a young married couple."

"You're telling me," she said, her lips trembling.

"You don't have enough to do; no wonder you get into mischief. And if you ask me, your husband wouldn't drink so much if he had anything else with which to occupy himself. Why don't you two rent a little house and make a fresh start?"

In her shallow blue eyes there was a sudden radiance. "If we only could!"

"Forget wild oats," I said bluntly, "and raise flowers and chickens – and babies for a change. You used to be in love with each other, I dare say."

"Yes! Oh yes!"

"Well, then you'd probably be again with half a chance."

"A chance! But that's all I ask, just a chance!" she cried.

I shrugged my shoulders, and she caught my arm, clung to me pleadingly.

"That's why I've got to have ten dollars! It's-it's my chance."

"I suppose someone's given you a tip on some broken-down race horse that can't lose."

"Neilson isn't broken down. He's sure to win, and the odds are twenty to one. Please, please, Miss Adams, if you knew! If you only realized! Two hundred dollars means the difference between heaven and hell to me."

"No fool like an old fool," I muttered and with a sniff took two five-dollar bills out of my purse.

"It's the seventh race at Latonia," she cried. "And God bless you!" She was gone, dancing down the hall with my ten dollars.

"That's the last I'll see of her," I told myself grimly, it having been my experience that the quickest way to be rid of people is to lend them money.

I was feeling cross. It had been a nagging day. A number of things had upset me. Before I started for Grace's room on the second floor I went over and jerked the shades down. The sun streams in my south windows half the afternoon. They look out toward the employees' entry at the rear of the hotel. Middleway between is a rusty fire escape which no one ever used except the insurance inspector once a year.

Although the entrance is from the corridor, I can reach the iron railing of the fire escape from the back window in my bedroom. As I started to pull down the shades I remembered I had hung an intimate piece of my wearing apparel on the railing to dry that morning.

Guests are discouraged from doing laundry work in their rooms, but I doubt if there was a woman in the house who did not wash out handkerchiefs and underthings. I did, and do, whenever I felt so inclined.

I had leaned out to recover my garment, which was skittishly flaunting itself in the breeze to the satyrish amusement of two pimplish youths in the building across the court, when I saw the waitress Annie come out the rear door of the hotel, walk swiftly along the paved alleyway, and set off down the side street. I stared after her, feeling a catch in my heart. She was such a forlorn young thing. I wondered why waitresses never have any family and backing.

Not that I am familiar with a number of the profession; only the girls I had met in the Coffee Shop all were rather pathetically on their own, so far as I could tell.

"No wonder they flit in and out like June bugs," I muttered.

It was then I noticed that a man had detached himself,

apparently from nowhere, and was unobtrusively following the girl. I had to look twice to make sure I was not mistaken. It was the insignificant little man in the mousy-grey suit, Mr James Reid, of New Orleans.

"So that's why the Adair girl glared at him as if she wanted to kill him," I said to myself. "The man's a masher. Who'd have thought it?"

Having lived around a hotel for years, I flatter myself that I can recognize the male flirt on sight. It was a jolt to my pride to discover that I had picked Mr James Reid as the last man on earth to annoy young girls with his misplaced attentions.

"I hope that Annie has sense enough to put the little shrimp in his place," I muttered angrily.

I had an unhappy conviction, however, that the child did not have much idea about wolves in sheep's clothing. It was a relief when, hanging far out the window for a better view, I saw a young man join her at the next corner, a young man who limped slightly and who wore what, even at that distance, I recognized as a worn pair of blue overalls and a battered slouch hat. They went off together.

She was clinging to his arm.

"At least she's got somebody," I remember thinking, "although he looks down on his luck, poor fellow."

In my perturbation I accidentally dislodged the object I had hung on the fire escape. I made a grab for it, but, still flirting coquettishly with the breeze, it sailed lightly down, bellied out a little, then playfully flung itself at a window on the next floor where, to my consternation, a masculine arm in white shirt sleeves reached out and captured it.

"Is this – or should I say – are these your pink bloomers, Miss Adams?" murmured a mocking voice.

Speechless, I stared down into the insolent grey eyes of Mr Stephen Lansing.

He grinned at me. "It would, of course, be more gallant to keep them as a souvenir," he said, "only how would we ever explain their presence in my room?"

"I-er-er..." I gasped. "The very idea!"

He laughed, rolled the bloomers into a bundle, and said, "Catch!" I am sure I made a ludicrous spectacle, leaning far out to receive against my capacious bosom the bulky package he tossed at me. I know my face was scarlet, for I could feel it.

"Young man," I said, "you are entirely too fresh."

"Ah, say not so," murmured Mr Stephen Lansing, placing his hand on his heart with an exaggerated gesture of concern and sweeping me a profound and highly sardonic bow before I pulled down my window shade with a jerk that all but detached it from its moorings.

4

I had absolutely no luck at cards that afternoon.

If I held anything higher than a ten-spot, my partner had nothing. Ella Trotter was high, and Ella is as offensive a winner as she is a loser. Several times I felt if she crowed another time about the grand slam she made on me redoubled, I should fly into a thousand pieces.

However, as usual when the game was over, it was difficult to nurse a grudge against Ella. Her sister-in-law, a dumpy little woman who hopes to get Ella's money when she dies, was waiting when we went up to Ella's room on the third floor. Ella loaded the poor soul down with her own hosiery and mine.

"I don't want to impose on you," I said.

"Nonsense!" snapped Ella. "Lou likes to do things for me."

Lou nodded feebly. She has been toadying to Ella for years, though it is my private opinion that Ella will outlive all her poor relations, if only for spite.

"I have a knitted bag," I explained. "There is a run in one side. I don't suppose you could mend that on your machine."

Lou looked dubious, but Ella gave her no opportunity to say so. "Of course she can. Go and get it, Adelaide."

I shrugged my shoulders. I still thought it unlikely that the bag could be mended, but, as Ella briskly pointed out, it could do no harm to try. I took the elevator upstairs. When I came back down the corridor I found Kathleen Adair and her mother waiting for the car.

"Did you ring?" I asked.

"Yes," said the girl curtly, looking at me with the hostility which I had noticed in her eyes before.

"What a beautiful bag!" cried her mother. "I adore colours."

She laid her hand caressingly on one of the green roses which stand out boldly even yet against the sapphire background of the knitted bag.

Kathleen Adair smiled. "I think in some other reincarnation Mother must have been a gypsy."

I said nothing and, flushing a little, Kathleen moved aside for me to precede them into the elevator. I observed that she stood between me and her mother on the way down. The girl has a complex, I thought. She seemed to feel that she had to protect that spineless little creature from everybody. I believed it likely that Kathleen Adair had been standing between the older woman and reality for a number of years.

I got off at the third floor. Ella's suite, like mine, is at the end of the back corridor, and I was in a hurry. Lou Trotter lived on the far side of town and she had to cook supper for herself and an invalid husband after she reached home. It gave me a turn to come upon Mr James Reid, of New Orleans, just outside Ella's door.

He flashed me a queer look, and I am sure my glance at him was highly suspicious, for he had the grace to go a little pink. I could think of no good excuse why he should be on that particular floor. He had, so far as I had been able to see, no acquaintances in the hotel, and his room was on the fifth. I had made it my business to glance over the register again that noon to find out.

"I-er-was looking for you, Miss Adams," he volunteered in a flat voice.

"For me?" I demanded blankly.

"This is yours, I believe."

He fumbled in his pocket and, glancing quickly, almost furtively, I thought, over his shoulder, produced my green spectacle case.

"Well," I said, "forevermore!"

He nodded. "I-er-found it."

I knit my brows and then I remembered. "Near the elevator on the fourth floor?" I asked.

He nodded again. "You must have dropped it," he stammered.

"I did," I admitted. "Or, at least, I dropped my purse just outside Mrs Lawson's door."

"That's where I picked it up," he said quickly.

I took the green spectacle case and thrust it into my handbag.

To tell the truth I was a little wrought up over its singular appearances and disappearances. I probably stared at Mr James Reid very hard, for he began to inch away down the corridor.

"Thank you," I called after him.

He bobbed his head and slid around the corner. Like an eel, I thought, listening for his footsteps in the front hall and hearing exactly nothing. It was then I discovered Lottie Mosby peeping through the crack in a door halfway down the corridor. Catching my eye, she closed the door swiftly, and no wonder. The Mosbys, like myself, roomed on the fourth floor. Certainly she did not belong, of all places, in the room where I had seen her. I felt slightly sick. So it was true what people intimated, I told myself. The Mosby girl was worse than indiscreet.

"Here the thing is," I said to Lou Trotter, "though I doubt if you can do anything about it."

She smiled faintly, wadded the knitted purse into the large shopping bag which she carried, and began hurriedly to put on her small shapeless black hat. Ella patted her arm.

"Tell Jim I'm sending him a crate of strawberries tomorrow," she said.

That was exactly like Ella Trotter. She can exasperate you to tears, but she always ends up with a generous gesture. By the time I left Ella's room I had nearly forgiven the way she chortled when she bluffed me out of a sound three no-trump hand that afternoon with a psychic bid of two spades when she had only the three of spades.

It is my custom to dress for dinner, though I never have more than two dinner dresses, black velvet in winter, black lace for the other seasons. I can remember when I thought that if I were ever free I would wear all the colours in the rainbow. But by the time my father died, after having been bedridden for years, I was past the age of furbelows.

As I recall, I was in the middle of my bath when I thought of the green spectacle case again. One usually thinks of things at the moment one's in no position to do anything about them. I had a dim recollection of having absent-mindedly dropped the spectacle case into the knitted bag which Lou Trotter carried off.

"Drat it!" I muttered. "It's all the fault of that annoying Reid man and his disconcerting habit of bobbing up in the most unexpected places with one's personal belongings."

It appeared to me that Mr James Reid had been in my hair all day. However, in this instance I seemed to have done him an injustice, for when I looked into my black leather purse to make sure, the spectacle case was there.

"Apparently my memory has become a bruised reed," I told myself in chagrin.

Picking up the case, I dropped it into the drawer of the bedside table where it belonged. "Now stay there, for heaven's sake!" I exclaimed crossly.

Mary Lawson was standing at the front of the lobby, staring out, when I came downstairs. I am sure she saw my reflection in the glass, but she did not turn around. She was drumming on the back of a chair as she had done after lunch, and suddenly I realized what was strange about her slender white hand. She was not wearing her emerald! It might not have been unusual in anyone else. Most women change their jewellery with their costume. But I had never seen Mary without the big green stone in its old-fashioned massive gold setting encrusted with diamonds. It was her engagement ring, and Mary was still passionately in love with her husband although he had been dead three years.

I had been fond of John Lawson myself. He was a fine, solid chap with all the sterling virtues. It is a pity he was killed before his time in an automobile accident during one of our infrequent

sleet storms one January night. For a while I feared that Mary
would never recover from the shock, but she picked up wonderfully when Polly first came to live with her. I remember thinking
at the time that the girl was exactly the tonic Mary needed. Now
it struck me she looked worse than ever.

"Having your emerald repaired, Mary?" I inquired casually.

She did not look around, but I heard her catch her breath. "Yes,"
she said quickly. "Yes, I am."

I had never suspected Mary Lawson of even the shadow of
deceit; nevertheless, I knew she was lying. I studied her face in
the glass. It looked drawn and pale. I could not understand it.
John Lawson had left his widow well provided for. I happened to
know that Mary depended on large annual gifts to charity to get
rid of her income. It did not seem possible to me that she could
be having money troubles. Other trouble I freely admitted. For at
that moment Polly drove up in front of the hotel with Mr Stephen
Lansing.

While Mary and I looked on, he helped the girl out of his flamboyant roadster, being very solicitous and much slower about
releasing her arm than was necessary. Again I heard Mary catch
her breath. Polly was gazing up into Stephen Lansing's handsome predatory face with every evidence of complete fascination,
and coming toward them down the street, looking grim and very
intense, was Howard Warren. I was sure that Polly had seen him,
the little minx! I felt positive that that was why she deliberately
widened her eyes at Stephen Lansing in her most alluring manner.

"Darling," she murmured, "thanks for the spin and everything."

Of course, these young things of today call everybody darling.

I understand it is supposed to mean nothing, but it meant a great
deal to Howard. He looked at Polly as if he could cheerfully have
wrung her neck, and then he transferred his dark gaze to Stephen
Lansing, who merely grinned.

Mary moved over to the door. "I'm waiting for you, Polly," she
called out sharply. "The Coffee Shop will be open for dinner in

ten minutes."

"Righto!" sang out Polly. "I'll be ready in a jiffy or sooner than that."

Her face was flushed. I supposed she had been drinking and shook my head. Howard was waiting for the elevator, but when Polly approached he turned abruptly and went up the stairs.

"Guess he figures I'm contagious; guess he'd walk miles to get away from me," announced Polly with what might have been a giggle and could have been a sob.

The elevator creaked slowly downward and the Mosbys emerged. He looked sulky and was far from steady on his feet. She seemed to have been crying. They were pointedly not on speaking terms. He scowled when she turned the radio on full blast. There was a swing band doing its worst by the air as usual.

"Swell dance music," murmured Lottie Mosby with a little laugh that tinkled like a lead nickel. "Anybody want to dance?" She glanced coquettishly at Stephen Lansing, who had stopped at the desk to collect his mail, but Mr Lansing ignored her as if it were someone else who had been giving her the rush only the day before. Biting her lip, she glanced away, and I saw her husband watching her in the mirror behind the cigar case. Something in his eyes gave me a start.

Cyril Fancher flung open the doors of the Coffee Shop and Sophie came out. She had a vase of flowers in her hands, intended for the desk in the lobby, and she was wearing a bright yellow lace dress which might have been becoming to a woman thirty years younger and sixty pounds lighter. I imagine I lifted my eyebrows, for Sophie threw me a defiant glance.

"Cyril adores me in yellow," she said firmly.

I sniffed. "You are the last woman on earth, Sophie Scott, whom I should have expected to go simple in your old age."

She bridled. One of the things neither Sophie nor her new husband could forgive me was the fact that I never was able to remember to call her Mrs Fancher.

"A woman is only as old as she feels, Adelaide," she said tartly, "and, thanks to Cyril's devotion, I feel gloriously young - reborn, as it were."

"Humph!" was my only comment.

People were drifting into the dining room for, had we but known it, the last peaceful meal we were to have for days. I stopped to ask a question of Pinkney Dodge at the desk. He did not go on duty till seven, but he was usually around earlier, having nowhere else to go, poor fellow.

"Did Neilson win in the seventh at Latonia today, Pinky?" I asked.

He gave me a startled glance and said, "He didn't even show."

No wonder Lottie Mosby had been crying, I thought. She was the kind of silly little moth for whom the gambling fires are made.

"I didn't know you were a race-track fan, Miss Adams," Stephen Lansing remarked with a grin.

I looked him up and down before I addressed Pinkney.

"The hotel seems to be filled with crude people lately," I said.

Stephen Lansing sniggered. "Ouch!" he exclaimed. "But I asked for it, didn't I?"

Making no reply, I turned and sailed into the dining room.

Annie, the little waitress, hurried over to take my order. She seemed, for some reason, to believe that in me she had found a friend. However, I saw Cyril Fancier watching her from under his long womanish eyelashes and so I did not engage her in conversation.

It was, as I have said, the last peaceful hour under that roof for days, but nothing happened on the surface.

The Mosbys ate their dinner without exchanging a word. Polly Lawson, having made a late appearance, chattered volubly with Mary, who looked almost ill as she sat there, playing with her fork.

Howard did not come down to dinner. I suppose he was avoiding Polly and I remember thinking it would serve her right if he had a date to go out with someone else. I kept watching the elevator through the side of the Coffee Shop which is all glass. I thought Polly was also watching, but Howard was not to be seen.

Hilda Anthony appeared, wearing a brazen scarlet taffeta gown slashed to the waist in the back. As usual, she had on her outlandish artificial eyelashes, but they were becoming to her, I have to admit. She could get by with the sensational better than any woman I ever saw. Mr Stephen Lansing came in behind her and paused at her table. She shook her head when he would have sat down beside her and glanced into the lobby where Mr James Reid was staring at her fixedly from the bottom step of the stair.

"Sorry," murmured the Anthony woman. I could not be sure but I thought she added, "Later."

With a debonair smile the insouciant Mr Lansing moved on. I saw him stoop and pick up something at the side of the Adair table, but Kathleen Adair looked around swiftly and frowned at him, and he flushed and passed by without a word. I glanced back at the stair. The little man in grey had once more disappeared as unobtrusively as he took form. The lobby was empty except for Pinkney Dodge slumped down at the side of the desk, waiting to go on duty.

"Drat the Reid man!" I muttered for the second time that day.

"One moment he's here, the next he's gone up in smoke."

Between seven and eight is the best time to find the guests of the Richelieu in. It is too early for people who have an engagement for the evening to have gone out. At that hour the lobby is full of loungers and, if the weather is at all fine, so are the big chairs on the sidewalk outside, and this was a lovely evening. My arthritis being what it is, I do not deliberately court damp spring breezes, but I did compromise by standing to the left of the front door where I could catch a breath of the night. It was, I recall, faintly perfumed with wet honeysuckle. A night for lovers, I thought, though I am not a sentimental woman.

Kathleen Adair escorted her mother to one of the divans. "I

don't suppose you'd feel up to a little walk," she suggested and added wistfully, "It is such a beautiful evening."

"My bronchitis, darling," the invalid reminded her in a soft reproachful voice.

"Yes, of course you couldn't, dear," she said.

She made me think of a small fluttering bird I had once held in my band. It had seemed to me when I let it go that liberty is the most precious thing in the world. I had passionately wished I could as easily open the bars of my own cage.

I did not realize that Stephen Lansing had come up to her until he spoke. "Isn't this your handkerchief, Miss Adair?" he asked.

He held out a lacy scrap. His face was quite red. For the first time he looked to me unsure of himself.

"You dropped it," he explained lamely.

He did not say where, but I knew then what he had picked up beside the Adair table in the dining room.

"Thank you," said the girl in curt tones.

He hesitated. "It's too grand a night to waste indoors," he murmured tentatively, for him almost timidly.

She flung him a scathing glance.

"I don't imagine it will be wasted by you," she said.

He flushed. "Wouldn't you and your mother enjoy a little drive?" he asked.

"With you?" she demanded scornfully.

"Why not?" he inquired with a smile.

It was an attempt at his customary flippant gallantry but it failed to come off. He was suddenly not half the insolent young sheik he generally was.

"You've made fools of most of the women in this house, but I'm not having any," said Kathleen Adair furiously.

He winced. "Sorry," he stammered and walked abruptly away.

I forgot I was not officially part of the scene. "Good for you, young woman," I said grimly. "If ever a man needed taking down, that is the man."

To my astonishment Kathleen Adair turned on me in a temper. "It isn't his fault if he sweeps people off their feet!" she cried.

"So that is how the land lies," I said, shaking my head.

She coloured painfully. "I don't know what you mean," she protested.

I turned away in silence. I dare say any girl in her position would have denied it, yet I knew in spite of the rebuff she had handed him that the child was in love, or, I hoped, infatuated was the word, with the dashing Mr Lansing.

Ten minutes later he and Polly Lawson left the hotel together.

I was still stationed at the front door when they went out.

"Do you stand an hour after dinner, Miss Adams, to preserve the figure?" he asked with a return to his usual impudence.

"Young man," I said severely, "it's been all of twenty years since I've had a figure worth preserving."

Not until he laughed did I realize that he had provoked me into speaking to him before a lobby full of people. "The graceless young scamp!" I muttered as he and Polly went on out.

Lottie Mosby must have been hanging around on his account, for as soon as he left she went over to the elevator and pushed the bell impatiently. She acted as if she wanted to ring it off the wall. Her husband was sitting back by the telephone booth apparently reading the evening paper, though I saw him watching her from behind it.

As I noted by the indicator, the elevator was stopped on my floor. It came down at last in its jerky manner, making no pauses on the way, and Howard Warren stepped out. His room is on the third. I wondered what he had been doing on the fourth floor. I thought he seemed out of breath as he hurried up to me.

"How's for taking in a movie, Miss Adelaide?" he asked.

I glanced at him in surprise. Howard is not a movie fan, neither am I, and as long as he had lived in the hotel Howard had never invited me to go places with him before. Not that I had expected him to. I liked the boy all right. I suppose he felt much the same toward me, but Howard and I had never been, in any sense of the word, boon companions. My sceptical glance appeared to disconcert him.

"I picked up some easy money on the seventh at Latonia this afternoon," he explained, "and I feel a celebration coming on."

Now it was utterly unlike Howard to play the races or do anything else foolish, and I had been fond of his mother. My face must have expressed my disapproval, for he tried to laugh the matter off.

"Plugging along, everlastingly on the job, never gets you anywhere," he said bitterly.

So that was it, I thought. Polly's scandalous behaviour had backfired on Howard. He looked very young and very unhappy and disillusioned.

In such a frame of mind people have been guilty of reckless acts which they regret the rest of their lives. I am not one to shirk my duty and I myself in a similar mood had once done something I have never ceased to regret.

"All right, Howard," I said. "The Palace it is, as soon as I get my wrap."

He clutched my arm. "It isn't cold out, and I have my car."

Behind the desk Pinkney Dodge had reached up and produced the key to my suite. Howard glanced at him angrily.

"This place is full of eavesdroppers," he said.

Pinkney looked squelched. "I didn't mean to offend," he faltered.

"I just thought if Miss Adelaide was going upstairs for a wrap, she'd want her key."

"I do," I snapped, taking it from him. "Thanks, Pinky. Howard is not quite himself tonight, I fear."

Howard shrugged his shoulders and rang for the elevator. Like Lottie Mosby, he acted as if he wanted to tear the bell off the wall.

I glanced toward the telephone booth. Young Mosby had disappeared.

It was exactly five minutes of eight, and the lobby was empty except for ourselves.

"I still think you won't need a coat," persisted Howard.

I was prepared to sit through a tiresome evening for the good of his soul, if necessary, but not to risk a needless attack of arthritis.

"Please let me be the judge of that," I snapped.

Sophie Scott went up in the elevator with me. "Have you seen Mr Fancher, Clarence?" she asked.

Clarence was extremely diplomatic. "Yes 'm," he admitted, looking unhappy. "I seen him a while ago on fourth, dodging around."

Sophie's face was all at once as yellow as her dress. "On fourth!" she exclaimed. The proprietor's suite is on the fifth floor. "What was he doing on fourth, and what do you mean dodging around?"

Clarence squirmed. "He was just sort of acting like he didn't want to be seen," he said.

"Ridiculous!" expostulated Sophie, but her nostrils quivered.

I am positive she had the same thought I did, the Anthony woman in Room 409! However, she would have died rather than admit it to me, poor old Sophie. I left her in the car when I got off on four. I had no doubt but that she would cross-examine Clarence the moment my back was turned.

To my annoyance the light was not on in the back corridor. Once around the corner from the shaded globe opposite the elevator, the hall was very dark. I am not as a rule nervous. Nevertheless, I felt uneasy that night. I remember shivering and telling myself that someone had walked over my grave.

I made up my mind to call the desk as soon as I reached my room and give Pinky Dodge a piece of my tongue for the management's carelessness in failing to put on the dome light in the rear corridor. I had, I recollect, considerable difficulty in locating the keyhole to my door and again I was conscious of an eerie sensation, as if a dank wind had blown down my neck. It did not help my temper on entering my bedroom to discover that the switch at the side of the door merely clicked when I pressed it.

"A fuse has blown," I muttered irritably. "Of all the nuisances!" Not for the first time I thanked my stars that the floor sockets in my sitting room were on a different circuit from that which controls the switches. Having occupied the suite for years, I could find my way in the dark, although it was pitch-black, the window shades still being lowered.

I progressed somewhat gropingly through the door into the other room, making for the lamp on the end table by the couch. I remember moving cautiously because I did not want to come up against the sharp edge of anything. I had a feeling that the table was farther away than it should be. Then my hands encountered something and I stopped dead still, my body turning to ice.

I had touched a man's arm. I could feel the rough material of his coat sleeve. For a second I was paralised and as I stood there, my throat closed with panic, an object swung gently against my face. It was a man's shoulder! At the same moment I became aware of a sound, of a slow steady dropping as of water. But it was not water, for my hands were sticky with it, horribly sticky.

To this day I do not know how I located the chain on the table lamp or how I found the strength to pull it. It seemed to me I lived years with the dreadful lashing of my heart before the light came on and I looked up from my blood stained hands into the pallid grinning face of Mr James Reid, of New Orleans, hanging above me from the cross arm of the chandelier with his throat cut from ear to ear.

5

I have always prided myself on being equal to the emergency. Nevertheless, after I made the horrible discovery in my sitting room, my senses ceased to function for several minutes. I must have put out the table lamp to hide the sight of that hideous grinning face, although I have never remembered doing so. Nor do I know yet how I got the door open and myself out into the corridor again. Not for some time did I realize that it was I who was screaming dreadfully.

"Stop it! Pull yourself together!" I was commanded by a brusque voice.

I came to enough to know that Mr Stephen Lansing was shaking me with a great deal of violence, but I could only stare vacantly up into his face, which was faintly illuminated by the glow from an open door down the hall.

"For heaven's sake, Miss Adams," he asked more gently, "what has happened?"

All over the floor other doors were flying open and people were crying out excitedly. It was then I became aware that the blood-curdling shrieks which were alarming the house had their origin in my mouth. I promptly shut it, though I had to clench my teeth.

"That's better," murmured Stephen Lansing soothingly, as if I were a feeble-minded child.

It is queer what irrelevant things will pop into one's mind at such times. "I thought you'd gone out with Polly Lawson," I remarked in an accusing voice.

It seemed to me he changed colour. "I came back," he snapped.

"If you must know everything, even at a time like this, I forgot something."

He glanced beyond me to where Kathleen Adair was staring at him from the doorway of her room and, flushing again, he went on crossly, "Would you mind telling me what the fuss is all about, Miss Adams? Did you think you saw a mouse?"

He grinned provokingly, and I took a deep breath. My wits were recovering from their paralysis. I drew myself up to my full height, which is considerable.

"I am not a woman to have hysterics over a trifle," I announced not only to him but also to the crowd which was rapidly collecting about us. "There is a man in my room."

"Incredible!" cried Stephen Lansing. "Surely you didn't let him get away from you?"

"Your levity is misdirected," I said frigidly. "The man is dead."

"Dead!" gasped someone behind me.

I nodded, and my voice rose a little. "He is hanging to my chandelier with his throat cut from ear to ear. Murdered!"

"Murdered!" wailed little Mrs Adair. "Oh dear!"

"Who?" asked Stephen Lansing quickly.

"He's on the register as Mr James Reid from New Orleans," I said, compressing my lips.

"Oh dear!" wailed Mrs Adair again.

Her daughter caught her as she crumpled to the floor.

"She's fainted!" cried the girl. "Oh, Mother!"

"Let me," said Stephen Lansing. "She's too heavy for you."

Her eyes defied him. "I can manage alone."

He paid no attention. Although she continued to glare at him rebelliously, he carried the frail, limp body of her mother into their room and laid her on the bed.

Cyril Fancher came running down the hall. "What in heaven's name is the matter?" he demanded, looking at me as though he felt sure, whatever it was, I was to blame.

"One of your guests has got himself murdered in my sitting room," I said bitterly.

For a moment I thought he, too, would faint. Behind him Clarence, the elevator boy, gave a squeak like a rat in a trap, and at the bend in the corridor I heard Lottie Mosby's shrill voice.

"Dan, Dan, where are you?" she was calling frantically.

"Get Sophie," Cyril Fancher told Clarence weakly. "And hurry."

I shrugged my shoulders. Sophie's new husband might be a romantic lover but he was no rock on which to lean in adversity. I have never seen anyone deflate so rapidly.

"Sophie will know what to do," he said, mopping his brow and giving me a very unhappy look.

"Let's hope so," I remarked dryly.

The Anthony woman, who was standing on the threshold of her room, looked me over venomously.

"There are easier ways of getting rid of the boyfriend than murder," she observed. "You should exercise more self-control, Miss Adams."

Ella Trotter, panting a little, was just coming down the hall. "If you are insinuating that Adelaide had anything to do with killing that – whoever's been killed – you belong in a straitjacket!" she cried.

Hilda Anthony laughed cynically. "Is that so?"

I am not a clinging woman, but I felt grateful for the arm Ella put about me. The corridor light came on suddenly, making us all blink. I had left my door ajar behind me, and we could see that ghastly figure swaying gently in the draft from the window.

"Good God!" cried Cyril Fancher, stepping across the threshold and then stopping abruptly, his hand flung up in front of his eyes.

"No one ought to go in there till the police come," said Stephen Lansing, returning from the Adair room where Kathleen had slammed the door behind him. "Don't they always tell you not to touch anything?"

Cyril Fancher backed out into the hall, beads of sweat on his upper lip. "Yes, that's right," he said feebly, glad of an excuse to escape, I thought.

Sophie, looking like a squat homely tower of strength, came puffing around the bend in the hall. "The police will be here in five minutes," she said crisply, as though murder were part of her daily regime. "Everybody go down to the parlour and wait for them."

"I knew you'd know what to do, love," murmured Cyril Fancher gratefully.

"What do you mean, wait for the police in the parlour?" demanded Dan Mosby truculently.

I could not remember when he had joined our group. He had evidently had another drink. His eyes were bloodshot.

Sophie, absently patting Cyril's hand, nodded. "The police want all of you to wait in the parlour," she repeated. "At least, till further orders."

"Why should the police be ordering us around?" protested Dan Mosby. "My wife and I are going to a movie."

"I think not," said Sophie.

Down the street we heard the thin eerie scream of a police siren coming nearer and nearer. Lottie Mosby clutched at her husband's arm and began to tremble from head to foot, and again I was reminded of a poor bedraggled little moth with singed wings.

"It isn't as if either my wife or I knew this bird or ever spoke to him," exclaimed Dan Mosby angrily.

"Is that so?" drawled Hilda Anthony again.

Her yellow eyes mocked him, and the little shivering figure, clinging to his arm, sobbed once – quite loudly – before she pressed the knuckles of her clenched hand against her lips.

"So far as that goes, none of us knew him," muttered Howard Warren.

I wondered how long he had been standing there in the shadow at the turn of the corridor. He met my eyes and glanced quickly away, flushing darkly.

"Somebody knew him well enough to slit his throat," Stephen Lansing reminded us brutally.

"Couldn't it have been suicide?" stammered Mary Lawson.

It occurred to me that, being on the same floor, Mary must have been one of the first on the scene, although until she spoke I had not noticed her.

Stephen Lansing shrugged his shoulders and said, "If he killed himself, he must have eaten the weapon."

"Why was the corridor light off?" I demanded of Sophie Scott. "No wonder, with such carelessness, crime is rampant in the house."

"I wouldn't call one murder in twenty years a crime wave," she answered tartly.

"Give it time," I replied with more truth than I knew.

"I suppose the fuse is out," said Sophie.

I shook my head. "All the other lights on the floor were on, it seems, except this one in the hall and the ones in my suite." I shuddered.

"I can understand why my chandelier might not work, but I can't figure what ailed the corridor light. It's all right now."

"The bulb was loose," volunteered Pinkney Dodge. "I got up on a chair and tightened it."

Stephen Lansing frowned. "You shouldn't have done that. There may have been fingerprints."

Pinky went white. "You mean the-the murderer deliberately unscrewed it? I-I never thought I might be-be destroying evidence. I was only trying to help."

Sophie gave him a scathing look. "You'd be more help on the job, it seems to me. Who's looking after the switchboard while you stand around, gaping at things that don't concern you?" Turning red, Pinky beat an ignominious retreat. "And tell Clarence to stick with that elevator and stop acting like a chicken with its head cut off!" Sophie bawled after him.

She turned to her husband, who was still white about the gills. "The rest of you go on down to the parlour. You guard this room, Cyril. Let no one in till the police come."

"I?" gasped Cyril Fancher. "But, love, I..."

He was saved from what he plainly considered an intolerable task by the arrival of the police. They came, two strong, in blue uniforms and brass buttons, with revolvers on their hips, their faces stern and inimical. And between them, firmly held by either arm, her cheeks as red as fire, marched Polly Lawson.

"Polly!" cried Mary weakly. "What on earth?"

Polly made a little grimace, although her lips were trembling. "I'm under arrest, Auntie, all but the handcuffs. Isn't that funny?" She tried to laugh, but she could not quite make it, and behind me Howard groaned and then stepped quickly forward.

"What kind of farce are you staging?" he demanded. "You can't think that Miss Lawson had anything to do with this hideous affair."

The first policeman shrugged his shoulders. "We're just cops, mister. We ain't hired to think. The chief of the homicide squad will be along in a few minutes. He's the guy who does the brain-work. All that's expected of us is to line up the suspects. The inspector will take you apart himself and see what makes you tick."

"Suspects!" snorted Ella. "Of all the tommyrot!"

"Yes 'm," murmured the second policeman in a bored voice.

"You watch the stiff, Sweeney," said his companion wearily.

"Don't let nobody touch nothing in that suite. I'll round up the rest of the crowd in the parlour. Tell the inspector I and they will be there when he wants them."

"You can't do that," protested Dan Mosby. "My wife and I don't even know the dead man's name."

"On your way, buddy," said the officer. "You too, lady," he

added to Ella, who snorted again.

He had not relinquished his hold on Polly's arm. Howard deliberately planted himself in the way, his face dark with anger.

"I insist you turn that young lady loose," he said fiercely. "She cannot possibly, even in your dumb minds, be associated with this."

"Oh yeah?" murmured the cop. "I may be dumb, mister, but not dumb enough maybe." He grinned sardonically. "Your girlfriend may not have no connection with this murder, but just the same the inspector will want to ask her lots a questions."

"Questions?" repeated Howard with a scowl.

The officer grinned again. "About how come we caught her, when we drove up, trying to get away down the alley with a bloody knife."

There was a terrible silence in which none of us seemed able to move or speak.

The officer produced something from his pocket, wrapped in a stained handkerchief. "Ever see this before?" he asked.

Howard's face set like marble, I smothered a groan, and behind me Mary Lawson gasped as if the breath had been knocked out of her. Polly flashed her a tremulous smile.

"Naturally they've all seen it," she said, trying again to laugh and failing miserably. "It's the ivory-handled paper knife from Aunt Mary's desk set. Tell them, darling, how it was stolen from our sitting room sometime this afternoon."

With a face so ghastly I shuddered, Mary Lawson tried to speak, only no sound came from her colourless lips, no sound at all.

"Oh yeah?" murmured the policeman again.

6

I have said the parlour at the Richelieu was a dismal place. It was, even before that April night when the police herded us in like bewildered cattle among the heavy black-walnut sofas and chairs with their dingy green velour covers to match the dark-green carpet.

The policeman who had brought us downstairs was soon joined by the one called Sweeney. It appeared that the inspector had arrived and taken charge of my suite and its gruesome occupant.

Sweeney and his companion, Hankins, contented themselves with seeing that we all stayed put with no opportunity for private conversation.

Not that any of us felt up to talking very much, although we did tend to drift into groups with some attempt at speech in careful undertones.

"Just take it easy, folks, and no whispering," advised one or the other policeman occasionally. "The inspector will want to be in on conferences, if any."

"How long does he expect us to stay cooped up here like-like geese in a pen?" demanded Dan Mosby furiously.

The officer shrugged his shoulders. "The inspector's busy. Fingerprints, flashlight pictures, all that."

"I suppose this is the police's idea of being clever," said Howard hotly. "Part of the third degree, leaving us to stew in our own juice till he gets good and ready to put on his act."

Stephen Lansing smiled. "We might as well make the best of it since here we are," he said and strolled over to where Kathleen Adair was hovering solicitously above her mother's chair.

The girl turned her back on him. "My mother isn't well," she told the first policeman. "She should be in bed."

"I'm all right, darling," murmured Mrs Adair, though she looked terrible.

Mary Lawson put her hand on her niece's shoulder. "Someone must have stolen the knife," she faltered.

"Oh sure," said Polly with a bright unsteady smile.

Howard cleared his throat nervously. "Of course, someone stole the knife," he said.

Hilda Anthony smiled unpleasantly. "Naturally! Even an amateur murderess is too smart these days to be caught red handed with the deadly weapon."

Polly glanced down at her small chubby hands and shivered convulsively. Wincing, Howard moved closer to her and glared at the Anthony woman. Ella Trotter clutched at my sleeve.

"There-there are stains on Polly's palm," she whispered in a faint voice.

I gulped and nodded. Neither of us could bear to look at Mary, who stood over by the window, staring blindly at the dark office building next door, her fingers twisting and turning over each other as if it were her hands that bore that terrible stain.

"It seems to me we should be on the scene, Sophie, looking after things," murmured Cyril Fancher, plucking at his underlip.

"No telling what's happening to the hotel."

Sophie sighed. "The police have their own ideas, love," she said soothingly. "We ought to thank goodness they were willing to let Pinky and Clarence carry on as usual."

Stephen Lansing stooped and picked up something off the floor. "You dropped your bracelet, Mrs Adair," he murmured.

The Adair girl pushed his hand away with a swift angry gesture. "That isn't Mother's," she said.

"It's mine!" cried Ella Trotter in a startled voice.

Stephen Lansing came across the room, dangling the glittering bauble on his middle finger. "It's a good thing I heard it click when it hit the floor," he said. "Someone might have stepped on it."

"But I haven't had the bracelet on in weeks," protested Ella.

"It's in my jewellery box – or I'd have sworn it was."

"Nonsense!" I said irritably. "Your memory is never reliable, Ella, except at the bridge table."

"Says you," snapped Ella, who has a regrettable weakness for what she calls smart cracks.

"My head aches," wailed Lottie Mosby suddenly. "I think I'm going to be ill. Oh, Dan!" She caught at his hand, and he put his arm about her.

His eyes were still bloodshot, but he looked sober, soberer than I had seen him in months. "Steady, honey," he said quite tenderly. "It's a rotten shame, but I'll take care of you. Don't you worry."

"Oh, Dan!" she wailed again, staring up at him as if she had had a glimpse of Paradise Lost.

Stephen Lansing offered the Anthony woman a cigarette which she accepted with a wry grin. "Too bad," murmured she, "that our late date was interrupted."

I saw both Polly and Kathleen Adair stiffen, but it was toward Kathleen the Lansing man looked, and at the expression on her face he winced.

"Isn't it?" he drawled, smiling at Hilda Anthony. "But there's always another night."

She shivered and looked over her shoulder. "I wonder," she said thoughtfully.

We waited almost two hours before the inspector deigned to transfer his attention to the parlour. I do not know exactly what I expected the chief of the Homicide Bureau to look like, but I was not prepared for the dapper young man in the smart checked suit.

He wore a blue foulard tie to match his eyes and he had round cheeks as smooth as a girl's and a cleft chin. He reminded me of a juvenile male lead in a stock company.

"Inspector Bunyan," he announced himself, surveying us all

pleasantly. "Sorry to have kept you waiting."

"I'll bet," muttered Howard.

Inspector Homer Bunyan, having taken his time about arriving, also took it about proceeding to action. He pre-empted the large library table in a corner which commanded the room, sat himself down on a straight chair, produced a fountain pen and a neat leather notebook, leafed through some pages which he had already filled, and finally allowed his ingenuous blue eyes to travel slowly over every face in the room.

"Get on with it, can't you?" growled Dan Mosby.

"Hang onto yourself," Howard advised him. "That's what he's trying to do, wear us down."

Inspector Bunyan regarded him leisurely. "Am I to assume that you have something to conceal, Mr-er-"

"Warren," snapped Howard. "And if I have anything to conceal, it's up to you to find it out."

Inspector Bunyan smiled. "Exactly."

Quite suddenly his blue eyes were less ingenuous, his round face shrewd, if not menacing. I never afterward doubted that Inspector Bunyan was a force, however belied by his appearance.

When he turned his gaze on me it was precisely as though it were a gimlet boring into my conscience. To my shame, I admit that my hands tightened on the edge of my chair and for a moment my mouth went terribly dry.

"Can you advance any theory – Miss Adams, isn't it? – Why this man should have come to his death in your apartment?" he asked.

I swallowed hard. "None whatever."

"You were not acquainted with him?" He continued to look at me. I had a feeling he was turning my thoughts inside out. It infuriated me to have my face colour painfully.

Pursing his lips, Inspector Bunyan hunted for a certain page in his notebook and added something to it with what struck me as offensive gusto.

He then transferred his attention to Sophie. It was some sat-isfaction to my self-respect to see that Sophie's plump face also turned a mottled red under his scrutiny and she appeared sud-denly far from happy on the love seat which she was occupying with her husband.

Inspector Bunyan referred to another page in his notebook. "You are the proprietor of the Richelieu?"

Sophie inclined her head, and Cyril, catching the inspector's eye, wriggled uncomfortably and then looked quickly away, his pale eyebrows twitching like the feelers of a caterpillar.

"What do you know about the late James Reid, of New Orleans?" demanded the inspector.

"Nothing," said Sophie.

"Except he registered here a week ago tomorrow," supple-mented Cyril, as if he were trying to curry favour with the author-ities by being helpful.

The inspector once more consulted his notes. I realized then that he had by no means been idle while we were waiting for him.

Each of us had our special dossier in that neat black notebook which we were all to come to dread before we finished with Inspector Bunyan.

"You never saw him before he registered here at the hotel?" asked the inspector.

"Never!" said Cyril with undisguised fervour.

The inspector frowned. "But you did tell one of your employ-ees, Mr Fancher, that the man never set foot in New Orleans."

Cyril gave a sickly smile. "He thought Canal Street has boats on it, like Venice."

"I see," murmured the inspector, making a series of minute hieroglyphics on Cyril's page.

Sophie swiftly came to his defence. "If we were accused of mur-dering someone every time we remarked upon a guest's conduct, we'd keep you busy, Inspector," she said dryly.

"I don't doubt it," murmured Ella Trotter with a sour smile.

Sophie bridled. "We don't gossip about our guests without cause, Mrs Trotter."

"I hope we can depend on that," said Ella, determined on the last word.

The inspector again allowed his gaze to rest pleasantly on one of us, then the other. "Some of you knew the dead man," he said in a voice that permitted no contradiction. When no one spoke, he went on softly, "Some of you knew all about him, why he was here, where he came from, and what brought him."

Still nobody spoke.

"It would save a great deal of unnecessary inconvenience if those who have any information about James Reid would voluntarily give it to the police. Rest assured" – his voice grew silkier – "before we're done we'll get it."

"The velvet hand in the iron glove," misquoted Howard in his most sarcastic manner.

The inspector smiled. "Did you know James Reid, Mr Warren?"

"No."

"Yet you were on the fourth floor between seven-thirty and eight tonight."

Howard grinned defiantly. "Was I?"

The inspector glanced at Lottie Mosby, who instinctively drew closer within the circle of her husband's arm. "Mrs-ah-Mosby," pursued the inspector, "were you acquainted with the late Mr Reid?"

"Of course she wasn't," growled Dan Mosby.

The inspector made a little gesture toward Lottie. "Please speak for yourself."

"No! I didn't know him!" she gasped.

"Are you sure?"

"Listen here," exploded young Mosby, "you can't bully my

wife. I won't stand for it."

Apparently he spoke to thin air. "You say you didn't know James Reid, Mrs Mosby. Yet you left a note in his box at the desk shortly before six tonight," said the inspector.

"I didn't! I didn't!" Lottie buried her face on her husband's shoulder, and he glared about him like a baited bull.

"That's a lie!" he cried. "I don't care who told you!"

"And where, Mr Mosby," purred the inspector, "were you between seven-thirty and eight tonight?"

"In the lobby, reading the paper."

"Except for ten minutes when you sneaked off up the stairs."

"That's a lie too."

The inspector, without debating the point, passed on to Kathleen Adair and her mother. "Perhaps you ladies are willing to admit to an acquaintance with the unfortunate Mr Reid?"

"No, of course not. Why should we?" asked the girl.

"He was seen this morning emerging from your room."

Kathleen Adair went white. I expected little Mrs Adair to faint again, but she merely stared at the inspector like a small bird charmed by a snake.

"If that man was in our room, we know nothing about it," cried the girl passionately. "We were downstairs in the lobby all morning. We can prove it by Miss Adams."

The inspector once more treated me to the gimlet of his eyes.

"You are quite sure you can shed no light on the man who was foully murdered in your suite tonight, Miss Adams? After all, something took him there," murmured Inspector Bunyan.

"I have already told you I did not know Mr Reid," I said with all the hauteur I could muster, which is, as a rule, no laughing matter, though in this case it made little, if any, impression.

"So you have," mused the inspector. "Nevertheless, he was familiar enough with you to return to you on a certain occasion one of your more or less intimate possessions."

It was my turn to stare helplessly at the inspector. "You mean my-my..."

I found it difficult to continue, and the inspector smiled at me gently. "Do you usually carry your spectacle case with you, Miss Adams?"

"No."

"In fact, almost never. Right?"

"Right," I said with a feeble grimace.

"Isn't it a trifle peculiar that this man, of whom you profess to know nothing, should have recognized a spectacle case which rarely, if ever, leaves your bedroom?"

I gave him a withering glance. "If you are trying to insinuate something scandalous, Inspector Bunyan, please allow me to tell you that my life is an open book."

"No wonder she's a disappointed old maid," said Hilda Anthony.

The inspector frowned and looked for the first time a little nettled, but the Anthony woman merely smiled mockingly when he surveyed her with mingled resentment and admiration.

"If it's my turn, Inspector," she said blithely, "I did not know the murdered man. I never spoke to him or he to me, and while the employees in this house are a bunch of snooping busybodies, I defy any of them to tell you the contrary."

"No," said the inspector with what I took for regret, "no one has said anything of the kind about you, Mrs-er-Anthony."

I sniffed. "But James Reid was watching her from the stairs while we were at dinner tonight."

She grinned at me. "Men always watch a pretty woman, Miss Adams, though of course you wouldn't know about that."

The inspector hastily consulted his notebook, a little as though he needed something to distract his attention from the Anthony's opulent curves. Apparently he came up with Stephen Lansing's name.

"You are a salesman, I believe, of cosmetics," he murmured.

Stephen laughed. "Guilty."

"Did you know the unlamented Mr Reid?"

"Nope."

"Positive?"

"Positive!"

The inspector made a little drawing on the side of the notebook.

"You were in the Sally Ray Beauty Shop from four to five this afternoon, Mr Lansing, demonstrating a new permanent-wave pad?"

Stephen Lansing's eyes narrowed. "Yep."

"At five minutes to five a man in the Sally Ray Shop called this hotel and got in touch with 511, the room occupied by Mr Reid, of New Orleans."

"And so?" murmured Stephen Lansing with a chuckle that rang anything except true to my ears.

"Did you telephone to Mr Reid this afternoon?"

"Nope."

The inspector sighed, slowly riffled through the pages of his notebook, and asked, "None of you cares to amend your statement? It will in the long run save you as well as myself a great deal of useless difficulty if you speak the truth, here and now, freely and without reservation."

No one said anything. The inspector sighed again and glanced lingeringly from Mary Lawson's drawn white face to her niece's bright twisted smile.

"It was the knife from your desk set, Mrs Lawson," he said very quietly.

Mary all but wrung her hands. "I haven't killed anyone!"

"And I didn't even know who was killed until I was dragged upstairs," Polly cried.

The inspector pursed his lips. "Yet you tried to run away with the weapon, Miss Lawson."

She was trembling. "Someone threw it out the window. I was on the sidewalk, waiting for Mr Lansing to return. All at once something clattered at my feet. It was – it was –"

"The knife from your aunt's desk set?"

"And there was blood on it. I got some on my hand. Then I heard the police siren and I-I lost my head and ran."

"Ah!" murmured the inspector. He waited a minute. "Can you prove you did not follow Mr Lansing back into the hotel, Miss Lawson?"

Polly's teeth were chattering. "Pinky was at the desk. He would have seen me."

"Mr Dodge says that at about a quarter of eight he was in the telephone booth, taking a long-distance call from Memphis, asking for a room reservation. He cannot swear who passed through the lobby at that time."

"But there were others in the lobby," cried Polly. "Miss Adams for one."

"I should certainly have seen Miss Lawson had she re-entered the hotel," I said indignantly.

The inspector regarded me thoughtfully. "Did you see Mr Mosby when he cautiously circled around you and made his way upstairs, Miss Adams?"

"No," I was forced to admit.

"Did you see Mr Stephen Lansing when he re-entered the hotel?"

"N-no."

The inspector shrugged his shoulders significantly, and Hilda Anthony laughed. "How it must gripe Miss Adams not to have eyes in the back of her head," she said.

"As a matter of fact," remarked the inspector wearily, "not one of you has an ironclad alibi from seven-thirty to eight, which is as near as we can fix the hour of the crime."

"How absurd!" I protested. "I was in the lobby continuously

from dinner until I discovered the body."

"Provided he was dead when you discovered him," murmured the inspector. "There seems to be quite a hiatus between the time you went up in the elevator and the time your screams aroused the hotel, Miss Adams."

"I-I was shocked, unable to scream, unable to do anything for some minutes," I stammered.

"Who wouldn't have been?" demanded Ella angrily.

The inspector made some little dots on his notebook. "How long would you say it was, Miss Adams, after you found the lifeless body of Mr James Reid swinging from the chandelier in your suite before you remembered to scream?"

"I don't know," I said shortly. "I had other things to think of than preparing a timetable for the police."

Again the inspector submitted us all to a prolonged scrutiny.

"Where were you, Mrs Mosby, during the fatal hour?" he asked softly.

"In my room."

"Alone?"

"Yes."

"On the fourth floor?"

"Y-yes."

"And you, Mrs Lawson?"

"Alone in my room."

"Also on the fourth floor?"

"Yes."

The inspector shook his head. "No," he said, "none of you who were present in the house at the time of the crime has an alibi for the suspect interval. That is why I had you detained, why I am compelled to regard each of you with more or less suspicion."

"Don't be a fool!" cried Dan Mosby furiously. "We didn't even know the man. Permanent guests in a hotel like this never pay any attention to transients. They're here today, gone tomorrow.

Why pick on us because a man happens to get knocked off in a public house in which we happen to live? Ten to one you'll find he was followed here by somebody who had good cause to kill him. Maybe he's a gangster or a sneak thief."

"No," said Inspector Bunyan, "he wasn't followed here nor is he a gangster or a sneak thief, and he didn't just happen to get knocked off. The man was coldly and brutally murdered by" – he paused impressively – "someone who has been living in this hotel for quite a while."

"Then the police know who he is?" I gasped.

Inspector Bunyan glanced at me curiously. "Don't you, Miss Adams?"

"What do you mean, by someone who has been living here quite a while?" interrupted Sophie tremulously. She tried to draw herself up. "We do not have murderers as house guests, Inspector."

He frowned. "The man was a private detective, Mrs Fancher."

"Detective!" she whispered.

Across the room Kathleen Adair put her hand over her mother's lips, and Lottie Mosby swayed.

"Yes," said Inspector Bunyan, "the late James Reid was head of a well-known private detective agency in St. Louis. I identified him at a glance."

"But what was he doing here?" I asked in a voice I hardly recognized.

The inspector picked up a yellow slip of paper off the table. "As soon as I recognised Reid, I telegraphed his office. This is their reply," he said.

He cleared his throat and then read in a clear concise voice the following telegram:

"REID ENGAGED BY UNKNOWN CLIENT FOR SECRET INVESTIGATION AT RICHELIEU HOTEL STOP CLIENT INSISTED ON KEEPING IN THE DARK STOP REID USUALLY WAITED WEEK TO HAND IN HIS REPORT STOP WE DON'T KNOW A THING EXCEPT

THEY SEEM TO HAVE GOT HIM FIRST STOP."

"Secret investigation!" gasped Sophie.

The inspector smiled wryly. "Reid's speciality was shadowing people, uncovering evidence for divorce suits and so forth. It's been suggested he was not above doing a little left-handed blackmailing on his own account."

"Blackmail!" I repeated weakly.

None of the others said anything. They were staring at the inspector or at the floor, their faces blanched, their eyes avoiding everyone else's.

"If you mean there has been anything going on in this hotel to justify blackmail, I don't believe it!" cried Sophie Scott.

"Don't you?" murmured Inspector Bunyan.

"You think James Reid stumbled onto somebody's guilty secret and was killed to shut his mouth," surmised Stephen Lansing shrewdly.

The inspector shrugged his shoulders.

"A private investigator comes high, Mr Lansing. Reid was not working for nothing. If it was worth important money to his unknown client to find out something, it was probably worth more to another person to prevent the truth from coming out."

"Oh!" cried Kathleen Adair. "Surely no one would kill a man to-to..." She choked, could not go on.

"Somebody did kill James Reid," said the inspector grimly.

"But he-he-"

"He was working in the dark, remember," murmured Inspector Bunyan.

"Who brought him here?" demanded Sophie angrily.

"One of you knows," said the inspector softly.

"You're screwy!" growled Dan Mosby. "If you want to find the guilty party, look among the transient guests."

"No transient guest is responsible for the man's presence in the hotel," said the inspector.

"How can you be sure?" I asked with a sniff.

"I wired Reid's agency a second time," he said with a shrug.

"I'll read you their answer:

"REID FIRST APPROACHED A MONTH AGO BY ANONYMOUS CLIENT STOP BUSY ON ANOTHER CASE AT THE TIME STOP ACCEPTED HANDSOME RETAINER AND AGREED TO REPORT ON THE JOB LAST WEEK STOP."

"Oh dear," wailed little Mrs Adair, "and we came here in search of peace."

The inspector smiled pleasantly, but his eyes narrowed. "That's why I'm advising all of you to tell everything you know," he said. "Murder, like measles, is highly infectious. Or should I say that when you begin to stir muddy water a number of ugly citizens rise to the surface?"

Stephen Lansing grinned wryly and said, "Taking Mr James Reid for an example, Inspector, it doesn't look as if it is very healthy to probe for other people's secrets in the Richelieu Hotel."

The inspector's blue eyes regarded him reflectively. "Am I to construe that as a warning, Mr Lansing?"

Stephen Lansing swept us all a mocking smile. "It might be well for all of us to bear it in mind," he said lightly.

"Murderers and blackmailers!" I groaned. "It sounds like a nice mess."

"It is," said Inspector Bunyan gravely.

And so it proved before we were done with it.

7

At least the police made no arrests that night. "I suppose they imagine if they give us rope enough we'll accommodate them by hanging ourselves," commented Howard bitterly.

Those of us who had been in the hotel between seven-thirty and eight were warned not to leave town until after the inquest, the date for which had not been set, and before he left the inspector sealed my suite. For an indefinite period – or so he said. I felt relieved. I was never to be in the place again, especially in the dark, without seeing that grisly, swaying figure, attached by its own suspenders to my chandelier.

"We can move you into the same rooms on the third, Adelaide," said Sophie ungraciously, "only I suppose you'll insist on having them redecorated first."

"Since living in this house, I've grown used to dwelling in the midst of my own dirt," I said coldly, "but I have a decided antipathy against inheriting someone else's."

"Then we'll just have to make what shift we can for a few days," said Sophie wearily.

"I suppose so," I murmured, none too graciously myself.

In the end it was decided to leave the bulk of my things where they were until the decorators had finished with my new quarters. Fortunately my wearing apparel and toilet articles were in the bedroom. Accompanied by Sweeney, whom the inspector had left in charge, and by Clarence, who kept rolling his eyes toward the closed door into the sitting room, I collected enough of my belongings to tide me over the ensuing week, hurriedly packed them in a couple of travelling bags, and, again accompanied by Clarence, went upstairs to the small bedroom on the top floor which had been assigned to my use.

The fifth floor, being next to the roof, is the least desirable in the hotel in the summer. It is commonly reserved for tourists or such of the employees as live in the house. However, the weather does not as a rule turn uncomfortably hot in our section of the country before May, and so I had made no objection to being temporarily installed on the attic floor. Nevertheless, it did give me something of a turn to discover that my room was 511, until recently occupied by Mr James Reid, not of New Orleans.

"Ain't nuff money in the mint to git me to sleep in here," said Clarence, shaking his smooth oiled head and edging hastily toward the door.

"How silly!" I said curtly. "The man's dead. He's done all the harm he can do in this world."

"Yes 'm, I hope so," said Clarence dubiously.

The police had already removed the shabby black Gladstone, the sole piece of baggage which the murdered man brought to the hotel. They had packed into it everything he left scattered about the room and taken it down to headquarters, and Sophie had sent a maid up to put the place in order. It looked as bare and impersonal as hotel rooms usually look when prepared for transient guests.

There was not even a scrap of paper in the wastebasket to remind one who had slept there last. However, I carefully examined the closet and the small shower bath and, for the first time in my life, got down, regardless of my stiff knee, and looked under the bed, finding exactly nothing for my pains. Apparently the police had gone over the ground with a broom and a magnifying glass and swept it clean of every trace of its late occupant.

"Don't be an idiot!" I scolded myself. "There isn't anything to feel creepy about."

Just the same I had an unpleasant clammy sensation up and down my spine as I unpacked and prepared for bed. I caught myself doing a number of unnecessary things to prolong the moment when I should have to turn out the light, such as washing out my princess slip and a pair of hose. There was nowhere in the tiny bathroom to hang so large a garment as my slip, but my old standby, the fire escape, was near at hand, though now I was on the opposite side of it. When I leaned out to drape the slip on the iron railing I was gratified to find that there was a full moon.

"At least it won't be pitch dark," I told myself and flipped off the bed light beside me.

The moon made quite a brave showing, shining in my window, and when I stretched out on the somewhat humpy bed I discovered that I was aching from fatigue. Every nerve in my body appeared to have been screwed up like a wire. However, I was never wider awake. I did not want to lie there, seeing pictures in the pale ghostly light of the moon. Only I was not able to close my eyes.

"Must be going into your dotage," I scolded myself.

I heard the town clock, three blocks away on the county courthouse, toll solemnly for midnight, then one and two. I knew I should be good for nothing the next day. Loss of sleep always makes me cross. I think sometimes that is where I acquired my crusty disposition, during those long lonely years when Father was ill and I sat up beside him night after night. It was difficult the next day not to snap at people from sheer fatigue, and those things get to be a habit, one you cannot break through later – or so I have found.

It must have been close to three when I finally dozed off. The last thing I remember thinking was that the moon was slowly passing over to the other side of the heavens, leaving me in a darkness which was growing blacker and blacker. The next thing I knew I was sitting straight up in bed, staring at the pale oblong which was the open window in the inky darkness.

There was not a sound. It was as if the whole world, like myself, was holding its breath in an agony of apprehension. Yet I knew someone was there, near me, only a few feet away, some unknown presence, waiting for my next move.

"Who is it?" I cannot describe the horror with which I produced that choked, almost unintelligible sound nor the panic which electrified me when I heard it. Whoever was in the room could no longer doubt that I was aroused. To this day I do not understand why I did not scream. Perhaps instinctively I knew it would be my last act.

"What do you want?" I quavered. "For God's sake, get it and go."

How I knew that it was the murderer, his hands already irrevocably stained with human blood, I cannot tell. Certainly I never doubted that I was at that moment nearer death than I had ever been in my life.

"Please, go," I gasped again.

There was a rustle, so close I could have reached out and touched it, then a whisper of movement, and a faint creak as the door into the corridor swung softly open. A shadow passed between me and the dim glow from the ceiling globe in the hall, the door swung noiselessly to, and I was out of bed, banging on the wall with the telephone receiver and screaming into the transmitter.

I admit I was excited but I did not, as I have repeatedly informed the people who waxed facetious about it, bite myself in the foot. I simply, in my vault from the bed, dropped the two prominent false teeth which I wear in the front of my mouth on a pivot and stepped on them, the result being a small but painful stone bruise just below my big toe. Naturally I limped for several days.

I think I must have been shrieking into the telephone for several minutes before Pinky Dodge managed to break in on me. "What is it, Miss Adams?" he cried tremulously. "For God's sake, what's happened?"

"Murduth! Fieves! Helpth! Helpth!" I continued to shriek.

I have neglected to state that the absence of my pivot bridge leaves a wide gap in the exact centre of my upper teeth through which my breath whistles in a highly irritating manner, distorting my speech so it is not surprising that Pinky had some difficulty understanding me. As a matter of fact, he was still pleading with me to make myself clearer when Mr Stephen Lansing, in a fascinating black brocaded dressing gown, bounded lightly through my window from the fire escape, resembling nothing so much, it seemed to me, as a sleek and handsome tomcat on the prowl.

"Seen another mouse, Miss Adams?" he demanded with that sardonic smile I was learning to associate with him.

His suave insolence had one recommendation. It never failed to restore my sanity. I became aware of my bare feet, especially my bunions, and of the row of false curls which it is my habit to pin across my forehead when I am dressed to receive people. I was by then sufficiently collected to shove them off the top of the dresser into a drawer and button my purple corduroy bathrobe about me before I answered.

"Thome one wath in my room," I said coldly.

"Again?" he murmured and gave me an exasperating grin. "It's getting to be a habit."

"He wenth out the door when I waked upth and spokth to him."

He eyed me thoughtfully. "Why the baby lisp? Or is that one of the wiles with which you lure your unsuspecting victims to your room, I mean den?"

"Young manth," I said, limping over to the bed and inspecting the floor beside it, "even in my youth I wath not possessed of lure."

"You wrong yourself," said Mr Stephen Lansing gallantly and then added in a sharper tone, "What on earth are you looking for?"

"My falseth teeth, if you musth know," I said bitterly.

He laughed but proceeded to get down on all fours and join in the search. "Is this ith?" he asked. "Great guns, you've got me doing it!"

He handed me the bridge which I popped into my mouth, but he did not at once get up. He was fingering what appeared to be a narrow slit in the carpet. We were, as it happened, in the anomalous position of Mr Stephen Lansing kneeling at my bare feet when, summoned by Pinkney Dodge, the policeman Sweeney burst into the room followed at a wary distance by an ashen-faced and trembling Clarence.

"As I live and breathe!" exclaimed Patrolman Sweeney disgustedly.

"A scene from Romeo and Juliet! And I thought someone was being murdered."

"It's no fault of the police I wasn't," I snapped, while Stephen Lansing, dusting his hands delicately, rose to his feet, his smile as imperturbable as ever.

"Attagirl!" he murmured to me sotto voce. "The best defence is a stout offensive."

I transfixed Sweeney with my most eaglish look. "Were you or were you not left here on guard?" I demanded.

He spread his hands helplessly. "I'm just one lone man, lady. I can be spread over so much territory and no more."

"And that's the sort of service we taxpayers receive for our money," I said bitterly.

"Spill it to the inspector when he comes," muttered Sweeney.

"He'll probably put my feet to the fire for hauling him out of his bed in the middle of the night. As if," he said, giving me a very unfriendly look, "as if I can help it if a maiden lady has a nightmare and thinks she's being killed or something."

"I assure you I am not subject to nightmares," I said haughtily.

I also assured the inspector of that fact when he arrived fifteen minutes later, only to have him shake his head.

"You can't be blamed for being over-imaginative, Miss Adams, after your shocking experience earlier in the evening," he said politely.

I was piqued. "There was someone in the room," I insisted. "I can't be too emphatic about it."

"You admit yourself that nothing's been disturbed," murmured the inspector.

I nodded and admitted it.

"If anyone was here, what was he after?" asked Inspector

Bunyan.

"Have you been informed, Inspector, that this room was formerly occupied by the late James Reid?" inquired Stephen Lansing, who had lingered with Sweeney and Pinky Dodge, the latter having put Clarence in charge of both the elevator and the switchboard, there being little, if any, demand for either at three-thirty in the morning.

The inspector frowned. "If you mean the murderer was looking for something his victim secreted here, he was wasting his time. My men went through this room with a fine-tooth comb."

"Looking for incriminating documents?" drawled Stephen Lansing sarcastically.

"Looking for anything incriminating," said the inspector and sighed.

"Without success?" The inspector shook his head wearily. "If James Reid got the evidence he was after, he wrote it in his head."

"Maybe the-er-murderer didn't know the police had been through this room," contributed Pinky.

I glanced at him in some surprise. It was unusual for the down-trodden little night clerk to vouchsafe an opinion of his own, but I suppose there is an amateur detective dormant in all of us. I confess I felt the faint stirring of such an instinct myself.

"He was undoubtedly after the papers!" I cried excitedly.

Stephen Lansing smiled. "Them good old melodramatic papers, so dear to fiction!"

The inspector did not look amused. "It is possible," he said slowly, "we are approaching this whole affair from the wrong angle.

If somebody really broke into this room tonight, there is a chance that James Reid merely stumbled into a trap set for another person.

"What do you mean?" asked Stephen Lansing, knitting his brows.

It made me nervous the way the inspector looked at me. "It's a striking coincidence that this alleged second act of violence should also have centred in Miss Adams' locality," he said.

The hair on the back of my neck crawled. "You can't believe that I – that James Reid was killed – that he was mistaken for me?" I asked faintly. "Or-or are you suggesting that I am his murderer?"

"Steady," whispered Stephen Lansing at my ear. "Don't let him get your goat."

"After all," murmured the inspector, "it's never been explained how the man got into your suite, Miss Adams. I believe you told Sweeney that both outside doors to the suite were locked when you entered it."

"So was that one when I went to bed," I remarked tartly, pointing to the door into the corridor.

"Being a private detective, Inspector," murmured Stephen Lansing, "mightn't Mr James Reid have been expected to provide himself with a skeleton key? They are supposed, or aren't they, to go hand in hand with pussyfooting investigators."

Inspector Bunyan languidly smothered a yawn. "My men searched the corpse for such a key, Mr Lansing."

"Again without success?"

The inspector for the first time showed traces of irritation. "The unanimity with which all our clews have come to nothing in this case, Mr Lansing, is a strain on the official mind."

"Skeleton keys, fiddlesticks!" I exclaimed disdainfully. "Nobody needs such a thing to enter either this room or my suite downstairs. Any fairly active person could climb in by way of the fire escape, as Mr Lansing did just now when I yelled for help."

Stephen Lansing groaned.

"I wondered," murmured the inspector softly, "how you happened to be on the scene so soon, Mr Lansing. Before my man Sweeney or anybody else arrived, I believe."

"Yep," said Stephen cheerfully, "as soon as I heard Miss Adams' siren call I clambered right up the old fire escape to the rescue, pronto – or even quicker than that."

"How fortunate," said the inspector, eyeing him curiously, "that you were already wearing your street shoes."

Stephen coloured. "I'm a bit of a night owl, Inspector. I hadn't, as you have also noticed no doubt, removed anything except my coat."

"Yes," said the inspector, "I had noticed."

"It was a mere trifle to slide into my dressing robe."

"I dare say," murmured the inspector. "Naturally, from our viewpoint, it's regrettable that in your precipitate ascent you have probably destroyed all traces of whoever preceded you up the fire escape."

"Isn't it?" drawled Stephen with a broad grin.

The inspector strolled over to the window and stared, rather hopelessly, I thought, at the rusty iron landing of the fire escape.

"The proper entrance is from the corridor," he observed, "but as you say, Miss Adams, any fairly active person could swing across to this window."

With pardonable exasperation I noticed that my slip was no longer neatly draped on the railing. It had fallen down and apparently been trod on once, if not often.

"What is that thing? A tent?" inquired Inspector Bunyan, peering over my shoulder.

"That," I replied with cold dignity, "is a piece of my wardrobe."

"Miss Adams uses the railing of the fire escape at her convenience as a-er-washing line, Inspector," Stephen explained.

"Up to now," I remarked bitterly, "we have not needed a traffic officer on the fire escape."

I made several futile efforts to reach the slip, but I could not quite make it. By leaning far out and practically standing on his head, Stephen Lansing recovered the missing article.

"It does look a little as if a herd of cattle had been driven over it," he acknowledged.

The inspector's eyes lighted. "Any footprints?" I wadded the slip up in my hands. "What do you think it is, a desert waste? Certainly there are no footprints."

The inspector scowled. "Another clew gone to glory!" he muttered.

Stephen Lansing laughed, and the inspector looked from one to the other of us with a gleam in his eyes which I did not fancy.

"There is, as you may or may not know, a legal penalty for suppressing evidence," he said in the silky voice which I was learning boded no good. "From-ah-six month's to-ah-three years in the penitentiary."

"I think," Said Stephen Lansing impudently, "you'd better turn your petticoat over to the inspector, Adelaide. He seems to have ideas about it."

I nearly dropped the object under dispute. "Adelaide!" I snorted.

He grinned. "Partners in crime should dispense with formality, don't you think, Adelaide?"

"I suppose," continued the inspector softly, "you didn't lose your petticoat climbing up and down the fire escape, Miss Adams?"

I glared at him. "Evidently you have no sisters, Inspector. This is not a petticoat; it is a slip with shoulder straps. One cannot lose it without disrobing, and I assure you I neither tonight nor any other night have undressed either partially or completely on the fire escape."

Stephen Lansing chuckled. "I wouldn't put it past you, Adelaide, if the occasion demanded it."

The inspector sighed. "Just the same, I think I'll take the slip along to put with the other exhibits in the case."

"Suit yourself," I snapped.

The inspector turned toward the door. "I believe after this, Miss Adams, I'd keep the window next the fire escape locked. In fact, if you don't mind, I'll have Sweeney attend to it immediately."

I put my nose in the air. "Still harping on my being a victim – or is it a murderess – Inspector?" I asked.

"One wonders," he said, lifting his eyebrows.

My face stung. "I haven't a grudge against a soul in the world, Inspector, and there is no one who either loves or hates me enough to kill me. It's been a long time since I've mattered that much to anybody," I said.

"Yes?"

"Yes!" I cried unsteadily.

The inspector shifted the bundle which was my rolled-up slip to his other hand and inquired, "Are you aware, Miss Adams, that when Kathleen Adair and her mother came to this hotel they asked to be put on your floor?"

I stared at him blankly. "The Adairs!"

Beside me Stephen Lansing seemed to freeze in his tracks.

"But I don't know the Adairs," I said weakly. "That is, I never saw or heard of them before they moved into the hotel a month ago."

"Nevertheless, they specifically requested to be placed as near Miss Adelaide Adams' suite as possible. Right, Mr Dodge?"

Pinky flushed. "Yes sir," he said, giving me a flustered glance.

"I can't understand it," I protested.

"Nor I," murmured the inspector. He turned to the door.

"Coming, Mr Lansing?"

"Directly!" sang out Stephen Lansing and then, dropping his voice to a husky whisper, he added fiercely, "For God's sake don't give them away!"

"But –"

"I don't know how they're mixed up in this, only I'd stake my life on the girl."

"Kathleen Adair?"

"Sh!" he warned me.

The inspector had put his head back in at the door. "I found this clinging to your slip, Miss Adams. The clasp seems to have been

stepped on by somebody on the fire escape. I presume it's yours?"
He was eyeing me as a cat eyes a mouse. "Or is it?" He held out
a pin, a large old-fashioned gold-and-black brooch pin such as
women used to wear at the neck of their frocks in my youth.

I do not know how long I stood there staring at the object in the
inspector's hand, while time unrolled its relentless curtains and
I was back in a dew-drenched garden one breathless June night
with passion and duty tearing my heart in two.

From a great distance I heard Stephen Lansing's voice, still
hoarse, almost desperate. "Certainly it's her pin. Isn't it, Adelaide?"

Our eyes met. "Yes," I said at last very slowly, "it's mine."

The inspector's lip curled. "Can you prove it, Miss Adams?"
Stephen Lansing caught his breath, but my voice was steady, perfectly steady.

"Yes, Inspector, I can prove it," I said. "Look on the back. You'll
find engraved there – you'll find engraved there *From Laurie to
Adelaide*."

Stephen Lansing was staring at me incredulously, but the
inspector, who had turned the pin over, sighed.

"Just so," he said and handed the pin to me.

"God love you!" breathed Stephen Lansing and followed the
others from the room, once more his smiling and debonair self.

Alone I stood for a long time, staring at the quaint piece of
jewellery which the inspector had found clinging to my princess
slip. It had been twenty-five years and ten months since I last saw
the pin, almost half my life. A long, long time, I thought, my eyes
blurred with tears. I knew then why the Adair girl from the first
had tugged at my heart, why something about her had at times
given me a spasm of pain.

"Oh, Laurie, Laurie!" I whispered, remembering the way
Kathleen had stared at James Reid in the elevator, as though she
would, if she could, have stricken him dead at her feet.

8

There was a pall over the Richelieu the next morning. People had a strained look about the eyes and a tendency to keep to themselves.

No one showed an inclination to discuss the affair uppermost in all our thoughts, yet it was impossible to ignore it. To Sophie's distress, the police had practically moved in upon us in a body. One was apt to run into a uniform in any of the corridors, to say nothing of certain strange individuals who wandered vaguely about, any one of whom might have been a new transient guest in the hotel but was more likely a plain-clothes man, snooping around to find out what he could.

"This is going to ruin me," cried Sophie tragically. "I've already had a dozen notices from people who intend to move out on the first."

I shrugged my shoulders. "After all, one doesn't exactly court the thought of being murdered in one's bed, to say nothing of not being able to step for fear of treading on the police force."

"The whole's thing's ridiculous!" stormed Sophie. "Can we help it if a private detective chooses to get himself put on the spot in our hotel? No doubt he had scores of enemies. From what I can discover, his reputation smelled to heaven. Not for a minute do I believe our regular guests are mixed up in it."

"According to the inspector..." I began.

"Stuff and nonsense!" snorted Sophie. "All the inspector has to go on is that telegram from the agency, and they could have told him anything. How do we know one of Reid's own crowd didn't follow him down here and kill him? Personally," she declared emphatically, "I think that unknown client business is a stall of the police."

And then she spoiled everything by adding in a strangled whisper, "It was you, wasn't it, Adelaide, who hired that fellow to come to the Richelieu?" I stared at her and I imagine my lips curled.

"No, Sophie," I said, "it wasn't I. But it has occurred to me that there are a number of things you must be anxious to know about your husband, including what he was doing slinking around the fourth floor shortly before eight last night."

"Adelaide!" protested Sophie in a horrified voice. "You can't believe I'd set a private detective onto Cyril!"

"That's the worst of an affair like this," I said wearily. "It turns everybody's hand against everyone else."

"Yes," said Sophie, both her chins quivering, "I suppose we'll end up by suspecting everyone of something, if not murder."

The inspector, in spite of his interrupted night, was on hand bright and early that morning and closeted himself behind closed doors in the parlour. From there he operated after the manner of a spider in a web. That is to say, every so often he extended a long arm in the shape of one of the uniformed policemen and brought in another fly for dissection. Sometimes he detained his victim for only a few minutes, occasionally the unhappy captive was put through a more prolonged grilling, but in every instance the subject came out of the parlour looking as if he had been run through a vacuum cleaner.

"It makes me sick," cried Howard Warren savagely. "He proceeds to accuse you of the most impossible things, and when you deny it he merely smiles cynically and goes on to something else."

I pursed my lips. "He seems to have acquired an astounding amount of information about us all in an incredibly brief time."

Howard glared at Pinkney Dodge, who was slumped down in a chair between the desk and the telephone booth, staring unhappily at the floor, his eyes red-rimmed from loss of sleep. Pinky usually went to bed as soon as he was relieved by Letty Jones at seven in the morning. I supposed, like the rest of us, he was too excited to retire. Now I know he was afraid, hideously, horribly afraid, poor Pinky!

"It isn't difficult to guess where the inspector gets his information with a male old woman camping at the switchboard," said Howard crossly.

Pinky flinched and gave us a pleading, almost tearful look.

"He-he's clever; he-he worms things out of you," he admitted in a shaking voice.

I felt sorry for him; I always had. I could well imagine that Pinkney, who had been successfully browbeaten for years, was no match for the inspector or anyone else with the authority to ask questions and demand an answer.

"No one can blame you, Pinkney, for telling the truth," I said. "The police are entitled to it."

"Thanks, Miss Adelaide," he said gratefully.

Howard flushed. "Pinky has no right to put his own interpretation on things which do not concern him." He again glared at the shrinking night clerk. "What if I did ask Miss Adelaide to take in a movie with me? Maybe it was the first time I ever invited her out, and perhaps I did try to persuade her that she didn't need a coat. That doesn't prove I was trying, for reasons of my own, to keep her from discovering the murder."

"Of course not," I faltered with a sinking feeling at the pit of my stomach.

Pinkney made a little humble gesture. "I didn't say any such thing to the inspector, Mr Warren. I swear it. If-if he put that interpretation on your conversation with Miss Adelaide, it's his own idea."

Howard looked a little ashamed of himself. "All right, all right," he said. "Skip it. Only if I were you, Pinky, I'd not forget that one man has already paid with his life for dabbling in other people's affairs in this house."

Pinky shrank back, and his hands began to tremble. "I don't want to make trouble for anybody and-and I can't afford to get

into trouble. My-my mother... If anything happened to me I don't
know what would become of her."

"Nothing's going to happen to you, Pinkney," I said soothingly,
"or to anybody else, let's hope."

"Yes, Miss Adelaide," stammered Pinky without conviction.

A stocky policeman approached and stood stiffly at attention.

"The inspector would like to see you, Mr Warren, in the
parlour."

"Again!" groaned Howard and, his face set and white, turned
toward the stair, kicking at a chair on his way.

There is no denying all our nerves were on edge that morning.
Being forcibly detained in any one place is in itself sufficient to
make the average person feverishly eager to be elsewhere, and the
inspector had prepared a list which one of his henchmen passed
around. The people on that list were not to leave the house until
further notice. We were, or so it said, to hold ourselves in readiness
for further examination by the police.

"As if we were on the chain gang!" growled Dan Mosby, pacing
the lobby floor.

At least he had not been drinking. For the first time in months
I was able to regard him with something like approval. In his cups
he was undoubtedly a bore. Sober, he struck me as a fairly decent
chap, making allowances for his obvious lack of breeding, which,
as I reflected, was quite probably his parents' fault.

His wife spent the morning, except for a brief trip to the parlour,
huddled in one of the big chairs at the front of the lobby, her small
common little face tragically white and absolutely expressionless
except when now and then her husband paused beside her. It gave
me a pang to see how hard she tried to smile up into his face, and
once when he patted her shoulder she turned and laid her lips
against his hand.

Neither Mary Lawson nor her niece came down to breakfast
that morning. Feeling uneasy, I telephoned up to their room about
ten o'clock. Polly answered in a bright flippant voice, trying to be

giddy about it all, although I was sure she had been crying.

"No, Miss Adelaide, neither of us is ill. We just don't crave food, if you know what I mean. However, after three sessions apiece with the inspector and more to come, or so he hinted, we're having a full morning. Isn't life just one long sweet song?"

Now I could not condone Polly Lawson's behaviour for the past two months, but suspecting her or Mary Lawson of murder was a cat of another odour, and my voice trembled with indignation when I said so.

"The inspector is more of a fool than I took him for," I insisted in conclusion, "if he seriously hopes to involve you and Mary in this sordid business."

To my surprise Polly's bravado abruptly deserted her. "I-I take b-back everything I ever said about you, Miss Adelaide," she faltered. "You may be an old fuss-budget in prosperity, but in adversity you're an angel."

It was a dubious compliment; nevertheless, it touched me. "Thank you, my dear, and I quite understand why you tried to run off with that dratted knife."

"Do you?" she whispered.

"Naturally your first thought was that, innocent as she is, being its owner, the police would be certain to think the knife implicated Mary."

"Yes," said Polly with a little sob.

"I should have done exactly the same thing in your place," I said firmly.

"I bet you would at that," she said and, after hesitating a minute, asked, "Have you seen Howard, Miss Adelaide?"

"The inspector sent for him again a few minutes ago," I said.

"Oh!" she gasped and then added huskily, "Did you say again?"

"Isn't it asinine?" I demanded. "I haven't the slightest doubt that while the police are wasting precious hours, interviewing perfectly innocent people, the murderer is busy successfully covering up his tracks. No wonder the city can't balance its budget."

"I guess so," said Polly in a forlorn voice.

"At least," I went on, "the way Howard championed your cause last night did my heart good. I should be very happy, my dear, to see you two bury the hatchet or whatever it is that has spoiled love's young dream lately."

Polly's voice trembled. "If I only dared!"

She hung up, to conceal her tears I was convinced, not far from tears myself. It has always seemed to me pathetic how often people hurt the ones they love. I did not know why Polly had deliberately wrecked her romance with Howard Warren, but at that moment nothing could have persuaded me that they were not in love with each other.

"Perhaps some good will come of all this yet," I muttered to myself. It seemed to me it would almost be worth it to bridge the breach between Howard and little Polly Lawson.

Needless to say, I was exasperated when about eleven Polly came down to the lobby, painted up like a red Indian, and, ignoring Howard, who eagerly started toward her, made straight for Stephen Lansing, who had for some time ostensibly been absorbed in a punchboard at the desk while guardedly watching Kathleen Adair in the mirror behind the cigar counter.

"Oh, h'lo," Polly sang out, giving him an impudent smile and pretending not to see the look on Howard's face as he turned away.

"Hello yourself," said Stephen Lansing, his wide grin displaying his very white teeth. "It must be telepathy. I've been wishing you or somebody just like you would come along."

"Really?" He caught her arm and turned her toward the entrance to the drugstore. "If one can't leave the premises, one might, don't you think, make merry on a stool built for two."

"And why not?" asked Polly, permitting him to install her in front of the soda fountain where they sat for some time, inhaling Coca-Colas through straws. Each of them, I felt sure, fully aware that they were plainly visible through the glass door into the lobby where Howard Warren sat, scowling ferociously at the cash register, while Kathleen Adair, with a stony look in her brown eyes, hovered about the chair in which she had installed her mother.

Little Mrs Adair looked downright ill that morning. Until then I had thought she was one of those invalids who "enjoy" poor health for the sake of being fussed over and waited upon, but I was compelled to revise my impression of the woman. It seemed to me she had aged overnight, as if all the planes of her small ineffectual face were threatening to cave in. There was fever in the way her irresolute, frail hands kept moving restlessly about, like a crumpled butterfly futilely beating its broken wings.

"Wouldn't you be more comfortable upstairs in bed?" I asked, strolling over to her corner.

She looked up at me, and her eyes were startling. "One feels safer in a crowd," she said in a thin lifeless voice.

I frowned. "Are you afraid?"

"Yes."

"But the man had nothing to do with us. His death is to be regretted, of course. However, if you want my opinion, I think it's all much ado about nothing," I said in a brusque attempt to reassure her, though by no means convinced myself.

She shook her head. "I am psychic. I sense things in advance. And I feel disaster, black disaster, hanging over us all."

"Rubbish!" I cried.

"It won't stop with one death," she whispered, that strange fateful look in her eyes deepening.

The girl glanced at me defiantly and, rising abruptly, went over to the cooler back of the elevator. She returned with a paper cup of water into which she had dropped a small white pellet taken from a glass tube in her purse.

"Drink this, Mother," she said, "and see if you can rest a little before lunch."

"Yes, dear," murmured the older woman like a docile child.

Apparently the pellet was a sedative, for after a time little Mrs Adair leaned back against the pillow which her daughter had placed behind the neat grey head and went quietly to sleep. The corner in which we were sitting was as secluded as it is possible to be in the lobby of the Richelieu Hotel, and I carefully lowered my voice when I leaned forward and turned back the frill on my linen blouse.

"This belongs to you, doesn't it?" I asked Kathleen Adair gently.

Her eyes did not lose their stony expression as she stared at the black-and-gold brooch pinned under my collar, but the cords in her throat jerked once, although she said nothing.

"It was found last night on the fire escape," I went on quietly.

Her face was as white as paper. "I – how could it have been found – there?" she gasped.

In my heart an old wound throbbed unbearably. "You have Room 411, don't you? Directly under the one I am now occupying, the one formerly occupied by-by-"

"Yes," she interrupted, wincing from head to foot.

She drew a long breath. "I remember now," she stammered. "I dropped the pin upon the fire escape yesterday afternoon when I leaned out the window to-to look at the at the sunset."

She must have known from my expression that she had trapped herself. The sunset is hidden from the view of anyone on the fire escape at the Richelieu Hotel by an apartment house across the street. For one long terrible moment we stared into each other's eyes and thought God only knows what thoughts. Then silently she reached out her hand for the brooch.

"I'm sorry," I said. "I'll have to keep it, for a while anyway. You see, I told the inspector the pin is mine."

Her lips quivered. "You did that for-for me?"

"And for the man whose name is engraved on the back."

She made an effort to pull herself together. "I-I don't understand."

"Laurie was your father, and your name isn't Adair."

She gasped. "You are mistaken."

"I gave that pin back to him years ago before he – before we... I suppose later he gave it to your mother."

She shook her head. "I bought it in a pawnshop," she said, openly defying me.

"Oh, my dear, you couldn't have bought Laurie's eyes in a pawnshop, nor his smile," I whispered.

"You are mistaken," she said again.

I put my hand on her arm. "Don't you realize I want to be your friend? I am your friend."

Her eyes were tragic. "I'm sorry," she said. "It's impossible."

I stared at her. "There isn't anything on earth I wouldn't do for Laurie's daughter!" My voice broke. "But for a combination of circumstances, which I shall regret to my dying day, you might have been my daughter."

"Don't!" she cried painfully.

"That's why you came here, isn't it?" I asked. "Because once your father and I loved each other. I loved him better than anything in the world except my sterile sense of duty, God help me! I'd like to think that Laurie told you to come to me if you needed a friend."

"Please, Miss Adams!"

"You did come here because of me?"

"No, I-I ..." She paused and drew an anguished breath. "Be merciful and drop the subject," she whispered.

"My dear, my dear!" I protested. "Won't you let me help you?"

"Maybe I – maybe I did plan to-to..." She was trembling. "It doesn't matter why we came to this awful place," she interrupted herself harshly, "because-because- No, Miss Adams," she said, rising to her feet, "you can't help me. No one can help me."

"My dear, my dear!" I protested again.

"Perhaps I thought you could when I came," she said bitterly.

"Perhaps I dreamed all sorts of silly dreams, but dreams don't come true. At least, mine never do and they never will."

"Child, if you are in trouble there is nothing I wouldn't do!"

"Trouble!" repeated Kathleen Adair with a dreadful smile. "Oh God, why was I ever born?"

I tried to catch her arm, but she twisted away from me and, her eyes blinded by tears, ran up the stairs.

9

We were all at lunch, including Mary Lawson, her face shockingly worn and haggard, when the inspector sent around another note.

We whose names figured on the list were to report to the parlour promptly at two o'clock 'for a conference.'

"Not content with mentally undressing us in private, he's now going to repeat the process with full benefit of audience," remarked Howard Warren bitterly.

The rest of us said nothing, but I caught myself glancing uneasily from one set face to another, hastily averting my gaze if I encountered anyone's eyes, conscious that the others were behaving in much the same fashion. I have said the worst feature of the affair was the way it set everybody against everyone else. By noon that day the pressure had become nerve racking.

"If certain people were forced to tell what they know, the rest of us could go on about our business in peace," growled Dan Mosby, again pacing the lobby floor while we were waiting for the hands of the clock to reach two.

I did not like the way he looked at Cyril Fancher, and apparently neither did Cyril.

"Are you throwing that insinuation at me, Mr Mosby?" he asked, his upper lip quivering.

"A hurt pig squeals," said Dan Mosby.

Cyril flushed. "I assure you –"

"Does the inspector know you were on the fourth floor last night, Fancher, very close to the time a certain party got his throat cut?" interrupted Dan Mosby.

"How do you know who was on the fourth floor at that certain time, Mosby?" countered Cyril.

Dan Mosby coloured darkly, and his wife put her hand on his arm. "Don't let's start quarrelling among ourselves," she pleaded.

"The inspector will get the truth out of us soon enough."

"You sound as if you had cause to fear the truth, Lottie," said Sophie with something that was almost a sneer.

The Anthony woman laughed unpleasantly. "Never have secrets, Mrs Mosby. They always come out on you in the worst spots."

Dan Mosby glared at both women as if he hated them. "My wife has no secrets," he said shortly.

"Is that so?" drawled Hilda Anthony.

"Neither has my husband, Mr Mosby," retorted Sophie.

Hilda Anthony looked Cyril Fancher over as if he amused her.

"Why must people be mean to each other?" whispered little Mrs Adair. "There's enough beauty to go around if only people would share it."

I had never heard Stephen Lansing's voice so soft. "Yes," he said, "beauty was intended to belong to everyone."

Little Mrs Adair smiled at him. "Of course," she said simply.

I noticed that Kathleen was staring at Stephen Lansing with wide eyes and when he smiled at her, rather shyly, I thought, she moved between him and her mother and continued to stand there, face averted, like a slim carved maiden on a golden shield.

It was precisely two when the policeman came down from the second floor. "The inspector will receive you now," he informed us stiffly.

While Howard and Polly had not exchanged a word since she entered the lobby that morning, he instinctively moved closer to her as we mounted the stair, and when the policeman had ushered us into the parlour Howard, doggedly refraining from looking at either of them, nevertheless took up his position directly behind Mary Lawson and her niece, who had sat down on one of the hard green sofas.

"This is an outrage!" protested Ella Trotter, breathing very hard. "I warn you, I shall write the mayor."

Inspector Bunyan, again encamped at the library table with the inevitable black notebook, smiled affably. "Please be seated," he said, as if we were about to have afternoon tea.

"Okay, Mr Bones," sang out Stephen Lansing flippantly, straddling a straight chair back of the other hard green sofa to which Kathleen Adair had assisted her mother.

"Some of you I have already talked to today," murmured the inspector. "Others," he continued, eyeing me with marked fixity, "I have delayed seeing until" – he referred to the notebook – "until I had more data to proceed upon."

Up to that moment I had felt relieved because the summons to the parlour, which I had expected all morning, had failed to materialize. Under the inspector's prolonged scrutiny, however, I was no longer so smug about my escape as I had been. It seemed to me the way in which he studied the page devoted to my activities was nothing if not portentous.

The inspector addressed me so suddenly, I started violently. "I am no longer inclined to doubt the presence of an intruder in your room last night, Miss Adams," he assured me. "Investigation substantiates your story."

"You might have saved yourself that trouble by believing what you hear," I said dryly.

He smiled. "I never believe anything I hear unless the facts corroborate it."

"He does it with mirrors," contributed Stephen Lansing with a derisive grin.

The inspector regarded him reflectively. "You'll probably be interested to know, Mr Lansing, that your impetuous dash to Miss Adams' rescue last night did not - ah - fortunately destroy all evidence of the fact that someone preceded you up the fire escape."

Stephen Lansing caught his breath. "How nice!" he drawled at last, looking slightly greenish.

The inspector next smiled at me. "Your present room was not the only one which had a surreptitious visitor last night, Miss Adams."

"No?" I asked weakly.

"Somebody," said the inspector, "in spite of sealed doors and windows and the presence of a guard in the corridor outside, succeeded in effecting an entrance to your former suite."

Stephen Lansing smothered an oath. "What the..." He subsided abruptly, knitting his heavy black brows.

The inspector looked him over deliberately. "You were about to say, Mr Lansing?"

"Nothing."

However, when the inspector once more bent his sleek head over his notebook, Stephen Lansing leaned closer to me and out the corner of his closed mouth made what to me was a completely mystifying statement.

"So it was you who brought that guy down here," he said.

When I stared at him incredulously, he shook his head and added with quiet bitterness, "Live and learn. I knew you were onto them, but no matter what they've done to you, I thought you were too good a sport, Adelaide, to set that kind of skunk onto two helpless women."

"Young man," I said tartly, "I haven't the faintest idea what you are talking about."

"Naturally you'd deny it," he remarked with appreciable disdain, then turned abruptly to the inspector. "You haven't told us, Inspector Bunyan, if the marauder – or was it the murderer? – helped himself to anything in Miss Adams' former suite."

"No," said Inspector Bunyan with a frown, "nothing was disturbed, absolutely nothing."

"Not even the floor?" demanded Stephen Lansing quickly.

The inspector frowned. "The floor? No, Mr Lansing, nothing

about the floor was disturbed."

"I don't get it," muttered Stephen Lansing, scowling at me.

"Neither do I" said the inspector, also scowling.

"What is this?" demanded Dan Mosby truculently. "A guessing contest? If nothing in the suite was disturbed, how do you figure someone got in?"

"The seal on the window –" explained the inspector wearily, "I might add that it was the window within reach of the fire escape was broken open."

"Those dumb cops of yours probably forgot to close the darned thing," said Dan Mosby with conspicuous rudeness. "Or maybe they thought it was a love letter and sealed it with a kiss."

"Please, Dan," whispered his wife, her eyes fastened on the inspector with such raw terror I felt a little sick.

Her warning, poor bedraggled little moth, came too late. Apparently Dan Mosby had succeeded in getting under the inspector's skin. The glance he bent on the other man made my flesh creep.

"He asked for it and he's going to get it," muttered Stephen Lansing, glancing at Lottie Mosby's small twitching face and then away as though he could not bear the sight.

"Last night, Mr Mosby," said the inspector in velvety tones, "you saw fit to deny that you went upstairs between seven-thirty and eight. Are you prepared to retract that statement?"

"Why should I?" retorted Dan Mosby, while the small quivering figure beside him began to rock with silent sobs.

"You did go upstairs, Mr Mosby. You were seen crouching on the landing between the third and fourth floors by two different people within five minutes of the discovery of James Reid's murdered body."

"So what?" asked Dan Mosby, turning white.

The inspector's lips curled. "How long have you been spying upon your wife?" he asked.

"I don't know what you mean," stammered young Mosby, then went on quickly, "Why should I spy on her?"

"There is an old saw, Mr Mosby, to the effect that a betrayed husband is the last person to know it."

Lottie Mosby moaned softly.

Clenching his fists, Dan Mosby sprang to his feet. "Damn you!" he cried. "You can't say things like that about my wife! Not if you have all the police on earth behind you."

"Oh, Dan," whispered Lottie Mosby.

"You have been suspicious of your wife for months, Mosby," said the inspector. "That's why you haven't dared stay sober. You weren't man enough to face the truth."

Dan Mosby was trembling.

"I don't know what you are talking about," he stammered.

"Was it you who hired James Reid to come to the Richelieu?" demanded the inspector sternly.

"If you mean, did I hire a dirty gumshoe to snoop on my wife, no! No!"

"But you snooped upon her yourself last night."

Dan Mosby swallowed painfully, and his bloodshot eyes turned desperately to that small shrinking figure beside him. "Honey," he said, as if he had forgotten everyone else, "I know you've been indiscreet, but, as God is my helper, I never suspected you of worse."

She could not speak. She could only go on staring at him, her eyes looking back at him from beyond the fires of her private hell.

"You do not know then, or do you, Mr Mosby," asked the inspector, "that your wife has been gambling steadily on the races for the last six months?"

"That's my business," growled Dan Mosby, but he had started violently at the inspector's question. "If I can afford it, what's it to you?" he demanded.

"But *can* you afford it?" pursued the inspector. "It is true you earn, or so I have discovered, around two hundred dollars a month. However, it costs you something to live, particularly in a hotel. And as I have taken the trouble to find out, your bank account has been non-existent since the first of the year."

"That's also my business."

"Naturally," the inspector admitted. "Nevertheless, the police are curious to know where, if not from you, your wife procured the two hundred dollars she has spent with the bookmakers this spring?"

Dan Mosby's face seemed to have shrivelled. "I don't believe it," he said at last, his eyes dull and old.

The inspector sighed. There was a laboured silence and then, hitching slowly to her feet, Lottie Mosby held out her small shaking hands to her husband in a gesture which broke my heart.

"It's true, Dan," she said faintly. "I have lost two hundred dollars to the bookies, and I – and I got the money from-from-"

"From the men who bought your favours behind your husband's back," said the inspector.

"Yes."

The word fell upon the silence of that room like a groan. It seemed to me its echo would never die. Slumping back into his chair, Dan Mosby covered his face with his hands, leaving her standing there, swaying a little, her eyes staring at him pleadingly though quite without hope.

"I kept thinking each day I'd win and – and be free," she faltered. "Free of the whole horrible business! I didn't want to be bad, Dan. I just got in and couldn't get out."

He did not lift his head or speak, and after a while she said sadly, "I didn't think you'd ever forgive me if you knew."

He looked up then, his face contorted with loathing. "Forgive you? I'd see you in hell first."

"Yes," she whispered. "I thought you'd feel like that."

"I can't stand much more of this," muttered Stephen Lansing.

"For God's sake," he cried to the inspector, "haven't you any mercy?"

But the inspector was a man hunter close to the kill. "You murdered James Reid, Lottie Mosby!" he said harshly.

"No, no!"

"It wasn't small fry like you he was after, but when he stumbled onto your wretched secret he tried to blackmail you, and so you killed him."

"Good Lord, Inspector," protested Howard Warren, "she's only a little scrap. She couldn't hang a man up by his suspenders to a chandelier, much less cut his throat."

"James Reid was a very slight man," said the inspector, "and the strength of a desperate woman would surprise you, Mr Warren."

"I didn't kill him," whispered Lottie Mosby.

The inspector produced a sheet of paper on which other small pieces of paper had been pasted. "This," he said, "is the note which Lottie Mosby left in James Reid's box at the desk a little before six yesterday afternoon." He held it out. "It will do you no good to deny it, Mrs Mosby. The experts at headquarters have identified your handwriting."

Her lips quivered. "I don't deny I wrote it," she faltered.

"It reads like this," murmured the inspector. " 'I have paid all I can. There isn't any more. But if you tell my husband about me, I'll get you and I don't mean maybe.' It is too bad from your viewpoint, Mrs Mosby, that when James Reid tore up your note he left the pieces in the wastebasket in his room."

Her eyes were unnaturally distorted, her voice frantic.

"I'm not going to hang for something I didn't do!" she screamed. "I don't want to die! Not until I've washed away my sins! I didn't kill James Reid, and I-I won't be the goat!"

She was out of the room before anyone guessed her purpose. The rest of us, shocked by her sensational outburst, began to mill about like stampeded cattle. The inspector, biting his lip, hurried out into the hall and barked rapid questions at two startled policemen.

"She darted up the stairs there," stammered one.

"After her!" cried the inspector furiously. "She's gone to her room on the fourth floor!"

Dan Mosby continued to sit with his head in his hands. It seemed inhuman to stay there, gaping at his misery. By twos and threes we drifted away. A police car roared up outside, and four more policemen swarmed into the hotel.

"Find her if you have to take the place apart!" I heard the inspector shouting.

However, at the end of fifteen minutes Lottie Mosby still had not been found. What with the police running hither and yon, peering in at doors, even opening cabinets not large enough to conceal a kitten, and with the guests in the house being pushed about everywhere while protesting bitterly against the violation of their privacy, it would be difficult to imagine a more confused quarter of an hour. No wonder that later nobody could give a coherent account of his movements during the fatal moments.

I recall, though I could not have proved it, that I was standing in the lobby, rehearsing in my mind the scathing terms in which I intended to inform Sophie Scott that I was moving out the minute the police lifted their ban, when I heard the thud, that single dreadful sound which still at times rings in my ears.

Nobody would believe, unless he felt it, that one slight body striking the roof over the employees' entry could shake an entire building from top to bottom. Of course, she was dead when they found her. I pray she never knew what hit her, poor little thing, lying face upward on the paved alleyway at the back of the hotel, her eyes staring up with a terrible bewilderment at the indifferent blue sky above her.

"Dead!" gasped Dan Mosby, kneeling beside her and gathering the small broken body into his trembling arms. "Oh, Lottie, Lottie! Why did you do it? If only you could come back, I'd forgive you. I'd forgive you anything, Lottie, if you'd come back."

Howard Warren, to whose hand I was clinging, was not ashamed to let me see the tears on his cheek. "She couldn't face it," he said thickly. "And who can blame her? Suicide is kinder than the hangman."

The inspector put a shaking hand up to his lips. "At least she's saved the state the expense of a trial," he sighed.

I glared about me. "If you ask me, she was practically hounded into a life of infamy," I said bitterly. "A little tolerance and understanding might have saved her. In my opinion her blood is on all our hands."

"Yes," said Ella Trotter, blowing her nose.

Hilda Anthony smiled unpleasantly. "If a few more of your old hens had a change of heart, the Richelieu might not be such a dismal hole to live in."

"Is that so?" I demanded, giving her a dose of her own bitters.

"You're accepting this as suicide and a confession of murder, Inspector?" asked Stephen Lansing, his face drawn and tired.

The inspector nodded. "That's how it'll go down in the record," he said and drew a long breath. "I don't mind confessing I'm glad to close the case. It had me going around in circles for a while."

"We can all rest easier to know that none of the rest of us is a murderer in disguise," murmured Ella Trotter, sounding very shaky for her.

Polly Lawson smiled weakly. "It was pretty terrible for us suspects," she said.

"Yes!" cried Kathleen Adair in a choked voice. "Thank God, it's all over," sighed Sophie, leaning heavily on Cyril's arm.

"Except," said Stephen Lansing quietly, "it isn't over."

We all gasped and stared at him.

"One of us is a double murderer," he said.

The inspector turned violently red.

"What are you driving at?" he demanded furiously.

"You are still going around in circles so far as this case is concerned, Inspector," drawled Stephen Lansing with a twisted smile.

"Explain yourself," snapped Inspector Bunyan.

"This poor girl did not kill herself. She is another victim. Somebody in this hotel is a double murderer."

"Impossible!" cried the inspector.

Stephen Lansing knelt by that small shattered body which Dan Mosby was still cradling in his arms and turned back the frivolous little lace collar about Lottie Mosby's childish white neck.

"Mrs Mosby," said Stephen gravely, "did not throw herself out of a window. She was hurled to the ground after she had been strangled to death."

He pointed to cruel livid marks, already turning dark, on the girl's thin young throat. Then his gaze travelled slowly around the group gathered about Lottie Mosby's crumpled body.

"She told us she did not kill Reid, but I think she knew who did," he said.

"Good God!" gasped Howard Warren. "Then she, too, was-was killed to-to..."

"Like James Reid, she was killed to preserve somebody's guilty soul," said Stephen Lansing and added gently, "God rest her poor stained soul."

10

It is the human instinct in time of stress to seek lights and a crowd, and so the dining room in the Richelieu was filled that night with haggard and sober faces, albeit nobody had an appetite. I suppose everyone felt as I did. The sight of food was a little sickening, yet anything was better than being cooped up alone in my room.

Lottie Mosby's pathetic body had been taken away by the police, its immediate destination the morgue, to lie, until the coroner's inquest, alongside that of James Reid, to me a horrible thought. Dan Mosby was in the hospital under a physician's care.

The shock of his wife's tragic fate had completed the havoc already wrought by liquor upon his none too stable temperament.

"Poor devil," muttered Stephen Lansing just before we all went in to dinner that night, "he's in a bad way. Mind temporarily a blank."

I sighed. "It's just as well. He'll have a long time in which to remember."

"At least," said Howard, "the police have eliminated him from the list of suspects, if he was ever really on."

"Yes," said Stephen, "Mosby's the only person in the house who has an alibi for the last murder."

Howard nodded. "He never stirred out of that chair in the parlour till after she struck, poor fellow."

I shivered again. I did not have to close my eyes to see that slight form hurtling downward onto the sloping narrow roof over the employees' entrance and then sliding limply off to the paved court below it.

"It seems to me," murmured Howard, glancing sharply at

Stephen Lansing, "that in this instance the murderer has overshot his hand. I mean, after all, it ought to be possible for the police to locate the window from which she-er-fell. There should be marks on the sill, wouldn't you think?"

Stephen frowned. "The police haven't taken me into their confidence," he said brusquely. "If you are out pumping for information, Warren, why don't you ask the inspector himself if he's located the room from which the girl was thrown?"

"Damn you, are you suggesting that I – that I ..." began Howard heatedly.

I made a testy gesture. "Tut, tut," I said, "all this is trying enough without our flying at each other at every opportunity like bantam roosters. You are unnecessarily thin skinned lately, Howard, and as for you, Mr Lansing, I consider Howard's question a perfectly natural one. I myself would give something to know if the police have any clue as to where Lottie Mosby met her doom."

"I don't doubt you'd like to know, Adelaide," said Stephen disagreeably.

"I don't in the least doubt it."

It was my turn to flare up. "Are you insinuating that I – that I..."

Howard laughed. "Now who's flying off the handle?"

Somewhat sheepishly I subsided, and Stephen gave us both a sardonic grin. "From now on, unless I'm greatly mistaken," he said grimly, "it's going to be every man for himself in this investigation and the devil take the hindmost."

I did not doubt it. One had only to glance around at the various tables in the dining room that night to feel the hostility which was rising to fever heat among us. Only a short while before we had been a normal group of civilized human beings, the majority of us rather better bred than the average, I should say, but under the threat of violence and personal danger we were fast reverting to the primitive, where self-preservation is the first law of the pack.

Nobody that night was disposed to meet anybody else's gaze frankly, and back of the furtive glances which we did exchange lurked suspicion and other vicious thoughts, their ugly heads reared in our eyes like serpents. It was painfully apparent from that moment on that not one of us trusted the other. Speech was guarded, unless betrayed by anger into virulent attack. If possible, people did not say what they were thinking. After all, two in that house had already paid with their lives for knowing more than it was safe to know. Yet if anybody did forget himself sufficiently to bring his ideas out into the open, he invariably went too far, as temper generally does.

I myself was no exception. Already worried and upset, it irritated me to the boiling point to find a new waitress installed at my table, a floozy young woman with hennaed hair and prominent hips which she had a habit of flaunting as she walked. She was not inexperienced – in fact, she seemed to know her business thoroughly; nevertheless, she was the grievance which broke the camels back so far as I was concerned.

I crooked my finger imperiously at Cyril Fancher, and when he approached, with obvious reluctance, I regarded him in a jaundiced manner over my spectacles and remarked in my most caustic style, "Of course, I am merely a guest, just one of those who pay the bills, and I realise a guest in this house is regarded by the management as a necessary evil with absolutely no rights in how the place should be run; nevertheless might I be so bold as to inquire what you have done with the girl Annie?"

To my utter astonishment Cyril Fancher turned white, as white as if I had accused him of murder or worse. "What do you mean?" he demanded in a quaking falsetto. "How dare you intimate that I have-have..."

I suppose he saw by my expression that he was behaving more than customarily like a fool, for he paused abruptly, bit his lip, and attempted one of his inane jokes, though his voice was still not quite steady.

"You surely don't hold me personally responsible, Miss Adams," he murmured, trying to look both arch and ingratiating at the same time, "for these little fly-by-nights who flit from job to job like Eliza – wasn't it? – skipping over the ice floes in Uncle Tom's Cabin."

"You should know by now, Cyril Fancher," I said sharply, "that no well brought-up Southern woman ever read Uncle Tom's Cabin or allowed that obnoxious book to be mentioned in her presence."

"Yes," he said, "I did know, only I forgot. Please accept my apology."

He gave me an obsequious glance.

"I suppose no offence can be taken where none was intended," I conceded grudgingly.

"Thanks," he said and started to move away, an expression of relief upon his face.

I frowned. "You still haven't told me what happened to Annie," I called after him sharply.

He looked back over his shoulder with a grimace.

"Nothing has happened to her so far as I know," he snapped.

"She simply informed me at noon today that she had found a better place and wouldn't be back."

"I hope she's right," I sighed. "So often these young girls seem to go from here to worse."

Again he stared at me with a startled face.

"What do you mean?" he stammered.

"What could I mean," I demanded impatiently, "except that waitresses appear to me to have a genius for popping off the griddle into the blaze?"

"Yes?"

I knit my brows. "There was that Gwendolyn," I said. "Didn't she get run over by a truck after she left here, trying to hitchhike her way to Hollywood?"

"I believe I saw something to that effect in the paper," he admitted in his noncommittal way.

I shook my head. "She was a silly chit," I said, "but you'd think even a Dumb Dora would know that a straight line is the shortest distance between two points or at least that southeast on the New Orleans highway is no short cut to Hollywood."

He shrugged his narrow shoulders. "I suppose if they had any intelligence to speak of, they wouldn't be hopping tables," he said.

"I suppose not," I agreed pensively.

This time he succeeded in making his escape, disappearing kitchen ward with a haste which gave me a feeling of acute satisfaction.

I did not like Cyril Fancher and I may as well acknowledge that it always afforded me pleasure to give him an uncomfortable moment. There was no one, in fact, upon whom I would rather have vented my spleen, and our little tilt had done a great deal toward clearing up my disposition. It enabled me to inquire the name of my new waitress with less acidity than might otherwise have been the case.

"Gloria, madam, Gloria Larue," she informed me blandly.

Nee Lizzie Brown or Jones, I thought to myself, eyeing her blunt nose and rouged mouth and the large knuckles of her reddened but capable hands.

"I see you also take after the movies," I remarked dryly.

She looked me over for a moment and then nodded vigorously.

"Ya-uss. All us girls do. Don't you?" she said with an enthusiastic smile.

I coughed. "Well, not exactly," I said. "As a matter of fact, I loathe them."

From that time on Miss Gloria Larue made no attempt to engage me in conversation although she was scrupulously careful about attending to my wants. I think she would have cut up my meat and spoon-fed me had I allowed her. I seemed to have been pigeonholed in her category as a mental deficient, a sad case though harmless.

Glancing about the dining room that night I did not feel any too complacent myself about the workings of my head piece, which I had been in the habit of regarding as an excellent bit of machinery.

It seemed to me that being in the very centre of things I should have had in my hands all the necessary threads to the intricate and sinister tangle in which we found ourselves involved at the Richelieu Hotel. If so, I was compelled to admit that I was too stupid to recognize them.

A number of curious things occurred to me as I studied my neighbours at the other tables. I was aware of queer undercurrents, of inexplicable divergences from the normal in the conduct of certain people, of puzzling incidents which I had seen or shared, but what it all meant I was at a loss to say. Nor could I find answers to the questions buzzing in my ears like a horde of mosquitoes.

"We can't all be guilty of murder," I thought irritably, striving to ignore the reason or reasons which I had for suspecting practically every person upon whom my eyes rested.

Polly Lawson and her aunt made a brave pretence at eating while carrying on a hectic conversation, although it was patent their thoughts were elsewhere. I frowned. Why had Polly run away with the blood stained knife? Why had that particular knife been used in the first place to slit a man's throat? Had the knife really been stolen from Mary's room the afternoon before the murder? And in that case why had Mary, when confronted by the police, failed to say so, after Polly fairly put the words into her mouth? I frowned again.

Over at the next table Howard Warren was scowling at his plate, carefully avoiding so much as a glance in Polly's direction and feverishly lighting one cigarette from the butt of another. It was unlike Howard to smoke or carry any other habit to excess. It had always seemed to me Howard was, if anything, a little too exemplary.

I remember saying once that he would be more human if his foot could slip once. There was no doubt that in the past two days Howard had changed. He was by no means the model of irreproachable propriety he had been.

I sighed. Why had Howard broken all precedents and invited

me to a picture show the night before? Why had he insisted, to the point of rudeness, that I did not need a coat? What possible motive could he have had for wanting me out of the hotel? For trying to keep me from going to my room? And what was Howard doing on the fourth floor that night during the half-hour when James Reid was murdered? "Keep this up, Adelaide," I advised myself sternly, "and you'll end in a private sanatorium with the rest of the imbeciles."

Hilda Anthony stopped Stephen Lansing on his way out of the Coffee Shop, detaining him at her table until she finished her after dinner coffee, smiling up at him through her absurd eyelashes like an odalisque, providing an odalisque is, as I have always believed, an oriental female without a vestige of shame. As usual, the Anthony woman had nothing to conceal. At least, her voice carried to every part of the room.

"Is it true, Mr Lansing," she inquired, "that the police are absolutely unable to account for where the Mosby woman went when she ran out of the parlour?"

Stephen shrugged his shoulders. "I don't know how the impression has got around that the police use me for a confessional."

She laughed. "Isn't there such a thing as gratitude? You saved Inspector Bunyan a nasty blunder. He'll have to admit that – or does he?"

"On the contrary," said Stephen with a grimace, "the inspector admits nothing. He does not deny that I precipitated matters. Only it was barely a question of minutes before the police would have made the same discovery for themselves, says he."

"Oh yes?" she scoffed.

Stephen grinned ruefully. "The inspector hasn't even given me a good mark for my bright powers of observation. I am still, right along with some other people, high up on the black list of potential murderers."

She looked puzzled. "Surely the murderer is the last person in the world who would have called the police's attention to his crime. I mean, he of all people wanted it to look like suicide. Or should I say her crime?" she corrected herself with a taunting light in her yellow eyes.

Stephen grinned. "Far be it from me to slight the fair sex, even when it comes to manslaughter."

"No," she said, "you wouldn't."

His face sobered. "Many a woman has been driven to murder and worse."

It seemed to me his glance flickered involuntarily to where the Adairs sat directly behind me, and, looking into the mirror, I saw that, while Kathleen did not raise her eyes from her fixed scrutiny of a salad fork by her plate, her cheeks had paled.

Hilda Anthony was still studying Stephen Lansing with a slightly baffled expression. "You haven't yet explained why the inspector has refused to scratch you off the list of suspects," she reminded him.

Stephen's lips curled. "The inspector was good enough to point out that, since the police were bound to stumble upon the truth eventually, it would be a very clever stunt on the part of the murderer to distract attention from himself by exposing the alleged suicide as another successful murder. To throw the inspector off the track, or words to that effect."

"That dressed-up little dude was never on the track," declared Hilda Anthony scornfully, "and, what's more, he never will be."

"Don't take any bets on that," said Stephen Lansing.

"Don't worry. I never bet on anything," she snapped, rising to her feet. "I leave that kind of sport to the well-known suckers. Any time I let a dollar get away from me the eagle screams."

They went on out together, followed by Howard's contemptuous gaze. I noticed that Polly bit her lip and scowled as they went up in the elevator together, but Kathleen's eyes were still fixed on her salad fork, although there was a white line about her mouth.

"Water will find its level," I thought to myself with vexed disdain and wondered why it should matter to me if Stephen Lansing was flinging himself upon the talons of a vampire.

I had never pretended to like his style and as between him and Hilda Anthony I imagined it would be difficult to choose the more skilful at that particular game. Nevertheless, I was unreasonably disappointed and I have never been the kind to delude myself.

"It's nothing to you," I muttered angrily, but I knew, in spite of everything, that I was beginning to have a sneaking fondness for the dashing young Mr Lansing.

I had even decided that a large part of his flippancy was a pose and, like a matchmaking old fool, I had fancied that the only woman he was seriously interested in at the Richelieu was the Adair girl.

Now, however, I made up my mind that when it came to a choice of playmates Stephen's only requirement was the more the merrier.

"Very likely Kathleen's indifference piques him," I told myself.

"He plainly is not used to being held at arm's length. No doubt his only object in pursuing her is to keep up his batting average."

Be that as it may, I was sure that to her he stood for more than that, much more, poor child. I sighed again. It had occurred to me, as to the inspector, that Stephen Lansing was by no means absolved from suspicion. There were a number of questions concerning that young man which bothered me.

What had Stephen Lansing forgotten and come back after the night James Reid was killed? Stephen's room was on the floor below, yet he had been the first by several minutes to reach me after I ran shrieking into the corridor. Who, if not he, had telephoned to James Reid from the Sally Ray Beauty Shop the afternoon before the man was murdered? How had Stephen Lansing happened to be almost completely dressed at three o'clock that morning, the same morning on which two rooms in the hotel had been visited by a mysterious intruder? And why had he been eager to destroy any clues which the intruder might have left upon the fire escape? I winced.

Mention of the fire escape brought me up against that which to me was the most heart breaking question of all. What had Kathleen Adair been doing on the fire-escape landing outside the room formerly occupied by James Reid? That she had been there I could not get away from. I was prepared to admit that my green spectacle case appeared, on one occasion, to have taken a promenade of its own accord, but I did not for a minute believe that my freshly washed princess slip had repeated the feat.

Kathleen had lied when she said she dropped the black and gold brooch while leaning out her window to observe the sunset. I could not bring myself to believe that Laurie's daughter was that damned soul who had stood beside my bed the night before. Nevertheless, by the evidence of the brooch, she had been on the fifth floor landing of the fire escape at some time or other, of that I was convinced. And she was in trouble, trouble which had made her run away from me that day at noon in an anguish of despair.

As I was rising from the table I came face to face with Sophie Scott, bustling into the dining room for her own dinner, a distressed pucker between her eyebrows which, since her marriage, she had taken to dyeing, with hideous results, need I add? As I have said, Sophie and I had not been on the friendliest terms after Cyril's advent into her life, but we had been once, and the look she threw me at this time was so hostile as to give me a decided turn.

"I do think, Adelaide, considering the stew we are in already, you might be more considerate than to hurt poor dear Cyril's feelings for no reason at all," she accused me with unconcealed bitterness.

"Poor dear Cyril shouldn't wear his feelings stuck out like a sore thumb," I defended myself tartly.

In spite of myself, however, I was touched to see that Sophie's eyes had filled with tears. "I realize you've always been prejudiced against him, Adelaide, simply because you don't understand Cyril. Poor boy, he's had such a thwarted life. Never till he married me did he know what peace and tenderness and security can mean."

"I don't doubt that," I snapped and then, staring at her curiously, I asked, "Just how much do you really know, if anything, about Cyril's past, Sophie?"

"Why I-I know everything, of course!" she cried indignantly. "I cannot imagine why you persist in trying to make out, Adelaide, that Cyril is of an evasive disposition. I'm sure he never attempts to conceal the facts about himself."

"Doesn't he?" I inquired grimly, thinking I had never known a person who could talk faster and say less about his past than could Cyril Fancher.

Putting her nose in the air, Sophie barged away toward the kitchen. I stared after her thoughtfully. There were several things which puzzled me about Sophie and her husband. What had he been doing on the fourth floor the preceding night almost immediately before I discovered James Reid's lifeless body, and was it Sophie who hired the private detective in the first place? Not for a minute did I believe she was satisfied, or ever had been, with the vague account which Cyril Fancher gave of himself.

What elderly wife with a younger husband would be? She had said that never till he married her had Cyril known peace and security. How much were they worth to him, I wondered, a chill playing up and down my spine. Was it Cyril Fancher's guilty secret for which James Reid and Lottie Mosby had paid so terrible a price?

Apparently Stephen had not lingered long with that brazen seductress, the Anthony woman, for when I came into the lobby he was just stepping out of the elevator and he had a slender long stemmed rosebud in his hand.

"How lovely!" cried little Mrs Adair, her wan face lighting with pleasure. "Such an exquisite pink!"

He paused beside the divan on which she was sitting and, rather self-consciously for him, held out the rose. "Wouldn't you like it?" he asked.

"Oh, thank you," she whispered with a radiant smile.

The girl made a swift passionate gesture of protest. "Don't take it!" she cried.

Stephen Lansing's eyes dwelt on her with strange intensity. "Why not?" he asked softly. "Your mother loves pretty things."

She shrank back but she did not speak. I think, poor child, she was unable to force her bloodless lips apart.

"Yes," said little Mrs Adair, "I love anything colourful."

She suddenly tucked the rose above the coil of bright bronze hair on her daughter's neck.

"There!" she said. "It looks perfectly beautiful."

I thought the girl was going to reach up and tear the flowers to pieces and I did not doubt she yearned to fling them into Stephen Lansing's face. But little Mrs Adair was beaming like a pleased child over her achievement, and slowly, by a tremendous effort, Kathleen Adair controlled herself.

"Doesn't it look sweet in Kathleen's hair, Mr Lansing?" asked her mother naively.

His eyes met Kathleen's, and it seemed to me hers were frantic with dismay.

"Yes," said Stephen Lansing, turning a little white, "the rose is lovely in Kathleen's hair."

His voice made a caress of her name, but, although her lips quivered, her expression did not soften, and for the second time I saw Kathleen Adair look at a man as though she would, if she could, have slain him with a glance.

"I told you, Miss Adams," murmured little Mrs Adair abruptly, "that there would be another death."

Tearing my gaze with an effort from Kathleen's ravaged face, I turned with a little shiver to the older woman.

"Thank God, we don't have that to look forward to any longer," I snapped.

Under my very eyes her small pale face grew thinner and more wasted. "Oh, but it isn't ended," she said. "Death is still all about us."

I tried to say "Nonsense!" only I could not get the word out, and in the breathless silence I heard Kathleen Adair whisper in a furious voice to Stephen Lansing, "If you betray us I'll make you pay if I have to follow you to the ends of the earth and back!"

11

It was Howard who a few minutes later brought us the latest bad news. "The inspector wants to see all of us in the parlour at eight fifteen," he announced with a grimace.

"What now?" I groaned.

Behind me little Mrs Adair murmured, "Oh dear!" and Polly Lawson glanced quickly at Mary and went quite white. The Anthony woman laughed unpleasantly.

"Thank the Lord, I have nothing to fear," she said with a significant glance at the faces around her on which chagrin or possibly a more poignant emotion was indelibly stamped.

"I notice the inspector has not omitted you from the list as yet," I pointed out.

She grinned at me. "The inspector likes to look upon a good looking woman, Miss Adams. Exasperating as it must seem to you, most men do."

I shrugged my shoulders. It had struck me that Inspector Bunyan had betrayed a little difficulty in tearing his eyes from Hilda Anthony's lush curves. Nevertheless, there were several questions about the lady which interested me and which I imagined the inspector had not overlooked. Why should she have lingered on and on at the Richelieu after she secured her divorce the year before? Admittedly a gold digger, neither pure nor simple, what had caused her to withdraw herself from circulation in a place which for her purpose appeared to be peculiarly arid? And why had Mr James Reid been staring at her from the foot of the staircase less than an hour before he was killed?

Ella Trotter nudged me in the ribs. "I wouldn't put murder or anything else past that brazen hussy," she remarked in a sibilant whisper.

I nodded wearily. If it were true that one of us was a double murderer, nothing would have comforted me more than to have the guilt pinned on the Anthony woman, only I had a presentiment even then that she was too careful of her own skin ever to thrust her beautiful neck into the hangman's noose.

Stephen must have read my thoughts, for he grinned at me wryly and whispered, "It would be nice, wouldn't it, Adelaide, if you could shove it all off onto the lady known as Lou."

I sniffed. "Your idea and mine of a lady differ."

"Oh, I don't know," he remarked airily. "Believe it or not, I have a few inhibitions myself, especially about women."

I did not deign to reply. It was then, I recall, a few minutes before eight and, as the climax to an already sad and depressing day, it had begun to rain, a chill drizzle, half mist, which drifted into the house in spite of closed doors and windows. It promptly started the little tickle in my bronchial tubes which in damp weather, unless checked, gives me an annoying cough.

When I cleared my throat the second time, Ella Trotter frowned at me anxiously. "If you don't want to come down with another crop of croup, Adelaide, you'd better get your fascinator," she said.

Stephen laughed. "I didn't know there was a female extant who still used those gimcracks."

"Young man," I remarked grimly, "there are many things which you do not and probably never will know."

"True, how true, Adelaide!" he murmured with a rueful smile.

At almost precisely that same hour the night before I had gone to my room to stumble upon the body of a murdered man. Though not a fanciful person, I must confess that it gave me no little relief at this time to discover, when I rounded the corner from the elevator, that the lights were burning quite properly in both corridors on the fifth floor, although somebody had left the door open which led out upon the fire escape and the hall was full of fog.

I slammed it to and bolted it. "The employees in this hotel have grown more slipshod every day since Tom Scott died," I muttered to myself, coughing as I fitted my key to the lock.

The atmosphere inside 511 felt equally thick, and when I opened the door the draft whipped the lank lace curtains at the nearer window out and in. I went over angrily and jerked the sash down. It was then, with a prickle at the base of my scalp, I realized that the other window, the one on the fire escape, was up a foot from the ledge.

Now I had been short with Inspector Bunyan early that morning when he suggested that I keep that particular window locked and I had sniffed audibly when a little later the policeman Sweeney came and attended to the matter himself at the inspector's instigation.

Nevertheless, I had never intended to spend another minute in that room without being quite positive that the approach via the fire escape was securely closed off.

It had been the first thing I looked to before I took my bath that afternoon, the last I glanced back at as I was starting down to dinner. On both occasions the lock on the window had been firmly in place and latched. However, the window was now undeniably open. It was with what I regard as pardonable uneasiness that I approached it and slammed it down. Not, I freely admit, until the bolt was fastened and the shade lowered did I recover from a deplorable weakness in the region of my knees.

"Apparently locks and bolts have come to mean nothing in this house," I told myself bitterly.

My crocheted shawl was in the closet. As Stephen Lansing had said, 'fascinators' went out of style many years ago, but one of the compensations of being past fifty is the privilege of being comfortable, regardless of style, and I have never found any better protection for a sensitive throat than my lavender throw. Nor is it too unbecoming with iron-grey hair and a florid skin, as I remember thinking after a cursory examination of the mirror.

Unlike many women, I have never spent a lot of time in front of a looking glass. As a rule I am more often disconcerted than pleased with such a survey. This night was no exception. I was in the very act of turning hastily away when I spied the slip of paper tucked in at one side of the mirror frame.

It was on plain brown wrapping paper, such as might have been torn off any bundle. No attempt had been made to even the ragged edges, the piece being roughly the size of an ordinary sheet of note-paper. In the upper left-hand corner there was a crude drawing, done with the stub end of a cheap hard pencil. The figure it represented might have been scrawled on somebody's outhouse or on the walls of a padded cell. It was so vulgar as to make me feel a little nauseated.

Beneath it, printed by the same stubby pencil, were these words: "Unless you want the police to hear all about the Adair wench and her mama, place one thousand dollars in cash in the water pitcher and leave it on the fire escape landing tonight at one o'clock."

I don't know how long I stood there, staring from that abominable thing in my hand to the aluminium ice-water pitcher with which each room in the Richelieu is equipped. Until that moment nothing could have convinced me that I should ever, under any circumstances, pay tribute to that most cowardly form of criminal known as the blackmailer.

Next to a kidnapper, it had seemed to me that human nature could stoop no lower. I had frequently and with great emphasis expressed my opinion not only of such vultures but also of the weakness of any person who permits himself to be victimized by the like. It had been my conviction, spoken in no uncertain terms, that every conscientious citizen owes it to himself and his fellow man to report such an attempt without delay to the police, no matter at what cost to himself. That I should fail to do so had never by any flight of imagination occurred to me, granting anyone had the temerity to blackmail a person of my constitution, which I had firmly doubted.

Now, however, with that ugly scrawl in my hand, I was discovering that one never knows what he will do in a given situation until confronted with it. Had the threat been to myself I should not have hesitated, although the thought of showing that lewd figure at the top of the note to man or woman made my cheeks burn.

But the threat was not to myself and it was fiendishly clever.

To carry it to the police was to call the inspector's attention to the fact that there was something to know about the Adairs, and, while I myself was sufficiently disturbed about them to dread such a result, the inspector, so far as I knew, had no cause for suspicion in that connection, thanks to the manner in which I had misled him about the black-and-gold brooch.

And so I discovered that I simply could not, in spite of my convictions, go to Inspector Bunyan with anything which would set him upon Kathleen Adair's trail. It was all very well to tell myself that I was letting Adelaide Adams in for a vicious chain of such levies and that to do evil in order that good may come is merely to pay the devil a toll. I could not take that salacious and horrible scrawl to Inspector Bunyan, any more than I could have picked up Laurie's little girl bodily and flung her to the wolves.

I did not know what tale the writer of the note knew which he could carry to the police; nevertheless, there was something wrong, terribly wrong, with the Adairs. I had no doubt of that. I told myself, when I went downstairs, that suppressing the note was as far as I meant to go. I was, or so I kept saying under my breath, positively not going to pay a thousand dollars or any part of it to a blackmailer. I merely believed in preparedness, I carefully explained to my conscience.

Pinkney Dodge gave me a startled glance when I told him I wanted to get into my locked box which is kept in the hotel safe, a service not extended to all the guests in the house but one Tom Scott granted me many years ago because I have a well-known penchant for keeping a fairly large sum of ready money on hand.

My arthritis being what it is, I do not always find frequent trips to the bank convenient or even possible.

"But, Miss Adams, this isn't the first or the fifteenth," protested Pinkney, and then under the asperity in my eyes he went on feebly, "I mean, it's unusual for you to want to get into the safe at odd hours."

"I don't suppose the world will come to an end," I remarked coldly, "because I have decided to wear my garnets tonight."

I might explain that in my safety box I keep numerous pieces of old-fashioned jewellery which belonged to my grandmother and my mother, though I seldom wear them for the very good reason that by the time they were handed down to me my skin had taken on that leathery texture to which the less notice attracted the better.

"I suppose not," murmured Pinkney, but he still looked upset after he had opened the big safe behind the desk and produced the lengthy and commodious steel box to which I possess the only key.

To my relief the buzzer on the switchboard began to whir and Pinky's attention was forcibly withdrawn from my manoeuvres. To abstract the slender Manila envelope and thrust it down inside the stiffly boned front of my corset took barely a moment. When Pinkney turned around I was removing the strand of garnets from the velvet case. Having announced my intention of wearing them, there was nothing to do except clasp the string about my neck.

"How beautiful!" exclaimed little Mrs Adair, reaching out her small frail hands as if she longed to caress the lustrous red stones which I felt sure looked sadly out of place against my sere and withered throat.

"The pity is," I said, gazing wistfully at Kathleen, "that they cannot adorn the lovely skin of some radiant young creature like your daughter."

"Yes," sighed little Mrs Adair.

"But I hate jewellery!" cried the girl.

It was true I had never seen her wear any except a massive hand-wrought silver bracelet which she was seldom without, although the top was crudely set with brilliants in a crescent shape and looked like the sort of arrangement which catches on everything.

"Nonsense," I said. "All women love jewellery, particularly girls your age."

"So I'm forever telling Kathleen," murmured her mother, squeezing her arm.

The girl winced as if the prongs of the bracelet had pricked her, as I have no doubt they did.

"I loathe jewels," she said in a passionate voice.

"Nonsense!" I protested again, quite crossly. "Of course you don't!"

At that moment Stephen Lansing interrupted us. "It's eight o'clock, ladies, and there's no percentage in keeping the inspector waiting," he said in his brusquest manner.

Kathleen Adair bit her lip. "Why does he persist in dragging Mother and me up there? He-he hasn't a thing on us."

She meant her voice to ring with conviction, only it dwindled away and there was a terrible anxiety in her clear brown eyes.

"I'm afraid," said Stephen Lansing curtly, "the inspector has ideas which he communicates only if and when it suits his purpose."

"Oh!" gasped the girl, as though she had asked for and received a warning.

The exodus up the stairs had begun. Catching her mother's arm, Kathleen followed, her gallant young shoulder drooping pathetically.

Stephen and I brought up the rear. "You never struck me as the sadistic type, Miss Adams," he said in a disillusioned voice. "I mean, I'd have expected you to grab up something and lay your enemy cold, if necessary. I never thought you'd lay with them as a cat does a mouse."

I was too dispirited to deny the allegation with my usual fire. "Young man," I said wearily, "I may seem a back issue to your generation, but I know my Freud. And though a soured and more or less disappointed old maid, I am not a sadist or any of those other abnormal freaks."

"Just the same," remarked Stephen soberly, "when we get to the bottom of this, if we do, I think we'll find someone who is or soon will be a psychopathic case."

I thought of that nasty piece of brown wrapping paper which I had torn to pieces before I flushed it down the drain in my room and shuddered.

"If you are insinuating that a maniac is loose in this hotel, I am prepared to agree with you," I said.

12

It had begun to rain in earnest by the time we were once more assembled in the parlour on the second floor to meet Inspector Bunyan. Nothing, absolutely nothing, I thought, was lacking to add to the gloom of that dreary bilious room with the raindrops splattering against the windowpanes and an occasional spiteful flash of lightning illuminating our drawn uneasy faces. Even the inspector, nattily dressed in black serge with a white pin stripe, looked tired and dejected and sterner than I had ever seen him.

"It's beginning to get on his nerves as well as ours," I muttered.

Stephen shrugged his shoulders. "He pushed poor Lottie Mosby across the frontier of safety to her death. Policemen are not paid to have tender consciences, but you may rest assured, Adelaide, that it will be many a day before the inspector frees himself of that responsibility. Naturally he doesn't want to make the same mistake twice."

I shivered. "You mean he-he-"

"It's his job to force the truth out of people," said Stephen tersely, "and you must admit that to tell all you know right now is not the most healthful indoor sport which the Richelieu affords."

I shook my head. "No, you can't blame people for keeping under cover if possible."

I was thinking of the Manila envelope inside my corset. Apparently Stephen Lansing was thinking of something else, for he slapped his knee impatiently with a folded afternoon paper and scowled irritably at the inspector.

"The devil of it is," said Stephen crossly, "no one can run with both the hounds and the hare, not, at least, forever."

My conscience pricked me. "Nevertheless," I said firmly, "it's the inspector's business, not ours, to drag the skeletons out of the closets."

He nodded. "Only if there's another murder…" His voice trailed off, and I regarded him with what I feel must have been a ghastly face.

"Great heavens, you aren't expecting this-this murderous spree to go on and on?" I stammered.

He shrugged his shoulders. "There never was a truer platitude than 'what a tangled web we weave when first we practice to deceive.' A murderer kills for greed or from fright, let us say, in the beginning; then he kills to save his neck. Finally he sees every man's hand raised against him and goes a little mad, I think. That's when he begins to kill promiscuously at the slightest threat of exposure."

The lightning flared, and I shrank back involuntarily from the abyss which Stephen Lansing's prophetic comment had revealed yawning at our very feet, nor do I mind admitting that my voice sounded very strange and husky.

"It's-it's outrageous for the police to keep us trussed up here till one by one we get our throats cut!" I cried.

He nodded grimly. "That's another responsibility which, unless I'm much mistaken, is adding to the inspector's grey hairs."

I gave him a searching glance. "If I were a young man of admitted bravado, with a twelve-cylinder car and no reputation for discretion to speak of, and danger threatened a young girl in whom I had professed a more or less quixotic interest, I'm afraid I'd show the-er-police a clean pair of heels, if the gods were so kind as to offer me a black and stormy night like this."

"Why, Adelaide," Stephen chuckled, "to think of a lady of your unimpeachable integrity trying to corrupt the morals of verdant youth."

"Unimpeachable be darned!" I exclaimed bitterly. "If you think I wouldn't sacrifice you or myself or anyone else for that child, you are quite wrong, young man."

He shook his head. "I don't get you, Adelaide. One minute I think you are unequivocally on our side; the next minute I decide you're one of the subtlest people I ever came up against." He scowled.

"As for what you have so immorally suggested, do you suppose for one minute I'd be hanging around here, waiting for all hell to burst loose, if Kathleen – if I could get her to go?"

I stared at him. "You've asked her? Already?"

He spread his hands helplessly. "I think I'm the last person on earth she'd trust herself with anywhere." He made a grimace.

" 'S funny, isn't it? Most women do trust me – too much."

"I don't doubt it," I snapped.

At this moment the inspector, having treated us to another dose of what Howard called 'stewing in our own juices,' looked up from his prolonged scrutiny of the black notebook on the table before him and bestowed upon us a pleasant smile which managed to have teeth in it, nonetheless.

"In case any of you have doubts as to whether Lottie Mosby fell or was pushed from a window in this house," he said in a level, incredibly emotionless voice, "let me state that the police have indisputable evidence that she was brutally murdered."

His words shocked us all, though they told us nothing new.

"Had we suspected Mrs Mosby's object in fleeing from this room," went on the inspector slowly, "we might have saved her; again, we might not have. At any rate," he said, staring straight before him, "we did not save her. She died, and her death puts a different complexion on the series of tragic events under this roof. As Miss Adams said, her blood is to some extent on all our hands, perhaps particularly on mine. For that reason, if no other," he added very quietly, "I shall not rest till I hang her murderer."

There was an oppressive silence broken only by the haunting wail of the wind and the tearful swish of the rain against the windowpanes.

"I am aware that not one of you has been frank or even honest with me," continued the inspector softly, transfixing each of us with an ominous scrutiny. "Perhaps had you done so, a second body might not be lying tonight on a cold grey slab in the city morgue."

It was a thought not one of us could face without a shudder.

The inspector allowed us an interval for his pronouncement to strike home and then he went on in that velvety tone which each of us was learning to dread for reasons peculiar to ourselves. "I have warned you before that you will save the police and your-selves considerable inconvenience by being quite frank with me," said the inspector. "I now warn you that unless you abandon your present dishonest attitude your cowardice may well cost another life or lives."

He paused; no one spoke. I do not think anyone moved or breathed or dared look at anybody else. My own eyes were fas-tened on that poisonous green carpet at my feet, but next to my skin the Manila envelope burned like a live coal.

"No one has any information to volunteer?" inquired the inspector gently, a flame at the back of his blue eyes.

The only answer was an angry flare of lightning at which we all started. "Oh, please," cried Mary Lawson in a strangled voice, "must you drag it out so? Can't you see we are all at the breaking point?"

"Hush, Aunt Mary!" whispered Polly, holding her aunt's shaking hands tightly against her breast. "For God's sake, pull yourself together, darling."

Slowly, inexorably, the inspector looked from Mary's ravished face to her niece's defiant blue-green eyes "Perhaps you will help us not to prolong this session, Mrs Lawson," he purred. "I do not doubt you can throw a light on at least one of the problems which have hampered and retarded the investigation."

Mary's colourless lips twitched, but it was Polly who answered in a passionate, reckless voice, "Don't be stupid! How could Aunt Mary know anything about-about these m-murders!"

"I wish I knew," murmured the inspector.

"It's dreadful for people to make each other so unhappy," wailed little Mrs Adair.

Kathleen put her arm about her mother, and the trembling older woman cowered against the girl's shoulder. Behind me Stephen sighed heavily. I had a feeling when he got to his feet that he had no idea what he intended to say, that his only object was to create a diversion.

"You have told us, Inspector, that the police are in possession of indisputable proof that Lottie Mosby was murdered," he said leisurely. "Do the authorities consider that proof their private property or might one inquire its nature?"

"One might, of course, inquire, Mr Lansing," murmured Inspector Bunyan with obvious sarcasm.

Their glances clashed, and then Stephen Lansing said harshly, "I do inquire."

Howard laughed disagreeably. "Here's your opportunity to practice what you preach, Inspector. After your urgent advice to us, you can't conscientiously refuse to bare your soul for the general good – or would you?"

The inspector's eyes dwelt upon Howard's sneering young face and then turned swiftly to Stephen Lansing. "I suspect you could hazard a very good guess, Mr Lansing, as to the room from which Lottie Mosby plunged to her death."

"You flatter me, Inspector," murmured Stephen with a sardonic grin.

It was then I had my unfortunate brainstorm. "Great heavens, was it – was it my old suite, Inspector?" I cried incredulously.

"Adelaide, Adelaide!" murmured Stephen sadly. "Of all dames the cleverest or the dumbest! Would I know which?"

The inspector was staring at me with an expression that tingled up and down my spine. "Why, yes, Miss Adams," he said, "it was from the bedroom in your former suite that that unfortunate body hurtled downward."

"Oh!" I gasped, feeling suddenly my full age.

"How extraordinary for you to have guessed it, Miss Adams," the inspector went on with chilling and unmistakable irony. "Would you mind explaining to my – ah – satisfaction how you so nimbly reached a conclusion which the police almost failed to reach at all?"

"I-er-it occurred to me," I stammered hoarsely, "that since your men looked all over the house for Lottie Mosby, presumably in every conceivable place, it was unlikely you could have missed her unless-unless... I believe the suite I used to occupy is supposed to be-er-locked and sealed. It-it occurred to me it was probably the last place the police thought of searching."

Even to my ears my explanation sounded extremely thin and halting, and I am positive my face looked the picture of hang-dog guilt. I was not surprised to have the inspector survey me with a skeptical lift of the eyebrows.

"Quite a neat piece of deduction, Miss Adams," he commented in his silkiest voice. "If it was deduction," he added cynically.

"Surely you wouldn't doubt Miss Adams' veracity, Inspector," drawled Stephen with one of his saturnine grins.

"When it is possible for people to walk through both the police and locked doors at will, Mr Lansing," said the inspector grimly, "one begins to doubt the veracity of one's own senses." He turned on me so sharply, my spectacles tumbled off my nose. "What took Mrs Mosby to your suite, Miss Adams?"

"I haven't the remotest idea," I assured him earnestly.

"She was after something," continued the inspector, scowling at his notebook. "It was, I have no doubt, evidence of her innocence, perhaps evidence of the murderer's guilt. And she paid for it with her life." He again transfixed me with a glance. "This is the third time that we know of in which an attempt has been made to recover something or other from a room you are occupying or have occupied, Miss Adams."

I bridled in self-defence. "Don't forget the room I am now in originally belonged to James Reid and he-he met his death in my former suite."

"Quite so, but that merely brings us back to the starting point, doesn't it? Why was he there to be killed?" I shook my head, and Stephen Lansing laughed mirthlessly.

"What is this strange and perilous attraction you have, Adelaide?"

I could only fall lamely back on my former retort. "I haven't the remotest idea."

The inspector regarded every person in the room in turn from over his locked hands on the table before him. "I am still to be met with stubborn silence, is that it?" he inquired softly. "No one feels the urge to be helpful?"

Once more his only answer was the melancholy sigh of the wind and the rain.

"I have one more warning to issue," continued Inspector Bunyan in a voice which made my blood run cold. "James Reid was strangled first, then he was hung up by his suspenders to the chandelier, and his throat cut from ear to ear. Lottie Mosby was also strangled before she was hurled out a window on the fourth floor. Murderers, as any criminologist will tell you, have a habit of adhering to a fixed pattern. The only way any of you, except the assassin himself, can be positive that you will not feel those cruel, clutching fingers squeezing into your own windpipe is to aid the police in every possible way to round up this madman before he snuffs out another life."

I think everybody present swallowed. I know I did, as if already I felt those ghastly hands about my throat. Stephen was the first to recover from the paralysis of horror into which we had all been plunged.

"Did you say madman, Inspector?" he asked.

"Hasn't it struck you, Mr Lansing," murmured the inspector, "that there is a touch of the macabre about this whole affair? Why, when he was already dead, should James Reid have been strung up like a fowl and his throat drawn from ear to ear? Why, when the breath had been choked out of her, should Lottie Mosby's lifeless body have been dashed to the ground and broken to pieces?"

"Couldn't the latter have been an attempt to palm her death off as suicide?" ventured Stephen.

"No, Mr Lansing, our murderer has proved himself too clever to underestimate the intelligence of the police in such a fashion.

He knew he had left the mark of Cain on his victim, a mark which was certain to come out at the inquest, if not before."

"You mean the fingerprints on the throat?"

The inspector nodded. "There is only one way to explain the savagery with which these two dead bodies were needlessly and cruelly mutilated."

Across the room the Anthony woman smothered an oath. "Bologney!" she cried scornfully. "As if we wouldn't know if there was a stray lunatic floating around among us!"

The inspector shook his head. "Unfortunately, Mrs – ah – Anthony, in the case of certain mental disorders, dementia praecox for instance, the degeneration of the brain is up to a certain stage extremely slow and not easily detected even by experts. According to psychiatrists, a person with such a disease may continue for an indefinite period to conceal his affliction, granting he is not subjected to a severe nervous strain. In that event, of course, he goes to pieces very rapidly. The interval between his being an apparently normal individual and the period when he becomes as rabid as a mad dog may be a matter of only a few weeks or even days."

The Anthony woman laughed harshly. "What are you trying to do, Inspector? Scare us into breaking down and telling our right names?" she demanded mockingly.

"I'm merely warning you that it might be wise for all of you who value your lives to tell not only your right names but everything else which you are, from motives best known to yourselves, concealing from the police," said the inspector soberly.

It seemed to me as his eyes circled the room that they lingered longest on Cyril Fancher, who shrank back into Sophie's bulky shadow.

"I am going to find out eventually," the inspector went on, his jaw tightening. "Make no mistake about that. But in the meanwhile, without your co-operation, I cannot guarantee that I will uncover the truth in time to save one of you, possibly more."

"Of all the tommyrot!" exploded Howard angrily. "Aren't you overworking your sense of the dramatic, Inspector? This isn't a lurid stage play where every time the curtain falls another victim has bit the dust. Why should your murderer kill again? After all, he isn't just doing it for fun, I don't suppose."

"No," said the inspector softly, "the murderer isn't killing for fun. In each instance he has, unless I misread the signs, struck to save himself. And that's why I know he'll strike again. I am not going to give up till I wrest his secret from him, and each of you possesses some part of that secret, God help you! Before you are allowed to betray it, the murderer will, if possible, put you out of his way as ruthlessly as he has already stamped out the two other people who threatened his safety."

"In that case, Inspector, aren't you being a bit obtuse?" demanded Howard with tight-lipped insolence. "I mean, after your warning, how can you expect any of us to tell you what we know? Providing, of course," he added unpleasantly, "that we know anything, which I fancy none of us intends to admit."

"There are two armed policemen at the door, Mr Warren," said the inspector with cool composure. "I myself carry a revolver. This is the only place in this house at present, I should say, where it is possible to speak the truth, the whole truth, and nothing but the truth, without fear of consequences."

"Is that so?" muttered the Anthony woman, glancing uneasily over her shoulder.

"You were saying, Mrs – ah – Anthony?" purred the inspector.

She gave him a derisive grin. "Nothing, Inspector. Not one blamed thing – to you."

The inspector sighed. "I hope you never have cause to regret that."

She tossed her head. "Don't worry. If yapping to the police is the only way to get your throat wrung, believe me, I'll die in my little old bed."

I shivered. "You might do that and still be strangled to death," I said, thinking of that evil presence which had stood within reach of me the night before.

"Exactly," said the inspector.

Hilda Anthony's lips parted in a sneer. "Sorry, Inspector. I just don't scare easily."

Howard grinned. "I'm afraid your big drama of the clee-utching hand has backfired on you, Inspector."

"Yes?" murmured the inspector, his eyes narrowing to needle points.

"Watch out for the fireworks!" Stephen Lansing muttered at my ear. "This is what he's been leading up to."

"If all you say is true," said Howard, looking offensively cocky, "only a fool would risk his neck by shooting off his mouth to you or anyone else at this stage of the game."

"You think so, Mr Warren?"

"Let the police do it," murmured Howard with the bitter flippancy which was quite new to him. "I mean, I can't see why we should be expected to do the police's dirty work for them. After all, you're the one, not I, Inspector, who's paid to take desperate chances, and the like of that, for the common weal or what have you."

"Nevertheless," said Inspector Bunyan very quietly, "I'll lay you a little bet, Mr Warren, that before we leave this room I'll get the truth out of you, at least."

Howard turned a sickly white; the edge had gone out of his bravado.

It flapped about him in shreds when the inspector went on,

"You were up on the fourth floor just before James Reid's body was discovered."

"Oh yes?" murmured Howard again, very shakily.

"You came straight downstairs and made a feverish and unprecedented attempt to get Miss Adelaide Adams out of the hotel."

"It's no crime to ask a lady to the movies."

The inspector went mercilessly on. "You did everything in your power not only to remove Miss Adams temporarily from the scene but, furthermore, to prevent her going to her room in the meanwhile."

"It was a warm night, and – and I have a closed car." Howard defended himself in a thick voice.

"Why was it so important to you, Mr Warren, to get Miss Adams out of her suite and keep her out at that particular time?" demanded the inspector in short angry tones like the strokes of a riveter.

"You're making a mare's-nest out of nothing, Inspector," stammered Howard. "I had no ulterior motive in inviting Miss Adams to a movie." He tried to grin. "At least, that's my story, and you're stuck with it."

"I don't think so, Mr Warren," murmured the inspector. "There are ways, you know, of enforcing authority, and it's never safe to spit in a bulldog's face."

He rapped sharply on the table in front of him, and a policeman stuck his head in at the door. "Arrest this man, Sweeney, and take him down to headquarters," said the inspector.

Polly uttered a little wail, and Howard, his assurance suddenly restored, grinned at the inspector. "Arrest me for what, Inspector?" he inquired nonchalantly. "One does have to have a charge to make an arrest, doesn't one?"

"The charge," said the inspector curtly, "is murder."

"Oh no!" Mary Lawson was on her feet, her hands held out in a pleading gesture, her face distorted.

"You can't arrest Howard," she cried wildly, "because-because-"

"For God's sake, Polly," cried Howard, "make her keep still."

"No," said Mary Lawson, "I've already kept still too long."

"Arresting me is just a bluff to force you to talk!" pleaded Howard.

She did not seem to hear. Her gaze was fastened on the inspector. She looked broken and old.

"You can't arrest Howard," she said, "because-because it was I who-who asked him to keep Adelaide away from her room last night."

"Oh, Aunt Mary, Aunt Mary!" wailed Polly, while Howard, his shoulders sagging, reached over the back of the divan and gripped her hands tightly and I stared at Mary Lawson, unable to believe my ears.

"Yes, Mrs Lawson?" prompted the inspector gently.

"Howard came up to the fourth floor to see me. I had sent him a note by-by Clarence on the elevator. You could have found that out if you had asked him."

The inspector smiled wearily. "I did find it out, Mrs Lawson."

"I told you it was a trap," groaned Howard, while Polly began to weep like a forlorn and bewildered child.

Mary's lips trembled. "I asked Howard to-to see to it that Miss Adams did not go to her room between eight and nine that night."

The blood was roaring in my ears. "Mary, my dear!" I protested in a choked voice. "If only you had taken me into your confidence!"

"And have your blood as well on my hands," said Mary, staring at her fingers.

"Did you take Mr Warren into your confidence, Mrs Lawson?" asked the inspector quietly.

"I took no one! No one, do you hear?"

"Yet the moment your niece saw that bloody knife from your desk set, she tried to run away with it."

"I tell you, neither Howard nor Polly has any idea what this is all about!" cried Mary, beginning to shake from head to foot with hysteria.

"I wouldn't be too sure about that," murmured the inspector.

"The knife was stolen hours before the murder, Inspector!" cried Polly. "I told you that yesterday."

The inspector shrugged his shoulders. "When did you last see the paper knife, Mrs Lawson? That is, before the police produced it, along with your niece, sometime after the crime."

There was a dreadful silence and then a sigh as, with a face like death, Mary Lawson gasped, "I don't remember."

"I remember!" cried Polly Lawson passionately. "Because about five o'clock that afternoon I looked for the knife to-to open a bottle of gin, if you must know, and-and it was gone."

The inspector eyed her thoughtfully. "You've gone to rather a lot of trouble during the past several months to put on a show of being a very wild young woman, haven't you, Miss Lawson?"

Polly coloured painfully. "I-I don't know what you mean."

The inspector smiled. "Just why have you so ardently desired to leave the impression on numerous occasions that you were drunk, when you weren't?"

"I don't know what you mean," she faltered again.

He shrugged his shoulders. "You seem to have consistently placed the cart before the horse. I mean, few young women deliberately strive to appear worse than they are."

"Polly!" cried Howard Warren.

She refused to look at him. "I don't know what you are getting at, Inspector," she said sulkily. "If I've gone out of my way to shock the prudes in this house it's because they make me sick!" She whirled on Howard. "That goes for you too, you old-old holier-than-thou!"

"Polly!" gasped Howard, looking as if she had struck him in the face.

The inspector appeared to have lost interest in both of them. His brows were gathered into a frown when he turned to Mary

Lawson again. His voice gave me a shock. It was utterly ruthless.

"And so as early as five o'clock yesterday afternoon, Mrs Lawson, you suspected you might have to kill James Reid and had provided yourself with the paper knife off your desk," he said.

Mary's eyes widened and widened in her drawn ghastly face.

"I-I..." she began.

"You don't have to answer questions which might incriminate you, Aunt Mary," interrupted Polly, scowling ferociously at Inspector Bunyan.

The inspector ignored her remark. "That's why you wanted to keep Adelaide Adams off the fourth floor last night, Mrs Lawson. You had a date on the fire escape with a man and you had cause to believe that James Reid was spying on you. Right?"

Her bloodless lips, after a struggle, parted. "I had an appointment on the – on the fire-escape landing, yes. That's why I wanted Adelaide out of the way. But, as God is my keeper, I did not kill James Reid."

"With whom did you have a clandestine appointment on the fire escape, Mrs Lawson?" pursued the inspector, while I stared at her aghast.

Of all the women in that house none I had thought was cleaner of the taint of scandal than Mary Lawson, whose heart I would have sworn still ached unbearably for her dead husband.

"I can't tell you," she said.

"You mean, you refuse to tell?" he demanded.

"I can't! I can't!" she cried wildly. "If it were only myself..." She broke off, bit her lip, and put out her hands in a little pleading gesture which wrung my heart. "If I could, God knows I'd help you, Inspector."

"You are compelling me to take a step I regret," said the inspector sternly. He turned to the policeman Sweeney. "Take this woman down to headquarters. Hold her there till I arrive."

"You are going to arrest Aunt Mary?" cried Polly desperately.

"You can't, you mustn't, Inspector! The-the disgrace will kill her!"

Mary Lawson shook her head. "It's not so easy to die as all that," she said bitterly. "One's body lives on and on; only one's heart dies."

"Ready, Mrs Lawson?" murmured the inspector gently.

Mary's face was like those you have seen of the martyred saints. "Yes, Inspector, I am quite ready," she said.

She was still smiling when she walked out of the room beside Sweeney, the brawny policeman.

13

"It's an outrage" protested Howard Warren. "What if Mary Lawson was-was meeting some man on the fire escape?" He swallowed painfully. "What if it was her paper knife which killed Reid? That's a long way from being proof of murder. No jury in the world would convict on such evidence."

With Mary's departure in the custody of the police the conference in the parlour had more or less automatically dissolved. Those of us who had been Mary Lawson's friends were at first too stunned by her arrest and then too distracted by it to remain static, even if Inspector Bunyan had not summarily dismissed us with the observation that he desired to follow his prisoner as quickly as possible to police headquarters.

"Of course, you realize that I'll get in touch with Mary's lawyer at once," Howard told him savagely. "We'll probably be on the scene by the time you are, Inspector. Just in case you're planning to try something like the third degree, since you haven't any other leg to get off on."

"Suit yourself, Mr Warren," murmured Inspector Bunyan with a shrug of his dapper shoulders.

Polly was having hysterics in Ella Trotter's arms in the corridor outside the parlour doors where we were all congregated. Setting his teeth, Howard went over to them and, laying his hand on Ella's arm, said, "Tell her – tell her there's nothing to worry about, Mrs Trotter. It won't take a good lawyer five minutes to tear the inspector's case to ribbons."

Polly did not lift her head, but her sobs diminished in violence.

Still gazing at a point slightly above her dishevelled red curls, Howard went on in a halting voice, "Tell her, Mrs Trotter, that Mary's lawyer and I will have her out on bond before midnight."

"Oh, thank you, Howard d-darling!" gasped Polly and then, when Howard in spite of himself reached out his hand to her, she turned away again and lifted her eyes pleadingly to Ella Trotter.

"Please – please – I don't want to talk to anyone or see anyone – *Please* can't you make everybody let me alone?"

Ella nodded vigorously. "Trust me to do that little thing."

She then and there carried Polly off to her suite and, having put her to bed on the living room davenport, mounted guard over both doors with an 'only over my dead body' expression which settled that. The rest of us, unable to conceal our dejection, trailed downstairs to the lobby where we collected in small scattered groups, talking in low tones if we talked at all but for the most part listening in leaden silence to the dreary monotone of the rain.

Howard Warren, not having stopped even to get his raincoat, dashed past us on his way to meet Mary's lawyer with whom he had made an engagement by telephone. I had known a day when Howard would not have risked spoiling the crease in his trousers, much less wet feet, in such weather. I sighed. He had no doubt been, as Polly said, a little on the holier-than-thou side at one time.

He was so no longer. Howard had gone human with a vengeance, and I had never liked him half so well.

His headlong course through the lobby, however, was checked by Stephen Lansing.

"About bailing Mrs Lawson out, Warren," he said with a frown, "do you think that's altogether wise?"

Howard stared at him. "Leave Mary down there at the mercy of those-those morons? Not one moment longer than is necessary!" he expostulated.

"There are worse things to be at the mercy of than the law, Warren," said Stephen Lansing, "as we should all be prepared to testify by now."

Howard paled. "You mean?"

"I think it's self-evident that Mrs Lawson knows a great deal."

"Why, you – you –"

"If you ask me," said Stephen Lansing gravely, "most of us could be in more dangerous places than securely locked up in jail for the next few days, particularly Mary Lawson with whatever it is she has on that conscience of hers."

"Damn it, Mary didn't kill that swine!" protested Howard fiercely.

However, as he went slowly out the revolving door of the hotel he had lost the major portion of his aggressiveness, and I think none of us was greatly surprised to hear a little before midnight that, after an interview with her lawyer, Mary had decided for the present not to apply for release on bond.

"We did succeed in wringing one concession from the police," said Howard when he returned, his face jaded though happier than when he left. "She has not been booked for murder. She's being held as a material witness, or so the inspector gave out to the newspaper boys." He smiled wryly. "At least we shan't have her served up in headlines with our breakfast for the whole town to gape at."

"Thank God!" I muttered.

Stephen nodded and said, "I don't believe for a minute that the inspector thinks Mary Lawson is a murderess." When we stared at him he added, with a gesture toward the stairs, "You notice he hasn't called off his dogs."

"On the contrary," snapped Sophie Scott. "You have only to try moving about, to see them poking their square heads around corners or from behind the doors of supposedly empty rooms, like roaches coming up out of the drains."

I did see a couple of uniformed men in my corridor, when a little after twelve our informal gathering in the lobby broke up and along with the others I trailed up to my room for a night toward which none of us, I think, looked forward with any degree of pleasure.

To tell the truth, it gave me more of a comfortable sensation than not when I opened the door to 511 to know that in the hall behind me the policeman Sweeney, evidently under special orders, was staring fixedly at the back of my head.

Even so, there was a bad minute when I stood there in the dark, fumbling for the light switch. I wondered if there would be time to scream if those two murderous hands clenched themselves about my throat or if one would be able to scream when face to face with that anonymous horror which needlessly mutilated the corpses of its victims with all the savagery of a perverted and diseased brain.

However, when my cold and trembling fingers on the second attempt succeeded in turning the switch, there was nothing in the room before me of a sinister nature except one tiny scrap of blank brown wrapping paper which I had overlooked when I flushed the others down the sewer. The mirror was innocent of lascivious notes.

The window on the fire escape was still closed and locked as I had left it. Nevertheless, my heart had a tendency to climb into my throat at the least unexpected noise, and it seemed to me I had never heard a night so full of weird creakings and stealthy footfalls and uncanny rappings.

"It's only the wind, rattling doors and windows," I told myself stoutly, but my blood pressure continued to mount steadily until I could feel the pulse under my ears pounding and hammering in my throat.

I remember thinking that an elderly woman whose arteries are no longer all they should be would probably prove an easy subject for strangulation, before I finally managed to pull myself together and, having removed my shoes and my outer dress, crawled into bed and, with more fortitude than one might suppose, jerked the chain which extinguished the table lamp beside me, plunging me into a blackness that took my breath away for a moment.

Under other circumstances I think I should have slept with my light on that night, but, feeling positive the policeman outside my door had received instructions to keep a close watch upon me, I was taking no chances. It was not part of my plan to be caught red handed in the undertaking to which, after having counted the probable risk to myself and made up my mind to damn the consequences, I had positively made up my mind.

It was just after the courthouse clock tolled once for a quarter of one that I stole out the side of my bed, taking care to avoid with my stocking feet the plank which I had noticed possessed a squeak. Inch by inch I eased up the window which looked out upon the fire escape.

The rain had again drizzled into a thin mist. Leaning far out, I deposited on the iron landing below me the aluminium water pitcher in which I had placed my packet of greenbacks, wrapped in an old silk handkerchief. Then, drawing my purple bathrobe about me and hunching my throat deeper into the folds of my lavender fascinator, I crouched down just below the window ledge in the mist and the dark, praying to heaven that I should not sneeze at the zero hour.

I had baited the trap; I had only to wait for a human rat to walk into it. The pocket of my bathrobe sagged under the weight of the small ugly automatic which, in a moment of aberration after a series of robberies in the city years before, I had allowed myself to buy. Not until later did it occur to me that I had no idea how to fire the thing, even if it was loaded - which to my knowledge it never had been.

I can only say for what it's worth that it had given me a sense of protection for years to know that the revolver was in my dresser drawer, and, now that I was coming to grips with a mad and ruthless slayer, the gun still comforted me in the illogical way women have about such matters.

The clock tolled for one, and then the quarter and the half-hour. The tickling in my throat assumed the proportion of a major obstacle. To keep from coughing required a part of my self-control, but not the major portion. It was not possible to see the water pitcher from where I huddled without lifting the top of my head and one eye above the windowsill. Having no desire to alarm my prey, I yielded to this temptation only when I could no longer by main strength resist it.

However, I was not trusting to my eyes. With the police camping in the corridor, off which opened not only my door but the entrance to the fire escape, there remained but one approach to the water pitcher, and that by way of the fire escape itself. And while my knees and my eyes are not what they were, my ears are preternaturally keen. I did not believe so much as a mouse could climb to within a few feet of my nose without my hearing him, no matter how cautious his ascent.

It was, as near as I can estimate, a few minutes of two when I heard the faint metallic click on the landing. Aha, I told myself, the villain approaches. In my excitement I totally forgot to be afraid – explain that if you can. Nothing at the moment mattered to me except the thrill of the chase. In fact, only my determination not to frighten my game away at the last moment enabled me during the next few minutes to keep my head down.

As eager as a stove-up old fire horse, I crouched there, waiting for the signal to pounce. To this day I do not know if I expected my proposed victim to drop dead at sight of me or what. There are times even yet when I become slightly hysterical at the thought of what would have happened had I actually confronted that distraught and frantic creature for whom I lay in wait. But there is a destiny which watches over children and idiots, for I did not confront him.

When next I raised my head the water pitcher was gone.

I could not and would not believe it. I was convinced my senses or the ghostly grey fog which swirled by in tatters on the shoulders of the wind was playing me tricks. There was one terrible moment when I wondered if it was my brain which was going to pieces under the strain, when I wondered if perhaps the inspector and Stephen Lansing were right in harping upon the strange coincidence with which from the first I had seemed to be the focal point for the murders at the Hotel Richelieu. I even wondered if one who was losing her mind might in a temporary fit of madness fling a woman out a window and cut a man's throat without, at her lucid intervals, recalling a single one of her horrible actions.

However, after a while I threw off the hobgoblins and rose creakily to my feet. The water pitcher was gone. How and where, I had no idea, but my common sense came to my rescue in what till then had been the most desperate minute of my life. I had set the trap and a human rat had filched the bait from under my very teeth, but there was nothing weird or supernatural about the episode. I had merely been outwitted by someone far more cunning than I.

For the first time it dawned upon me how clever the blackmailer had been in his choice of the aluminium water pitcher as a silent partner in his nefarious business. Not only were they easily come by and practically unidentifiable, being a part of the equipment of every room in the hotel, but they each had a narrow rigid handle.

There was no other way to explain the metallic click and the way in which the pitcher had apparently taken wings and floated itself away.

"He has a fishing tool of some kind," I told myself bitterly, "or some sort of long rod with a hook on the end. He simply hooks the handle of the pitcher and draws it up or down or out or in, as the case may be."

My chagrin at the way I had been outwitted was equalled only by my, I contend, quite natural desire to get my own back. The loss of my thousand dollars was the least smart to my pride. Otherwise, my knees being what they are, the last thing I should ever have attempted was to clamber through my window and out upon the fire escape. I had some notion, I think, of peeping under drawn shades upon a malignant creature, gloatingly removing my greenbacks from my favourite silk handkerchief, which I had never intended for a cravenly blackmailer.

I still insist, regardless of Ella Trotter's gibes on the subject, that I should have succeeded in wriggling my rather corpulent body through the opening without too much difficulty. As I have bitterly pointed out, I must indeed have been at least halfway through for my writhing's to have discharged the revolver in my pocket.

Yes, it went off, as empty guns have a trick of doing at the most inopportune times. Went off with the most deafening explosion and an acrid puff of gunpowder, which promptly flew up my nostrils like a cloud of brimstone. Naturally I sneezed, went into a violent fit of coughing, and completely lost my balance.

That is why when Stephen Lansing again bounded up the fire escape in his brocaded dressing gown it was to discover me hanging out my window by my knees, in the manner of the famous three toed sloth, upside down, with tears streaming down my cheeks as I clutched the rungs of the fire escape and indulged in a series of asthmatic wheezes, while in the pocket of my purple bathrobe a small fire blazed merrily up.

"Good God, Miss Adelaide, make up your mind!" he gasped. "Are you trying to hang yourself? Or shoot yourself? Or burn yourself up?"

"At-choo! Glug!" was the only response to which I was equal at the moment.

He groaned. "One might know, Adelaide, you'd be no sissy even at suicide."

"Young man," I spluttered weakly, "I only hope I haven't killed anyone else – Atchoo!"

He stared at me with a convulsed look on his face, and I explained crossly, "It was that dratted gun in my pocket. It went – atchoo! – it went off for no good reason."

At this point, with some boosting on Stephen's part, I managed to work my way back into the room, where he joined me, continuing to stare at me very strangely while he beat out the blaze in my pocket which the gun had set off, and we both, as if by mutual consent, ignored the furious banging on the door which was the policeman Sweeney, trying to effect an entrance with, I admit, justifiable excitement.

"Open up, or I'll shoot the lock!" he thundered at last in what was unmistakably an ultimatum.

Giving me a rueful glance, Stephen Lansing shrugged his shoulders, crossed the room, noiselessly turned the key, and flung the door open so suddenly Sweeney all but fell in upon his prominent beak.

"What the..." he snarled, wildly swinging an enormous service revolver in all directions as if he were shadowboxing a whole army of criminals.

"You two again!" he exclaimed, stopping short and staring from one to the other of us with a sour expression. "Where's the corpse?"

"I regret to disappoint you, but no gore has been shed, if one accepts the feathers of the old grey goose," remarked Stephen in his suavest manner.

"Feathers!" repeated Officer Sweeney in an exasperated voice. "Whatcha giving me?"

"Feathers, feathers, everywhere, and not a lulu bird in sight," murmured Stephen, airily pursing his lips and waving a couple of pale grey feathers into Sweeney's outraged face.

It was then I perceived that the bullet from my gun had found sanctuary in one of the pillows on the bed, as evidenced by a neat blackened hole in the starched slip.

"There is only one hole," Stephen pointed out softly. "The-er your shot, Adelaide, seems to have buried itself in down."

"Thank providence!" I cried devoutly.

Officer Sweeney glared at me. "And what might you have been doing firing a shot at all?" he demanded.

"Well," I said tartly, "I might have been practicing for a beauty contest."

Patrolman Sweeney flung me an embittered glance. "Only you wasn't," he snapped.

"No," I admitted wearily, "I wasn't."

"I guess you might just as well save it for the inspector," said

Sweeney. "Only I warn you, after routing him out of bed for the second night in succession you two had better make it good."

To say that I experienced no enthusiasm at the prospect of presenting the inspector with an explanation for my, to say the least, peculiar actions on this occasion presents an entirely inadequate picture of the way I cudgelled my brain during that uncomfortable half-hour while Stephen and I waited for the inspector's arrival.

The turmoil had aroused everybody in the hotel, but Sweeney ordered the others back to their rooms.

Stephen and me he marched downstairs to the lobby, practically by an ear. There he left us in charge of two gawky and extremely nervous young policemen who were, I gathered, the cubs of the force. I think Sweeney himself wanted an unobstructed opportunity to search my room. I believe he expected to find no less than two murdered bodies piled up in my closet, if not under the bed.

Before he left us I heard him mutter to one of the fledgling cops, "If you want my opinion, she's a werewolf, and he" – indicating Stephen – "is her pet pup."

"Gosh!" breathed the young policeman, his knees betraying a tendency to clash together like castanets.

"I never had such a shock, Miss Adelaide," said Pinky from behind the desk. "As soon as I heard the shot I was certain somebody else had been murdered, and when Clarence squalled down the elevator shaft that the disturbance was in your room I nearly fainted right on my feet."

I took a long breath. "As it happens, the fuss has all been for nothing, absolutely nothing, Pinky. I took my revolver to bed with me, for a precaution, as I often do," I explained mendaciously, "and in some manner I managed in my sleep to-er-discharge a bullet into one of my pillows."

That was the story which I repeated firmly and without embellishment to the inspector after he came, not, I think, that he believed it for a second. However, he was unable to shake my testimony.

I was a little shocked at the facility which I had developed for telling the most abandoned lies without a twinge of conscience, a talent which had lain dormant in my make-up for fifty-odd years, no matter what Ella Trotter has to say on the topic.

"And you, Mr Lansing," murmured the inspector with a jaundiced gleam in his eye, "just how did you happen to appear once more with such remarkable ease and celerity in Miss Adams' room? Passing, it would seem, right through locked doors and windows, to say nothing of a two-hundred-pound policeman."

"Just like the daring young man on the flying trapeze, tra la," murmured Stephen impudently.

The inspector's face turned faintly purple.

"I forgot to mention, Inspector Bunyan," I interposed hastily, "that I had left the window on the fire escape open."

"Contrary to my recommendation?"

"I'm afraid so," I admitted feebly.

"Either you are a phenomenally fearless woman, Miss Adams," said Inspector Bunyan ominously, "or you have sufficient reasons of your own for feeling immune to the murderous attack of the dangerous criminal now at large in the Richelieu Hotel."

I shivered. "I -er-am a fatalist, Inspector," I murmured, more or less at random. "You know, what is to be, will be, and all that kind of thing."

"Believe it or not," added Stephen Lansing solemnly.

The inspector favoured us with what to me was a distinctly disconcerting look. "And once more, Mr Lansing, when Miss Adams trumpeted her appeal for help, you were fully attired, at two o'clock and past of a black and rainy night," he said with what I can only describe as a snort.

Stephen smiled brightly. "I was playing solitaire in my room, Inspector, on the third floor. I think I have remarked to you before that I am a bit of a night owl."

"Quite so," murmured the inspector. "Only it had slipped my mind till now that the owl, although a synonym for benignant wisdom in literary circles, is actually a bird of prey which prefers to do its hunting – and killing – at night."

Stephen grinned. "Have it your own way, Inspector."

Apparently satisfied that he had got all he was going to get out of us, the inspector let us go at last, taking the precaution, however, to send the two embryo policemen up in the elevator with us, presumably to rob us of an opportunity for private conversation.

The inspector might have known that Stephen and I were more than a match for a couple of amateur Hawkshaws.

Without turning his head, Stephen out of the corner of his mouth said, "Thanks, Adelaide. I'll do you a good turn someday."

"As if you haven't once or twice already," I exclaimed, apparently addressing the farther corner of the elevator cage.

"Gosh," murmured one of the fledgling policemen, "I always heard that crazy people talk to themselves."

"Till tomorrow, light of my eyes!" cried Stephen gaily, sweeping me an elaborate bow when the elevator stopped at his floor. "Granting we both live to greet another dawn," he added with what might have been a warning and could have been a threat.

It was all very well for him to treat the matter facetiously, but both of us knew he had not been playing solitaire in his room when he plunged out upon the fire escape to my rescue. I may have been as good as standing on my head at the time, yet I had distinctly seen the window from which he vaulted, pausing only to slam it to behind him. It was the window in the bedroom of my old suite on the fourth floor. And that was not the worst of it.

As Stephen Lansing neared the top of the iron staircase, staring incredulously at my, to be quite fair, strictly undignified situation, our gaze fastened at the same instant upon something lying on the landing at the level of his chin. I cannot even yet explain how I contrived, in the midst of my frantic scramble to maintain my equilibrium five stories above the earth, to get my hands on that bedraggled pink rose first, nor could I doubt from the look on Stephen Lansing's handsome face that for one tense moment he had an almost irresistible desire to remove at least one complication from his path forever by wringing my neck without further ado or possibly just by loosening my tenuous clutch on security, a simple feat considering my position at the time.

"It's getting so in this house, death, like taxes, is just around every corner," I told myself after I had closed and locked my door behind me.

The window upon the fire escape, thanks to Officer Sweeney's carelessness, was still standing wide open, the curtain flapping dismally in and out. Clenching my teeth, I went over, jerked the window down and bolted the latch. Not until I had carefully lowered every shade and, as an extra precaution, had hung one of my felt hats over the keyhole did I remove the rose from the top of my stocking where the thorns had pricked my game knee unmercifully for the past hour.

"You fool! You doddering old fool!" I accused myself unsteadily.

"As if there aren't a million pink rosebuds in the world!" But it was no use. My own eyes confounded me. Curled around the stem of the rosebud was a bronze hair which gleamed in the light in the chandelier above my head.

"Then Kathleen was on the landing, God help us all!" I cried, putting my hand to my throat which seemed to have closed up with dismay.

It was then I noticed for the first time that the string of bright red stones was gone from about my neck.

14

I come now to the third and last day in our reign of terror, a day which was to be written in letters of blood on the consciousness of all of us, a day which left a streak like a white ribbon in the thick black hair above Stephen Lansing's left temple, a day from which I emerged with a permanent tic in the muscles of my right eye.

We were a sober and lugubrious group that morning after Mary Lawson went to jail. Judging from the apprehensive faces, as one after the other the guests of the Richelieu straggled into the Coffee Shop for breakfast, no one felt the easier in his mind for her arrest. The tension had, if anything, increased. People said little and, where possible, kept their eyes down. You could have spread the nervousness in the atmosphere with a trowel.

The only exception was the waitress, Miss Gloria Larue. She, at least, was walking on air. She did not confide the cause for the lilt in both her eyes and her hips to me, having, as I have noted before, apparently made up her mind that my lack of enthusiasm for the talkie heroes and heroines put me beyond her personal pale.

However, I heard her burbling over to the Adairs at the table behind me.

"It's the chance of a lifetime," she explained breathlessly. "All I've ever asked is the opportunity to strut my stuff where it'll do the most good."

"I think it's wonderful," said little Mrs Adair. "There's something inspiring in the thought of a beautiful girl like you being on the air. Beauty was meant for the enjoyment of the whole world."

"Thank you, ma'am," said Miss Gloria Larue complacently.

Kathleen's voice sounded odd. "You are quite certain this – this offer is on the up-and-up?"

"Listen," said Gloria Larue indignantly, "big broadcasting stations don't send you notices, asking you to appear at a specified hour for an audition, unless they mean business."

"I suppose not," murmured Kathleen uncertainly.

"I guess they heard about me singing at the last Union Waitresses' ball," Gloria went on blissfully. "Everybody there said I was a riot but" – her voice trembled slightly – "I wasn't right sure they weren't poking fun at me. You see, I've been on my own since I was sixteen, and a feller sort of gets used to taking it on the chin when he's got nobody but himself to back his play."

"I hope it turns out splendidly for you," said Kathleen kindly.

"When are you leaving?"

"Right after lunch today. There's a Memphis bus at two-thirty, if I don't decide to-to thumb my way."

I sighed and made a mental note to leave more than my usual tip beside my plate. In fact, I was fumbling in my purse for two half-dollar pieces when I saw Cyril Fancher frowning at me through the mirror from the Adair table beside which he had pulled up with a tight look about his mouth.

"Haven't I warned you before, Gloria," he said, "that we do not hire waitresses to annoy the guests with their conversation?"

"But we don't mind," expostulated little Mrs Adair.

However, after a glance at Cyril Fancher's forbidding countenance, Miss Gloria Larue shouldered her tray and, sniffing audibly through her short snub nose, departed kitchen ward.

"Poor child," I muttered to myself. "I hope she gets a break for once. The underprivileged female so seldom does."

It was, I recall, a Thursday, the day my laundress brings my week's washing home. That is why, directly after breakfast, I ascended to my room. Carrie was waiting for me. She and Laura, the maid who was cleaning up my quarters, were talking volubly before I opened the door, but they hushed up quickly enough when I entered. I am accustomed to the secretiveness of the staff. There is nothing they do not know about the guests, but they never discuss it except among themselves which is just as well.

Pocketing her wages, Carrie shuffled out the door. Laura, having finished, was about to follow when I halted her on the threshold.

"Something seems to have-er-happened to my water pitcher, Laura," I said. "Please get me another."

"Yas 'm," said Laura stolidly.

However, when she returned a few minutes later, carrying the typical hotel pitcher which she deposited with an ungentle thump on my bedside table, she muttered something about her mammy having always told her that little pitchers have big ears, "but I never knowed twellately they had feetses."

"What's that you're mumbling, Laura?" I demanded sharply.

She gave me a sullen glance. "I jest said, it's funny how one minute dey is a water pitcher, next minute dey ain't. But I bin telling folks all year this here house is hoodooed. Reckon they's beginning to believe me."

My heart was thumping against my side. "Have other people in the hotel mislaid their water pitchers, Laura?"

Her underlip poked out. "Yas 'm. I clean up room, pitcher where he belong on table, next morning no pitcher. I git de guest another one. Sometime dat day old pitcher bob up, maybe by the trash barrel in the service hall, maybe jes' setting on the stair."

I might have known, I told myself bitterly, that the performance of the night before was too smooth not to have been staged before.

"Just whose water pitchers, Laura, have-er-behaved in this provoking manner?" I inquired.

She gave me a curious look, and not for the first time I wondered if there was anything about any one of us which the old maid did not pack under her cap.

"Well," she said at last with obvious reluctance, "there was Miss Polly's pitcher three-four times last winter, and Miss Mary's acts up about every week. And den there's that poor little Mosby gal, only she's daid now, and dat Miss Crain what packed up and left so sudden-like last week, and several others I disremember, because they hadn't been here long and they sort of got out, too, in a hurry."

"Mary and Polly and Lottie Mosby!" I gasped in a stricken voice.

"Yas 'm. Mr Mosby mighty near took the roof off about it," said Laura sulkily. "Like I could help it if de water pitcher loses hitself, and Miss Mosby has a weeping fit over a lot of little torn-up pieces of brown paper what she wouldn't 'splain to him about."

Laura was still mumbling to herself when she went out. Because my knees felt very weak, I tottered to a chair and practically collapsed into it. So I was not the only person at the Richelieu who had received a scurrilous brown note, nor was I alone in having, like a gullible fool, complied with its instructions. I knew then why Mary Lawson was in financial difficulties and I felt sure that the appointment she had had on the fourth floor landing of the fire escape the night James Reid was murdered was not with a man but had to do with an aluminium water pitcher.

"Only what has Mary, of all women, ever done to land herself in the clutches of a blackmailer?" I asked myself in a baffled voice.

I never doubted from then on that blackmail was being practiced on an extensive scale at the Richelieu Hotel and had been for some time, but I was convinced that one of the victims had tried to turn on his persecutor. For that, I felt positive, was the secret of James Reid's presence in the house. He had been retained to ferret out the secret of the blackmailer's identity. Retained by Mary Lawson, I told myself with conviction.

"That is what she meant when she intimated that her hands were stained with his blood," I sighed. "She brought him here to his death, poor Mary."

I was also able for the first time to account to my satisfaction for the reason why Mary had wanted me out of my rooms between eight and nine on that fatal night and why James Reid should have been murdered in my suite of all places.

If, as I suspected, Mary Lawson had been ordered by the

blackmailer to place a sum of money in her water pitcher and leave it on the fire escape that evening, it was perfectly plausible, or so I thought, that James Reid, like myself, had considered the trap set and concealed himself in my old quarters next door in order to nab the culprit in the act. Only the dastard had proved too clever for him also, for it was his own neck upon which the trap snapped.

I shuddered. "I shall have to tell the inspector everything," I concluded with a groan. "No matter whom it involves. Hanging is too good for such canaille!"

I was distracted from my painful thoughts by a brusque knock at the door and upon opening it was startled to find Kathleen Adair on the threshold.

"I brought them back," she said in a bleak voice.

I stared blankly at the neat white box she held out to me.

"Didn't you expect me to?" she asked and added with a bitter smile, "No matter what you think of us, you might at least give me credit for returning everything I could."

I did not answer. I couldn't. I could only go on staring at the coil of lustrous red garnets in the box which she had thrust into my hand.

At last the girl said in a halting stammer, "She doesn't mean to steal, you know. She's good, really good. You've got to believe me. It's just that-that she thinks beauty is everybody's birth right and she can't bear for the people she loves to be without it."

My lips were so dry I could barely move them. "Your-your mother takes things?" She nodded drearily. "Only you were right; my name isn't Adair, and she isn't my mother."

"Thank God!" I whispered to myself.

"I don't remember my mother, and my father died three years ago. He had been ill for a long while and out of work. I don't know what we should have done except for-for Mother." Her lips quivered.

"I call her that because it makes her happier than anything."

"My dear child!"

"We had rooms at her house. After Father fell ill, we couldn't pay, only she wouldn't let us leave. She has a tiny income but she is quite alone in the world and she's never been strong. She said we were all she had to live for."

"She was in love with your father?" I stammered.

She nodded and I suppose she read in my eyes the question I dared not ask, for she said, "He was never in love with her. I am sure you know, Miss Adams, the only woman my father ever loved."

"He must have loved your mother."

She shook her head. "He would never have married her if you hadn't driven him away from you," she protested and then went on with a reproach which cut me to the quick, "How could you when he loved you so?"

"I was blind and stupid, my dear, and unfair both to him and to myself," I faltered. "My father was a hopeless invalid; he had been for years. I convinced myself I had no right to sacrifice Laurie's youth, as well as my own. There was a girl visiting friends of his. He showed her some small attentions, through common courtesy. I was half ill from long hours by a sickbed.

"I told Laurie that lengthy engagements like ours wore all the glamour off a love affair. I said we'd both be happier free. I said I'd got over caring for him. I taunted him with the visiting girl and handed him back his ring and the brooch he'd given me. The next day he – they were married and left town. I never saw him again."

"You broke his morale. He never seemed to care about anything. It ruined his life."

"And my own."

"Maybe you hated him for marrying my mother, but he always loved you," she said sadly.

"I have only myself to blame, Kathleen, for wrecking our happiness. Though to this day there are people in town who will tell you that Laurie Yorke jilted Adelaide Adams because she was too dutiful and noble a character to sacrifice her ailing father to her lover."

"He did tell me to come to you if ever I needed a friend," she said softly. "He told me just before he died."

"My dear, my dear!"

"But when I met you," she whispered, "you were not the Adelaide he described to me, and I-I was afraid."

I winced. "Duty ate up twenty of the best years of my life, Kathleen, and left me a hateful and disagreeable old woman."

"You are not! You're infinitely kind, only by the time I found you out," she said with a little sob, "it was too late."

"It's never too late for you and me to be friends, Kathleen."

She shook her head. "Do you think I'd drag anyone else down into my private gutter?" she asked fiercely.

Her eyes fastened on the bright red stones which I had tossed upon the table. "If it's your mother, dear, perhaps I can help," I stammered.

Her eyes filled with tears. "I've told you before. No one can help – no one."

"It's a disease, isn't it?" I asked gently. "They call it kleptomania, I think."

She nodded. "When she's well, she can sometimes throw it off, but if she's ill or worried, she can't seem to help herself."

Our eyes met, and with a sinking heart I recalled what the inspector had said about the disastrous results of subjecting a diseased or degenerating brain to a severe strain.

"When my father was ill," went on Kathleen, so low I could barely hear, "she was terribly distressed about him. She could not bear for him to do without things, little luxuries and – and delicacies, you know. Every time she went out she brought him out of season fruits and flowers and-and other things. He was too ill and I was too young to wonder where the money came from."

"You mean she picked them up wherever she could?"

"Her fingers are never still; haven't you noticed?" I nodded, my mouth again terribly dry.

"For all they are so frail," said Kathleen sadly, "they can slide into your pocket and out without so much as touching you."

"It seems incredible!"

"You didn't know when she lifted the garnets off your neck last night under the inspector's very eyes?"

I shook my head weakly.

"I tried to bring them back at once," she said, "before you missed them, but the window on the fire escape was locked."

"That's when you lost the rose out of your hair," I said huskily.

She flushed. "I didn't want to take it. That man – Stephen Lansing – knows."

"About your mother?"

"Yes, and" – she swallowed painfully – "I haven't told you the worst. She's been in the penitentiary."

"That fragile little creature!"

"It wrecked her health. She isn't going to live very long, and there's nothing the doctors can do. That's why..."

She broke off and then went on almost hysterically, "I'd rather die than see her go back to that place!"

"Back?"

"She was released on parole. We were not supposed to leave New York state, only she... It was merely a question of time till she took something again. Then she'd have to go back, and I couldn't stand it."

She put her hand up to her trembling lips. "I thought if I came here and you liked me, it might-might – I was aware that you are a wealthy woman, Miss Adelaide, and I imagined that if you – if you fell for me, you'd probably give me lots of beautiful things. It isn't pretty put in words, is it?"

"Oh, my dear," I cried, "you are welcome to everything I have in the world!"

"You don't have to believe me, but I'm not as despicable as I sound," she said unsteadily. "Mother never takes things for herself. It's only that she wants the people she loves to be happy. That's how they caught her back home. As long as she stole only little things, she got by, but I was in my last year at school. She wanted dreadfully for me to have as pretty clothes as my classmates. So she-she took an expensive painting from the city museum and sold it. It was insured, and the detectives traced it to her. They-they sent her up for five years, but she was paroled two months ago on good behaviour."

"My poor child!" I cried.

"I never knew about her until they arrested her. It nearly killed me." She eyed me defiantly. "Perhaps you think I shouldn't have had anything else to do with her. Perhaps you think I'm tarred with the same brush or I wouldn't have anything to do with her now. But she did it for me. For my happiness, as she thought. She'd do anything for me. Everything she's taken in this house has been something colourful or beautiful which she believed I'd love to have. She-she's like a child about colours."

Polly's pink jabot, the Anthony woman's red box, Ella Trotter's gaudy bracelet, and my bright green spectacle case! I checked them over in my mind and groaned to myself.

"It's kept me busy," said Kathleen Adair with a ghastly smile, "trying to slip things back without being seen."

In my heart there was cold panic. "I can understand how, if her fingers are as dexterous as you say, she might be able to-er-abstract things from one's person when one was unaware," I stammered.

"But I do not for the life of me see how she got Polly's pink jabot, for instance, out of a locked room."

Kathleen smiled tremulously. "You could hardly imagine it. She can flit up and down stairs and fire escapes like-like a humming-bird. And she uses an umbrella to reach things through windows and transoms, one of those umbrellas with a crook for a handle."

"God save us!" I cried, thinking of the aluminium pitchers.

Kathleen, her lips twisted, had risen to her feet. "Now you

know why I couldn't ever let you have anything to do with us."

"My dear child..." I began.

But she interrupted me. "Any day, any minute, we are liable to be arrested for our past and future crimes," she said bitterly and walked out of the room.

15

When I came downstairs little Mrs Adair was sitting on the rear divan, staring vaguely out the lobby windows, her pale irresolute hands wavering about like small restless dragonflies. Kathleen was nowhere in sight. I had an idea she was in her room, weeping her eyes out. It was one of the few times I had known her to relax the vigilance which she constantly maintained over her foster mother.

"Poor child," I thought, "I don't know why she isn't a nervous wreck."

It was my not unnatural instinct to avoid the Adair woman. Pathetic she might be and was, but, to put it as kindly as possible, she was not normal. I had from the first thought her singularly foggy as to her mental processes. Now, to look at her, knowing what I knew, filled me with an almost overpowering aversion for the poor feckless creature that she was.

"Which is no more or less than Kathleen has been facing for months and even years," I reminded myself sternly.

For in spite of her tender and passionate defence of the unfortunate woman whom she called Mother, I had read in Kathleen's tragic eyes the same nausea which, after her confession, the sight of Louise Adair inspired in me. The habit of years is not easily broken, however, and I had been well grooved in the uncomfortable path of duty. So I did not, as I felt inclined, avoid the part of the lobby where Mrs Adair was sitting.

Instead I forced myself to drop down on the divan beside her. I had some quixotic notion of serving Kathleen. I recall thinking with decided grimness that I should prove a more than adequate watchdog in her absence. Thus doth conceit invariably precede a crimp in itself?

"What a beautiful design, Miss Adams," breathed little Mrs

Adair. "Such lovely colours!" She put out her hands like an eager child and patted the rose and gold and amethyst yarns which I was knitting in a crisscross pattern against a cobalt background.

"It's an afghan which I'm making for the orphans' home of my church," I said stiffly, biting my lips to keep from snatching it out of reach of those small fluttering caressive hands.

Howard Warren was lounging over the desk, scowling at the morning paper. "You're lucky to have something to do to keep you from going gaga, Miss Adelaide," he said bitterly. "I suppose you know that the inspector has sent around another note. None of us is to leave the house until he arrives."

"And when would that be?" I inquired with a sinking heart, recalling miserably that I had sworn, no matter whom it involved, to make a clean breast to the police.

"Only God and the inspector know," said Howard, shrugging his shoulders. "Though I believe that dumb cop Sweeney did say directly – whatever he meant by that."

Stephen, who was punching the nickel slot machine with unnecessary violence – or so it seemed to me – laughed shortly. "Time is the least of the inspector's worries," he remarked dryly. "Or I should say our time. You'd think it would occur to him we have jobs."

Howard flashed him a hostile glance. "But then your job has never bothered you a lot, has it?" he asked.

"You think not?" drawled Stephen.

"At least you've always taken the time to splurge around," said Howard unpleasantly.

"Miaow!" cried Polly Lawson, who had just stepped out of the elevator.

Ignoring Howard's pleading eyes, she walked over to Stephen and put her hand on his arm. "How's for letting me into your game?" she asked.

"Swell!" exclaimed Stephen gallantly, making room for her, while Howard, turning perfectly white, again buried himself behind his paper.

To my surprise Hilda Anthony had also gone literary on us that morning. She was sitting on the other divan, facing me, apparently absorbed in one of the flyspecked dime novels that may be purchased at the magazine stand in the hotel drugstore for a quarter.

It was the first time I had ever seen her read anything. Not till later did I recall that, although she must have sat there for nearly an hour, I never saw her look up or turn a page.

Little Mrs Adair quietly closed her eyes, leaned her head back with a wisp of a sigh and – or so I thought – drifted off to sleep, in spite of the noisy laughter and blatant repartee which Polly and Stephen Lansing were bandying back and forth. I was not surprised that it got on Howard's nerves. It got on mine, and I was not in love with the girl and had grave misgivings about the man. I remember thinking that I should enjoy shaking both of them, and I do not doubt that Howard felt even more violent about the matter.

"Punch, punch, punch mit care," chanted Polly. "Punch in the presence of the passenjaire!"

"Yowsah!" exclaimed Stephen, snapping his fingers.

"If that's wit, they can bottle my portion," growled Howard, ostensibly addressing Pinky Dodge but making sure his voice carried to the offenders.

Pinkney, slumped down before the switchboard, lifted a harassed face. He had relieved Letty Jones at the desk for a few minutes while she traipsed into the drugstore for her mid-morning coke, a disgusting habit, as I have frequently remarked in Letty's hearing.

"Were you speaking to me, Mr Warren?" asked Pinky in his vague way.

Turning scarlet, Howard snapped, "Who else would I have been speaking to?"

Pinky flushed. "I'm sorry," he faltered. "I'm afraid my hearing is failing a little."

"That's the whole trouble," I observed. "Just when one begins to have sense enough to live, one starts coming unstuck."

"Yes," said Pinky dully.

Howard, more, I thought, to cover his confusion than anything else, pointed derisively to a prominent caption in the paper which he had been reading. "Some people never learn," he said. "Listen to this: 'Man Feeds Tame Tiger Raw Meat and Pet Finally Turns and Chews Master's Arm Off.' You'd think," muttered Howard, "any imbecile would know better."

"The ingenuity with which the human race can mess itself up really should be utilized," I commented, acidly regarding the alluring smile which Polly Lawson was bestowing on Stephen, as if she did not know that she might as well be sticking red-hot barbs in Howard Warren.

"The little minx!" I fumed to myself, wondering how she could be so ungrateful after the way Howard in every emergency had snatched up his trusty sword and tripped himself upon it in her defence.

I have tried many times since, without success, to recollect just how long afterward it was that, still without raising her sleek blondined head, Hilda Anthony addressed me. I can only say that the circumstances were so startling, they drove everything else out of my mind. As I later explained over and over to the inspector, I simply could not swear who was near me in the lobby at the time, because the group was constantly shifting, or whether anyone was in earshot, providing, as I supposed then, that little Mrs Adair was actually asleep.

I had all I could do as it happened to retain possession of my own faculties. For not only did the Anthony woman when she opened her lips not lift her head, she kept her face hidden behind her book and her voice was so low I failed to locate it at first.

"For the love of God, Adams," she said, "keep on with your knitting and don't look at me."

I started when she spoke, but I did not glance in her direction, thank heaven, because it seemed to me her voice came from behind me, the book acting as a sort of backboard to deflect the sound, I suppose.

"What's the matter, Miss Adelaide?" queried Pinky Dodge, staring at me curiously. "Did you hear something?"

"No, I-I stabbed myself with my-my knitting needle," I stammered feebly.

"I see," he said with a faint smile and added humbly, "I used to often, stick myself I mean, when I tried to darn and sew on buttons. But I'm better at it now."

Poor Pinky, I thought. It seemed to me if frustration could have a body it would look precisely like Pinkney Dodge, another burnt offering on the exacting knees of that barren goddess, Self-Sacrifice.

The buzzer sounded, and Pinky bent over and placed the headpiece of the switchboard over his ears. That was why all I could tell the inspector later was that, of the various people in the house, Pinky Dodge was the only person who could not possibly have heard the rest of what Hilda Anthony said to me.

"I've got to see the inspector, Adams. I've got to! And if anybody catches on, it will be just too bad for me, and I mean permanently."

She paused again, and the cold sweat popped out on my hands, in which the afghan was tightly clenched.

"I know you hate me, Adams," she went on bitterly, "but you're a woman, and you'd throw a drowning cur a rope, wouldn't you?"

I managed slowly and painfully to pull my knitting needle in and out, purling one, dropping two stitches in my agitation, but, thank God, continuing to knit.

"I'm being watched, Adams. I have been since last night – every step I take, every move I make. I've got to act – and act fast – if I save myself. What a fool I was to think I could feed a-a – Get word to Inspector Bunyan, Adams, secretly, if you have a heart. Ask him to meet me in the parlour at eleven-fifteen, not before or after. Get it? Tell him to bring his gun along and for God's sake not to be late."

I purled two more, my hands clammy.

"You will, Adams?" asked Hilda Anthony's tortured voice.

My lips were stiff. "Yes! Yes, certainly!" I cried. With a shock I realized that I had spoken aloud and that Cyril Fancher was standing right behind me, though how long he had been there or where he came from I had no idea.

I swallowed hard and repeated wildly, "Yes, certainly, I sent for you, Cyril!"

He stared at me as if, not for the first time, he questioned my sanity. So far as that goes, I doubt if there was one of us who during the previous twenty hours had not entertained grave suspicion about the mental health of every other one of us. I know I had thought more than once that there was something degenerate about Cyril, with his womanish hands and long-lashed, evasive eyes.

"You sent for me, Miss Adams?" he repeated in a baffled voice. "But this is the first I've heard of..."

Remembering what Stephen Lansing had said about the best defence being a stout offensive, I attacked swiftly. "Yes, I sent for you, and I must say you took your time about it," I interrupted in my most withering accents.

He gulped and tried again. "But this is the first I knew of -"

"Never mind," I protested haughtily, rising to my feet and praying that my legs would sustain me. "It's my own fault if I haven't learned by now that the only way to get things done in this house is to take them up with Sophie."

"But –"

"Where is she?" I demanded coldly.

"In-in her room, I think, but..." However, I was already headed under full sail for the elevator.

Behind me Hilda Anthony, as I could see in the mirror beside the desk, continued to stare fixedly at her novel, and over by the front door Stephen chuckled.

"For ways that are eccentric, recommend me the dear Adelaide," he murmured mockingly.

It occurred to me that, having broadcast my destination, it would be well to carry out my announced intention. Just in case, I thought with a shiver, someone had read more than I believed possible into that strange and sinister little one-sided drama which Hilda Anthony and I had enacted in the lobby.

Sophie was indeed in her room. I heard her voice before I had time to knock on the door. She was sobbing over and over, "Oh, Cyril! Cyril! If you would only confide in me! I'd forgive you. I'd forgive anything you've done, my poor boy, if only you'd tell me what the trouble is."

She went off into a smothered fit of weeping, so desolate it chilled my heart. Despite the cleavage between us, my old affection for Sophie and Tom Scott was not entirely dead, and I lacked the courage to intrude upon her grief. My face very sober, I stalked down the hall to where the policeman Sweeney was standing on one foot and his dignity outside the door to Room 511.

"It's absolutely the limit of something or other for the inspector to keep us penned up like this, as if we were all a bunch of low criminals!" I cried indignantly and borrowed a leaf from Ella Trotter.

"I shall write the mayor a note, and I shall expect you, my good man, to deliver it."

"Say, lady!" he expostulated. "You can't ..."

I was shooing him ahead of me into my room, taking care to leave the door wide open behind us. "I want you to watch every word I write," I announced firmly. "A witness is important, or so I've been led to believe, when dealing with politicians, no matter how prominent."

"Listen, lady..." I snatched up a piece of paper and a pen from the desk, giving him no chance to finish. "Your honour," I declaimed in my most ringing tones while writing vigorously, "As one of the major taxpayers of this community, I demand, not request, that you pay a visit at once to the Richelieu Hotel and remove forthright and without a quibble the objectionable individual who is at present in charge of police proceedings here. Signed, Adelaide Mills Adams."

As my pen moved with hectic speed over the page Patrolman Sweeney's gaze followed it, his agate eyes growing wider and wider; but, to allow the devil his due, the man was more of an actor than I should ever have given him credit for.

"Of all the tomfool notions," he said with every evidence of soul searing disgust. "Listen, lady, if the mayor paid attention to all the crackpot letters he received, he'd be fit for the booby hatch."

"Nevertheless," I informed him loftily, "you are going to deliver this note into his honour's own hand, my good man, or-or I'll make it my business to –"

"All right, all right," he muttered in a bored voice. "Just keep your shirt on, lady, and I'll do anything."

Scowling wrathfully, he pocketed the folded paper which I handed him and, still scowling, marched out the door and down the corridor toward the elevator.

"There," I informed myself exultantly, "I defy anyone to see through that stratagem."

I believe I have said that there is the germ of an amateur detective in all of us. Certainly I have never felt prouder of anything in my life than of the subtle manner in which I had contrived to convey Hilda Anthony's message to Inspector Bunyan without, as I had every reason to believe, having given either her or myself away.

Needless to say, the words which I penned under Policeman Sweeney's starting eyes in no particular corresponded with those I dictated aloud. They said in essence that the Anthony woman was scared for her life and ready to break the case and requested Inspector Bunyan to meet her in the parlour at eleven-fifteen, and for everybody's sake to come armed and on the dot.

It was, I remember, a quarter of eleven when I returned to the lobby, my heart hammering against my ribs. Hilda Anthony was standing near the front door, staring out at the bright April sunshine and the freshly washed spring world. Smothering a yawn, she tucked her book under her arm without once glancing in my direction.

"Of all the dopey places to be stuck in!" she remarked in her usual blasé and disdainful manner. "Darned if I don't get a tube of amytal tablets and sleep the blasted clock around."

She strolled on into the drugstore, and Stephen Lansing smiled cynically. "Queer how people always get sore at the clock for their own sins," he said and tossed his black slouch hat at the face of the large Western Union timepiece which hangs directly over the desk.

"Look out, you clown!" cried Howard. "Now see what you've done."

Stephen laughed. His hat had lodged on the top of the clock where it stayed until, assisted by Polly, he climbed upon a chair and after varied exaggerated manoeuvres finally succeeded in dislodging it. Hilda Anthony, a small package in her hands, sauntered back through the lobby. "Good night, all," she cried flippantly, "and pleasant dreams."

I did not like her, but I was compelled to admire the poise with which, stifling another yawn, she walked languidly into the elevator, her exotic face expressing nothing except listless ennui. The elevator creaked upward, and I sank back upon the divan, suddenly aware that I had been painfully and in a state of complete funk holding my breath. It was then I discovered that both little Mrs Adair and my afghan had disappeared.

"So much for the wonderful watchdog you turned out to be," I told myself crossly, trying to remember if I had seen either the lady or the shawl since my return to the lobby.

Polly Lawson decided to go to her room and 'powder the old nose,' as she explained brightly. Stephen Lansing walked over to the elevator with her and then carelessly, as if by an oversight, got in beside her and was slowly borne upward. Howard, scowling ferociously, did not linger long about stamping off up the stairs.

It seemed to me, watching the creeping progress of the minute hands of the clock, that I had never seen the lobby so deserted.

There was, at eleven-fifteen, exactly nobody there except myself and Letty Jones, who was scratching her chin with the end of the stubby cedar pencil tied to the old-fashioned register while she stared pensively straight at me.

"Why doesn't the inspector come?" I asked myself feverishly.

And then the hands of the clock were pointing to twenty minutes after eleven and from the second floor over my head came a woman's scream, a scream of such piercing agony that I cowered like a whipped animal. That it was Hilda Anthony I seem to have recognized instantly. I was halfway up the stairs when she screamed again, one long-drawn-out shriek of such intolerable anguish, I stumbled and nearly fell.

She was lying on the floor by the grate, her once-exquisite face horribly repeated and magnified in the convex mirror over the mantel.

Her face was exquisite no longer. Acid was eating the chiselled features and running down onto the throat where there were cruel marks, already turning livid.

The head was oddly twisted over on one shoulder, the arms bound to the side, the eyes sightless, burned like the once-lovely face to a raw red mass of exposed tissue. But she was not quite dead when I knelt beside her, for her body quivered horribly for an instant and then went limp, while through her terribly disfigured ups bubbled a bloody froth.

"So he is up to his old tricks," murmured the inspector behind me. "Not content with breaking her neck, he had to destroy her fatal beauty."

I was sobbing uncontrollably. "Why, why, in God's name were you late?" I wailed.

"I am not late, Miss Adams. It is now exactly sixteen minutes after eleven."

"But the clock in the lobby!" I protested.

"The clock in the lobby has been turned up at least ten minutes."

"Oh!" I gasped.

"It is obvious what happened," said the inspector grimly. "The murderer, having advanced the hands of the clock, lay in wait for his victim here. Behind those window drapes, I should say. The moment she came within reach he flung that rug about her, winding her up in it till she was as helpless as a mummy. Then, having broken her neck, he poured the contents of a bottle of acid down her face."

"Oh! Oh heavens!" I whispered.

For not till then had I realized that the thing wrapped about Hilda Anthony's lifeless body like a winding sheet, the thing which the inspector called a rug, was my rose and gold and amethyst afghan.

16

I do not know about the others, but I did not appear in the Coffee Shop that day for lunch. I was till nearly two being grilled, like a sardine between two thin slices of toast, by Inspector Bunyan and the local chief of police, who, in the emergency, came to the aid of the party. I have never admired short, fat, pompous men, and so far as I could judge, the chief's only contribution to that prolonged and hectic conference in the parlour was a highly annoying trick of pulling his underlip out at frequent intervals and letting it fly back with a disconcerting "Pish!"

Others were summoned into the presence, questioned and dismissed, sometimes to be resummoned and questioned again; but Inspector Bunyan's interest in me went on and on. If he was temporarily engaged with someone else, I was politely though firmly requested to remain at the inspector's disposal. Steadily refusing to turn my head toward the spot where Hilda Anthony lay so horribly dead, I sat rigidly upright in one straight cane-bottomed chair until I felt positive I should wear the imprint so long as I lived.

When I was finally informed with ominous curtness that I might go 'for the present,' it was all I could do to totter into the elevator and point for down.

Although officially the Coffee Shop at the Richelieu is supposed to stay open until two, Cyril Fancher was just locking the doors when I stepped into the lobby. He knew of course, because everybody knew, that I had been to all intents and purposes in the custody of the police all during the luncheon hour; nevertheless, giving me a dour look, he strolled past me without a word. Had I been myself, I should have told him in no uncertain language what I thought of his cavalier treatment of one of the hotel's best-paying guests. However, I was too exhausted and depressed even to take a

crack at Cyril, which speaks volumes, and I had no desire for food.
The very thought made me a little ill.

"Tough going, eh, Adelaide?" murmured Stephen, strolling
over to the divan on which I had slumped down.

I nodded feebly. I have had to be a self-reliant person, but just
then I felt old and forlorn and helpless. I dare say my eyes looked
it, for Stephen put his hand on my arm.

"Brace up," he said gently. "Keep the old lip upper stiff or words
to that effect."

There had been a time when I should have resented both his
affectionate tone and the small caressing gesture, but not in my
then low state of resistance. I am forced to admit that, while I've
never had any patience with clinging vines, I even reached up and
clutched his hand.

Continuing to pat me in a very soothing manner, Stephen went
on cheerfully, "What you need, Adelaide, is something to back up
your ribs."

"I'm not hungry," I said wearily. "Privately, I doubt if I ever
shall be again."

"That clinches it," he said. "When a stout guy like you starts
weakening in the pinches, he requires fodder in a hurry and
plenty of it. Come on, Adelaide, here's where for once in your life
you perch on a stool in the old drugstore like the rest of the little
floozies and consume large quantities of soup and coffee, to say
nothing of a litter of hot dogs."

I grasped at my old manner. "Young man," I said sternly, "I
never ate at a counter in my life. In my opinion, no well-brought
up lady does. And I consider hot dogs an abomination to the eye
and an insult to the stomach."

My bluster had lost its bite. At least, it completely failed with
Stephen. Still smiling cheerfully, he proceeded to escort me into
the drugstore, where to my amazement the soup tasted remarkably good, as did the hot dogs with a liberal application of mustard.

Stephen's grey eyes twinkled when I disposed of the second

one, but he did not avail himself of his opportunity to rub my nose in it.

He merely grinned and asked softly, "Feeling better, Addie, old thing?"

I had never expected to permit Mr Stephen Lansing to employ the diminutive of my name, but I may as well confess that, after having been treated like a human pariah for several hours, it was comforting to be chummy with a fellow creature.

"Yes," I said with a sigh, "I'm feeling better, though I'll probably eat my next meal in the county jail."

"As bad as that?" he inquired with a frown.

"According to the inspector," I said, sighing again.

"Just what does he think he's got against you, Adelaide?"

Drearily I outlined the inspector's case. "From every possible source of evidence I was the only person, outside the police themselves, who knew about Hilda Anthony's date in the parlour or that she intended to welsh. It appears that I was slightly too ingenious about that note to the inspector. I seem, in fact, to have very cleverly knotted the noose about my own neck. At any rate, I'm left holding the bag, all by myself, as it were. Moreover, I was practically discovered in the act by the inspector himself; at least, according to him, I was hovering over my victim when he arrived. And-and it was my afghan."

"So you go and drape it all over the spot marked X for fear the police will fail to regard you with suspicion," said Stephen dryly. "Bosh! Phooey! Or what have you?"

"The inspector believes we are dealing with a very subtle criminal, as you ought to know," I reminded him in a resigned voice.

"He thinks it an extremely cunning finesse on my part to plant so obvious a clue against myself. He points out that every schoolboy nowadays has read enough detective stories to conclude that anybody in the cast is more likely to have committed the murder than the one who left his cuff link so conveniently on the scene."

"But if you were in the lobby when the Anthony woman

screamed, you have a cast-iron alibi, Adelaide. As that wall-eyed Letty Jones can testify if she will."

"Letty Jones is not only wall-eyed," I replied bitterly, "she goes into a coma every time she gets the chance on duty. And Letty's sworn statement deposes that she had not been paying the least attention to me or anything else in the lobby for some moments before Hilda Anthony screamed, at which time Letty went all over faint – or so she says – and closed her eyes tightly, a habit she has, or claims to have, in thunderstorms and other crises. When she opened them, says she, she was alone. For that reason she cannot swear that I was not in the lobby when she heard the scream, but she is able to be very definite about the fact that I was not there a few seconds later."

"Hell!" remarked Stephen feelingly.

"Quite so," I agreed with emphasis, although I do not in general practice approve of profanity.

Stephen grinned and began to chant in an atrocious British accent that allegedly comic song which was so popular in cheap English music halls some seasons ago.

"Miss Otis regrets that she cannot dine with you tonight,

because, cheerio, she has a date to be lynched this afternoon."

However, when I winced in spite of myself his smile faded and he said earnestly, "Don't let it get you down, Adelaide. The inspector only looks like a fool. He knows as well as I do that, regardless of your pose, you're too tender hearted to kill the proverbial gnat."

I shrugged my shoulders. "I doubt if a one of us, including the inspector himself, knows how much we know or has the faintest idea what it means."

He coloured. "Did you tell him about-about..." He paused and looked unhappy.

"About the rose on the fire escape and what window you bounced out of last night?" I asked and shook my head.

"No," I said, "there are a number of things I haven't told the inspector yet. Including the remarkable way in which you rang the lobby clock with your hat this morning. I haven't told him for the adequate reason that, quite early in the session upstairs, he informed me that, things having reached the pass they have, he'd ask the questions and I could speak when and as spoken to."

He drew a breath of relief, and I went on unsteadily, "But I shall have to tell him everything, Stephen. Right away! As soon as I can bring myself to demand his attention."

"Yes?" he drawled, knitting his heavy brows.

My voice was pleading, almost tearful. "One can't go on indefinitely, letting people be killed off as though – as though they were flies being swatted; not if one can do anything to prevent it."

"Are you developing scruples at this late date, Adelaide?" asked Stephen in a hard voice and then added with a curl of his wide sardonic mouth, "Well, you know the risks as well as I do. So if you think its healthy let your conscience be your guide."

Our eyes met, and for the second time in less than twelve hours I could not for the life of me decide if his mocking grin conveyed a warning or a threat.

At that moment Letty Jones, regarding me with resentment, put her head around the door which led into the lobby. "There's a man to see you, Miss Adams," she announced with a sniff.

It always provokes Letty to have to put herself to any trouble for the women guests at the Richelieu. Men are different. Letty belongs to that class of females which titters and gushes over everything masculine and thinks nothing too inconvenient to do for the lords of creation – which is what she would call them.

"A man to see me?" I repeated with a frown.

Letty sniffed again, nodded and withdrew, while Stephen with a chuckle assisted me off the stool on which, considering my bulk, I had been somewhat precariously mounted.

"I didn't realize you had another gentleman friend, Addie," he murmured with his old impudence.

As I came into the lobby Letty looked up from her rapt contemplation of the inkwell on the desk and shrugged one shoulder toward a young man, standing barely inside the front door and looking embarrassed in clean, though faded, overalls. I stared at him blankly. I had never to my knowledge seen him before, nor did I place him even when, advancing to meet me, he betrayed a slight limp.

"Miss Adams?" he inquired. I nodded, and he went on in an apologetic voice, "I know I haven't any right to bother a lady like you and I realize I'm not dressed fit for a place like this. But" – he swallowed painfully – "Annie told me how kind you was to her."

"Annie?"

"My wife, the-the girl who waits table here."

"Your wife did you say?" I demanded in a puzzled voice.

He flushed. "She never told nobody she was married when she took the job. You see, I-I'm a lineman for the telegraph company, but I happened to have a little accident the other day. Twisted my ankle, mowing our front lawn, and I've got to lay off for a while. And-and Annie and me have had a lot of expense lately, her father's death and all, and we're trying to pay for our little house out on Biddle Street. Annie thought it would help a lot if she could get something to do till I go back to work, so she-she-"

"Palmed herself off as a single girl," I said, frowning.

"It's not easy for a married woman to get a job since the depression," he explained ruefully.

I was weakening, but I still retained my suspicions.

"And what might all this have to do with me?" I asked.

Little haggard lines leaped out on his sober homely face. "Annie said you was kind, kinder than anybody here," he stammered. "And I-I thought... Something's happened to Annie."

"Something's happened to her?"

"She didn't come home yesterday afternoon. She didn't come home last night. She-she hasn't been home since-since yesterday morning."

He was staring at the cap which he kept turning over and over in his hands, but I had seen the terror in his eyes. Poor young fellow, I thought to myself and was amazed that I could have been so deceived in a girl. Until that moment I would have sworn that the timid little waitress I had known was the last woman on earth to desert her shabby, though obviously decent, young husband.

"I'm sorry," I said as gently as I could. "I know nothing about your wife except that she told Mr Fancher, the manager of the Coffee Shop, she was leaving yesterday for a better position."

His voice was thin with distress. "But she didn't leave."

"What?"

"I've always walked to and from work with Annie." His lips trembled. "I walked to work with Annie yesterday morning and yesterday afternoon I waited for her down on the corner, but-but she never came."

My sympathies went out to the poor young husband. "I'm afraid your wife has-has..." My throat felt thick. "Annie undoubt-edly had her reasons for not telling you that she was giving up her place here," I said uncomfortably.

His eyes opened wide. "But Annie and I told each other every-thing. She never had a secret from me in her life, ma'am. Why why" – he was clutching my arm in his eagerness to convince me – "she even got me to teach her the Morse code, and often when we are around other people we telegraph little messages to each other. You know, tap them out with our knuckles on a chair or a table. We think it's cute, 'cause nobody else is any the wiser." His fingers tightened on my elbow. "I can't believe it. My Annie wouldn't leave me for another job or-or another man or anything."

"But she hasn't been here since she went off duty at lunch yes-terday," I persisted.

He was trembling. "I tell you, she never left here."

I stared at him incredulously. "But –"

"I was watching for her."

"I know, but –"

"I could see the employees' entrance from where I stood."

"Perhaps so, but –"

"She never came out of the hotel."

It was then I had my second brain storm, one that came so close to costing me my life that I can scarcely bear to think of it even yet.

"Merciful heavens!" I gasped, grasping the back of a chair to steady myself.

I have said I never forget anything, though I may mislay it for a while, and I was recalling many obscure and curious incidents which had puzzled me at the time but to which I had been unable to find the key; only now they were falling into a pattern, a pattern so sinister it made my brain reel.

"Have-have you reported your wife's disappearance to the police?" I faltered.

He paled. "Then you, too, think something awful has happened to her?" he whispered.

I could not speak, and he put his hand to his quivering mouth.

"I haven't done anything," he gasped, "except walk the street up and down, up and down, between here and the corner, watching for her – for her to come out."

I was trembling all over. There were a dozen things I wanted to do at once. I flung a distracted glance at the lobby clock. It was a quarter after two. The Coffee Shop had been closed for over twenty minutes. It was then my right eye began to twitch with an acute attack of nerves which it has never got entirely over.

"Wait here," I cried, shoving Conrad Wilson down into a chair. "Don't stir till I come back. I want to take you to Inspector Bunyan, but-but there's something I must do first."

If only I'm not too late, I thought as I hobbled swiftly through the lobby and out the back into the long corridor which separates the kitchen of the Richelieu Hotel on the left from the Beauty Shop on the right. I dare say I looked pretty much like a wild woman when I thrust my head in at the door where Belle, the dishwasher, and Gene, the chef, were just removing their greasy aprons, preparatory to going out for a few hours before time to start dinner.

"That girl – that waitress Gloria! Has she gone yet?" I demanded jerkily, because I still could not seem to draw a full breath.

Gene stared at me in astonishment, but Belle did not turn a hair at my unprecedented intrusion behind the scenes.

"No 'm, she ain't gone, Miss Adams," she said, calmly untying her apron.

"Thank God!" I whispered.

"The other girl left right at two," Belle went on, "but dat Gloria's quitting, so she had to wait till Mr Fancher brung her check."

"Oh!" I wailed, the stitch in my side growing more pronounced.

"Where is she?" Belle glanced at me curiously. "Down in the dressing room, I guess, taking off her uniform. Leastwise I ain't heard her come up yet."

I had forgotten that, because of limited kitchen space on the first floor, there was a dressing room of sorts in the basement of the hotel which the waitresses in the Coffee Shop were permitted to use when they changed into street clothes or vice versa.

"She went down to the basement?" I gasped.

"Yas 'm."

"And you haven't heard her come up?"

"No 'm."

For an instant I heard Gloria Larue's voice as distinctly as I had heard it at breakfast that morning. "When a feller's got nobody but himself to back his play," she had said, "he gets used to taking it on the chin."

My heart was beating in great furious throbs as I turned back to the corridor. It all fitted, fitted perfectly, into a horrible pattern.

I knew at last why so many of the waitresses whom Cyril Fancher employed were on their own with no one to inquire if apparently the earth yawned and swallowed them. I knew, too, why he had discouraged them from talking to the guests, and why they never stayed long at the Richelieu, and why they had all been young and fresh and pretty.

"Please, God," I prayed as I stumbled down the corridor, "let me be in time."

I had been in the basement of the Richelieu many times, but not by way of the narrow staircase which opened off the rear hall between the door into the kitchen and the employees' entry. There is under the lobby a large concrete storage room for trunks and so forth to which I had often descended in the elevator when I had winter furs to put away in mothballs or summer frocks to take out of tissue paper.

I had previously seen for myself that the dark passage to the west of the elevator in the basement ran back toward the rear of the house, and I knew, of course, that there had to be a boiler room and such in the nether regions of the basement. I also, as I have said, had some vague knowledge that the waitresses' dressing room was down there somewhere.

However, I had never had any occasion to go farther back than the elevator stop, and as I started down the rear stair I had no idea of the layout or where I could expect to find the room to which Gloria Larue had gone. But to my relief both the steep steps and the corridor below were well lighted by a powerful drop bulb on the landing of the staircase which halfway down made an abrupt right-angled turn, so that while you were facing east when you started down, you were headed due west on the second flight.

I had no difficulty locating the entrance to the boiler room. It was well to the front of the basement, though at that distance from the bulb on the landing the corridor was dim and shadowy. Nor did I have any trouble discovering the dressing room. As I came around the bend in the stairs it was directly before me, next to the laundry chute. The door was closed, but I could hear the water running in the lavatory.

"Thank God," I cried, "she's still there!"

At that instant the powerful lamp above my head went out, plunging me into a blackness so intense I could not have seen my hand before me had I had the strength to lift it. I believe my heart, the very blood in my veins, stood still. For a second I could not move, I could not even think.

I was conscious of stealthy footsteps near me, nearer and nearer, and of a ghastly panting like some animal, but whether from below or above I could not tell for the roar of my blood in my ears.

And then with a choking sound that was an aborted shriek, I whirled around, flinging my arms out to ward off that nameless horror converging upon me. The next instant those dreadful squeezing hands were at my throat, grinding, clawing, digging deeper and deeper into my windpipe.

17

Slowly the shooting red lights in my congested eyeballs began to wink out and the agony in my cramped lungs to subside. I gulped once, twice, and then started to fight for air with a weird strangled sound which made my ears ache.

"Take it easy, Adelaide," said Stephen from somewhere quite near me.

It was still pitch dark in the basement, but the sound of his familiar and solicitous voice broke down my last defences and precipitated the hysterics on the verge of which I had been trembling ever since I realized what had most likely happened to poor Conrad Wilson's Annie.

"Oh! Oh! Oh!" I shrieked, and then again, like a fire siren, "O-oh! O-oh!"

"Steady, Adelaide," murmured Stephen, close to my shoulder, and put his arm about me. "You've been too grand a soldier to blow up when we're on the spot. Hang on!"

I proceeded to do just that, flinging both arms about his neck and trying desperately to hang onto him and my sanity at the same time. And that was how the inspector found us when, having turned on the light from the switch at the head of the stair, he plunged down the basement steps, a drawn revolver in his hand, mate to the one which the policeman Sweeney was flourishing as he stumbled breathlessly after his superior.

"Tableau!" murmured Stephen Lansing.

The inspector stopped so abruptly, his henchman had to sit down violently on the steps to keep from stumbling over him. From the landing they stared down at us in the corridor below, now garishly illuminated by the drop light on the stair.

"Aw," said Sweeney disgustedly, "it's just them two up to their playful little tricks again."

The inspector, however, was staring with a shocked expression at the angry dark-red marks on my throat.

"What's happened to you, Miss Adams?" he asked tremulously.

I had by this time sufficiently recovered myself to release my strangle hold on Stephen's neck and was attempting to look dignified and at the same time pin back in place the row of false curls which somewhere in the encounter had become detached from my forehead and was draped about my aquiline nose.

"I should think it's self-evident what happened to me, Inspector," I said tartly.

Behind me Stephen chuckled. "Hamlet is herself again."

"The murderer attacked you!" cried the inspector.

"Someone or something certainly attacked me," I said, wincing as I felt of the sore and aching muscles in my neck.

"Who is he? Did you see him? Where did he go?" The barrage of questions was shot at me by the inspector and Sweeney, both simultaneously and separately.

"I don't know is the answer to everything, so far as I'm concerned," I said wearily. "He-it-the light went out suddenly and-and – I don't even know whether he crept toward me down the stairs or up them from the basement. He was just there, somewhere near me, panting like a wild beast, and then – and then his hands were grinding the life out of me."

"This here is a two-way switch," announced Sweeney, who had been poking his flashlight here and there into shadowy corners.

"It can be turned off from the top of the stairs or down here at the foot, whichever switch you happen to be at."

"And a lot of help that is," murmured Stephen Lansing sarcastically.

The inspector scowled. "Just where did you come in on this, Lansing?" he inquired.

Perhaps I have neglected to state that since Hilda Anthony's tragic death that morning the inspector had shed his polite nicety of manner and reverted to a startling brusqueness, reminiscent of the hard-boiled detectives I have so often encountered in mystery novels, the kind who chew savagely on unlighted cigars and glare at the suspects with unmistakable ferocity while snarling unprintable epithets through their discoloured teeth.

"I came in just as you did, Inspector, by the door on the lobby floor," said Stephen smoothly. "Barely in time, in fact, to aim a flying tackle at Miss Adams' assailant which, I regret to confess to the lady, knocked her end over end down the staircase."

I understood then why I felt so alarmingly sore and bruised in a region of my anatomy which until that time I was not aware had been attacked.

"The-er-murderer," continued Stephen, "took advantage of the mêlée to scuttle away into-into... I have no idea just where he did scuttle away to, Inspector."

"Oh yeah?" murmured Sweeney.

"Surely if you were on the landing, as you must have been to knock Miss Adams off it, Lansing, your ears told you whether the murderer went upstairs or down."

Stephen grinned at me. "Miss Adams is a bit on the hefty side, Inspector, begging your pardon, Adelaide. And she does everything thoroughly. I mean, when she falls, it's rather like the Tower of Pisa coming down. You should have been able to hear the commotion upstairs."

"I suppose you are cognizant, Lansing, that there is no apparent reason why it couldn't have been you who first strangled Miss Adams and then pitched her down the stairs?" demanded the inspector.

I caught my breath. After all, I had told Stephen Lansing that I was going to the police with all the information which I possessed and he had as good as warned me that such a move was not healthy.

"Don't be ridiculous, Inspector Bunyan," I stammered. "Why

should Mr Lansing have tried to kill me one minute and then do all he could the next to save my life?"

"That fall of yours, Miss Adams, was enough to wake the dead," said the inspector dryly. "After it came off, Stephen Lansing's only hope was to reverse the act before the police got here and allow himself to be discovered in the role of your rescuer."

"Granting," put in Stephen, "that it was I who strangled her in the first place."

"I'll say we grant it!" sang out Sweeney lustily. The inspector nodded. "You have never rung quite true to me, Lansing."

"Isn't that just too bad?" drawled Stephen.

"There remains the fact that you did call up James Reid from the Sally Ray Beauty Shop the afternoon he was murdered and threaten to knock his block off if he did not stop his infernal snooping."

Stephen changed colour. "So you know about that," he said somewhat lamely.

"The more I consider you, the queerer you look to me, Lansing."

"Do tell!" murmured Stephen sweetly, but it seemed to me a little uneasily.

"Always fully dressed and first on the scene at any hour of the night!" continued the inspector in a tone of unconcealed scorn.

"Bounding up fire escapes like a Leaping Lena!" muttered Sweeney by way of reinforcement.

"Can you give any legitimate excuse for how you came to be in the basement at the moment Miss Adams was attacked?" demanded the inspector sternly.

Stephen grinned. "Incredible as it seems, Inspector, I had a hunch."

"A hunch!" repeated the inspector, looking outraged.

"That Miss Adams, of whom I happen to be rather fond, was barging straight into a chunk of trouble, and so I made up my mind not to let her out of my sight."

"You admit you followed her down here," said the inspector ominously.

"I was just in time to see her coat-tail swish through the basement door when I came out of the lobby, Inspector. My hunch caused me to quicken my steps. I have never fancied basements when there are murderers around. I had no more than closed the door behind myself when the light went out in my face. I must have stood there for a second or two, blinking but otherwise quite motionless.

It was then I heard Miss Adams choking for breath on the landing and took my flying tackle into the unknown."

"Do you seriously expect me to fall for such twaddle?" protested the inspector.

"Yes," cried Sweeney belligerently, "do you think I and the inspector are prize jackasses?"

"I wouldn't say you were exactly prizes," murmured Stephen with his most provoking grin, though I thought he looked pretty pale about the gills.

"Something has occurred to me, Inspector," I said, drawing a long breath, "which should settle once for all if it was Stephen Lansing who attacked me."

"Yes, Miss Adams?" murmured the inspector sceptically.

"I have just remembered that I bit my assailant."

"Bit him!" cried the inspector in a scandalized voice.

"You would, Adelaide – or the like of that," said Stephen with a faint chuckle.

"I twisted my head around and fastened my teeth in his arm a little above the wrist," I went on with a shudder.

"Blow me down!" gasped Sweeney.

"It brought the blood, Inspector, because just before I lost consciousness, I-I tasted it, hot and salty on my lips."

"Did I say she was a werewolf," exploded Sweeney, "or did I say she was a werewolf!"

Stephen was rolling up his sleeves to above the elbow. "Not guilty, Inspector!" he cried, his eyes again beginning to dance as he extended two smooth muscular brown arms.

The inspector stared from one to the other of us with an exasperated scowl. "That's either a remarkably well-thought-up yarn, Miss Adams, for the spur of the moment, or a peculiarly fortuitous set of circumstances for Stephen Lansing," he said sarcastically.

"However, I don't imagine without proof you'd expect me – or a jury – to credit it."

"I have proof, Inspector," I replied coolly and pointed to my chin on which there was a slowly drying crimson stain.

"You will have to admit," I remarked with a sniff, "that while I have been choked and otherwise promiscuously knocked about, the skin on my body is unbroken. Or would you prefer to have a policewoman examine me to make certain?"

The inspector groaned, and Stephen Lansing laughed. "Checkmate!" he said and added flippantly, "No hits, no runs, no errors, Inspector. Your side's retired."

The inspector flung up his hands with an exasperated gesture, and Patrolman Sweeney, not bothering to conceal his disgruntled expression, began again to throw his flashlight into the shadowy corners of the basement.

"I don't see how even a werewolf," he grumbled, "could bite a man hard enough to make him leak blood all over the place."

"What!" shouted the inspector. "Give me that flashlight."

Not from the minute the murderer's hands closed about my throat until that thin blade of yellow light fell upon the thick scarlet trail, leading from near the foot of the basement stair to the door of the waitresses' dressing room, did I remember my mission in that evil-looking place.

"The girl!" I gasped. "God forgive me, I forgot her!"

The inspector stared at me as if at last he was sure I had lost my senses, and Sweeney muttering "Bats in the belfry, and how!" put his blunt fingers to his temple and revolved them in an elaborate circle, but Stephen, turning deathly white, seized my arm and began to shake me violently.

"The girl? What girl? For heaven's sake, say something!" he cried.

I do not quite know how he expected me to speak with my chin waving in the air like a banner, but I finally managed to gasp, "The waitress, Gloria Larue, from the Coffee Shop! She-she came down here to-to change her clothes and-and she hasn't come up again."

Before I finished, Stephen was pounding on the dressing-room door. It was locked, which delayed him only a moment. Putting his broad shoulder to the upper panel, he lunged like a battering ram.

There was a rending crash, a screech as the lock tore out of the decaying wood of the frame, and then he was inside with me at his heels, after having accidentally, or maybe not quite accidentally, tripped Patrolman Sweeney with my broad Cuban heel as I brushed by him, leaving him, as it happened, hors de combat on his hands and knees like a gigantic half-opened jack-knife against which Inspector Bunyan came up with a thud which temporarily unhorsed the two of them.

The dressing room was empty.

It was a bare, depressing room with whitewashed concrete walls and floors. A dingy skylight near the ceiling shed a sepulchral light from the paved alleyway behind the hotel. There were two narrow steel lockers, the doors sagging open, the locks rusty and broken; a soiled towel dangling limply from a nail by the tin lavatory over which hung a peeling looking glass; and absolutely nothing else except the thick red splotch just over the threshold at which Stephen Lansing was staring with sickened eyes.

"Oh!" I cried. "I can't bear any more!"

I turned away, putting my hands up to shut out the sight. In front of me Officer Sweeney, still breathing stertorously, came to an abrupt halt and Inspector Bunyan forgot the furious remark he had been about to make, as they, too, spied that sinister patch of crimson at their feet.

"So he got her also," said the inspector huskily.

"Jees!" quavered Sweeney.

Stephen, his face a mask, pushed me aside to reach the corridor again. "Glory! Glory! Where are you?" he shouted.

"Dead women tell no tales," muttered Sweeney with a gloomy nod, absent-mindedly massaging his skinned knees.

"Glory, for God's sake!" shouted Stephen again. "Give me a sign!"

"I tell you ..." began Sweeney, tenderly rubbing his bruised palms.

"Keep still, you fool!" cried Stephen fiercely.

"Say," protested Sweeney, "I and the inspector – I mean, the inspector's the guy who gives the orders around here."

"Keep still, flatfoot!" growled the inspector.

Sweeney glanced at him incredulously and then, looking highly abused, gingerly felt of his battered port side and lapsed into injured silence.

"Glory! Glory!" cried Stephen again. "Answer me!"

And then we heard it, that faint scratching sound no louder than a mouse nibbling in the baseboard; only in the concrete basement there was no baseboard. To give the inspector his due, it was he who first located the packing case behind the furnace, along with a lot of other empty wooden boxes and crates, piled up there to be burned as trash, I suppose; but this case was not empty.

Gently Stephen lifted that doubled-up figure out of its hiding place. Cursing softly under his breath, he tore off the soiled towel which was twisted between Gloria Larue's teeth and tied behind her head. Still cursing, he untied the towel knotted about her wrists and the other one around her ankles. I might say here they were the regulation Hotel Richelieu hand towels of which at least a hundred went down the laundry chute to the basement every day.

"By heaven, Glory, if they've hurt you..." cried Stephen,

clenching his fists.

She smiled weakly and, in a voice I had never heard before, said, " 'Sall right, Chief. I can take it."

"Chief!" exclaimed Sweeney hoarsely.

"Chief!" I gasped.

"Chief?" repeated the inspector, looking very odd.

Stephen did not pay us the least attention. "For heaven's sake, Glory, I warned you that the phony notice from the radio company was the signal for the pay-off," he groaned. "Why-why didn't you watch your step, my dear fool?"

She shrugged her shoulders. "Just thought I was smart, Chief, a heck of a lot smarter than I am."

"And so walked right into his clutches," said Stephen bitterly.

"Everybody has his lapses," she admitted with an abashed and tremulous grin. "I knew as soon as I got the notice of the alleged audition, the stage was set, but I-I made one mistake." She shivered. "And but for you it would have been my last one. I thought I was safe as long as the pistol in my hand was levelled on Cyril Fancher."

"Cyril, yes!" I cried huskily.

She did not look at me. "I had always believed," she said in a puzzled and resentful voice, "that of all the yellow skunks on God's green footstool the yellowest is the white slaver."

"White slaver!" whispered the inspector.

Stephen Lansing and the level-eyed girl whom he called Glory had no time to waste on anyone except each other.

"I learned," she said with a rueful frown, "that even a skunk is dangerous when the rope starts to coil around his neck."

"Yes," said Stephen grimly. "So what?"

"The minute he told me to wait in the dressing room for my check I knew what to expect."

"Yes, yes! Go on."

"I changed my clothes and then I stood to the left of the door, my gun in the pocket of my coat, my finger on the trigger."

"All right! What happened?"

"He must have seen by my face that I was onto him or else some-thing else had got him on the run, for he came in at the door fight-ing. I mean, I never had a chance to fire the gun. I never even had a look at him. His fist shot out. Five thousand stars exploded in my head. When I came to I was tied up like a parcel-post package." She shivered. "Consigned to the furnace sometime late tonight, I think."

"God knows I hope there is a special hot spot reserved for him in hell!" cried Stephen Lansing, gritting his teeth. "To have let him slip through my fingers when I practically had him hog-tied is the bitterest dose I've tried to swallow in a long and lousy career."

"He can't have got far, Chief. You'll catch him yet," she faltered.

"After we've exposed our hand! Be your age, Quacky," he mut-tered bitterly, at which the inspector and Sweeney exchanged a surreptitious and highly triumphant glance.

The girl's shoulders drooped. "I'm sorry I spoiled everything for you."

Stephen laid his hand with rough affection on her arm. "Good Lord, kid," he cried, "I'm not blaming you. You said he came in the door fighting. Something tipped him off."

He glanced around at us for the first time and at sight of my stricken face paused and shook his head, "Adelaide, Adelaide, what did you do to flush the game?"

I swallowed. "Nothing, unless he saw me talking to Annie's husband in the lobby."

"Annie!"

"The-the waitress who disappeared yesterday."

His face greyed. "Disappeared? But she can't have! I mean, he would never have tried to sell her down the river. She has a home and a husband, someone to raise a row if she drops out of sight. I know, because both James Reid and I at various times followed her to find out."

"But Cyril didn't know," I stammered. "She passed herself off on him as a single woman."

"God!" groaned Stephen Lansing. "And I was that sure she was safe, I never even tried to keep an eye on her."

There was an aching silence, and then in a small voice Inspector Bunyan inquired, "Would you mind telling me what this is all about, er-Mr Lansing?"

"Special Agent Lansing," corrected the girl with a snap, "of the United States Service commonly known as G men."

"God!" exclaimed Policeman Sweeney in an awed voice.

"And my assistant and good Girl Friday," said Stephen with a faint smile, "Miss Gloriana Quackenberry."

"It's my real name, Inspector," said the girl in answer to the astonished incredulity on his face. "Because why? Because nobody would wish such a handle on themselves."

"I suppose not," stammered Inspector Bunyan.

"As for what it's all about, Inspector," said Stephen Lansing with a sigh, "for nearly a year the federal government has known that a traffic in young girls is being conducted in this section of the country. The shipping point is New Orleans, where they are loaded in crates on ships bound for the Argentine and ultimately for one or another house on the South American water front."

I shivered uncontrollably.

"We managed to intercept one of the shipments," Stephen said grimly, "but the shippers had been tipped off. The human cargo was dead when we got to them."

"Oh!" I gasped.

"We succeeded in striking the trail of another of the victims in transit. She wrote a note and threw it out of the blind truck in which she was being transported to New Orleans. But long before it reached us she was tossed out on the highway and the truck backed up over her."

"Gwendolyn!" I cried. "The waitress who was supposed to

have been killed accidentally, hitchhiking her way to Hollywood!"

Stephen nodded. "She had no people. At the place where she roomed they did not even know where she worked last. We were pretty sure what had happened to her, but the only thing we had to go on from there was a table napkin in her possession with a laundry mark which we were able to trace to the Richelieu Hotel."

"Oh!" I gasped again.

"That's why I've been here for the past month, Inspector, or scouting around in the near-by towns, supposedly demonstrating cosmetics." He made a wry face. "Actually checking up on the twenty or thirty girls who have disappeared in this vicinity during the past year."

"Twenty or thirty!" I whispered.

"Besides the table napkin, I had no reason, Inspector, for believing that the pickup was being operated from this hotel, except another hunch," said Stephen, again smiling faintly.

"Yes sir," said the inspector humbly.

"To be quite frank, my immediate superiors thought I was wasting my time, as did a number of other people." He flashed me a wry smile. "Wasting my time on a lot of silly women! As if," he said with a grimace, "one can turn up a ground rat without digging into the dirt around him."

"Yes sir, of course," said the inspector.

"Until day before yesterday it even seemed to me I had been terribly busy chasing a pipe dream. Having spaded into the private history of every woman in the house, I discovered nothing remotely resembling what I was seeking, with the exception of the poor Mosby girl, who was a side issue. Then overnight hell began to pop. I suppose when he killed Reid he needed money, and plenty of it, to cover up. Or maybe he planned to make one last big haul for a quick getaway if things got too hot for him. Anyway, he took on Glory here, whom I had had hanging around for weeks, begging for a job in the Coffee Shop, and I believed the trap was set."

That had a familiar ring. "But he was too cunning for you," I faltered.

Stephen Lansing sighed. "Yes."

Policeman Sweeney slowly closed his gaping mouth and gave his burly shoulders a little shake. "I still don't see how he could have done all that bleeding from one little bite in the wrist," he murmured plaintively.

Special Agent Lansing glanced ruefully at his assistant. "You said everybody has his lapses, Glory. That poor Annie is mine, and, God help us, in our business a mistake is nearly always fatal."

"You mean, it-it's her blood?" I cried.

He nodded, and, thinking of that pitiful young husband whom I had left upstairs, I began to weep heartbrokenly, while Stephen put his arm about my shoulder and murmured huskily, "Would I could mingle my tears with yours, Adelaide."

18

It developed that the inspector, in the very act of racing to my rescue, had planted several policemen at the head of the rear stairs, also at the elevator – the only exits, as he thought, to the basement.

That explained the smug expression on his face when Stephen Lansing bewailed the escape of his quarry. Undoubtedly the inspector had visions of covering himself with fame by a smashing victory at the expense of the federal man. However, the guards stationed at the proper entrances to the basement had nothing to report except that no one, not even a cockroach, had attempted to get by them.

It did come out that, shortly before I screamed, the bell on the elevator rang from the basement, but Jake, the day man, insisted that when he descended in the car there was nobody there, although he waited a few minutes, waited, in fact, until my blood-curdling shriek scared him out of his wits. When he came to, both he and the elevator were shaking with fright on the lobby floor.

The policemen, stationed at that point, corroborated Jake's testimony. He had been, they admitted, entirely alone when he brought the car up from the basement. I believed the inspector toyed with the idea for a while that Jake himself might be the culprit. Jake has barely sense enough to tote heavy suitcases in and out of the hotel and to push the lever on the elevator for up or down.

Fortunately for him, Ella Trotter was able to swear that Jake was taking her up to her floor when the bell rang in the basement. She heard him grumbling something about there being ghosts in the cellar, because they were always ringing for the car but nobody was ever there. Ella herself glanced at the light numbered 'B' in the row of signals. As she stared at it, it winked violently, proving that at that very moment someone was savagely punching the bell beside the stop in the basement.

"Then he's still here somewhere!" cried the inspector, looking bitterly disappointed and quite savage.

"Not that bird," muttered Stephen morosely.

The inspector, summoning more policemen, insisted, none-theless, on making a painstaking search of every nook and cranny under the Richelieu Hotel. Stephen, obviously not at all optimistic of the outcome, joined the searching party, and I, beginning to feel very sore and hoarse, decided to leave them with it. Accompanied by Miss Gloriana Quackenberry, who was somewhat the worse for wear herself, I ascended, with many twinges and a tendency to wheeze, to the upper regions of the house.

Poor Conrad Wilson was still sitting where I had left him in the chair by the lobby door, his face as dull as if a light had gone out behind it. I went over and tried to murmur something consoling, only I am sure he did not hear me or even know I was there.

After a while a policeman came who said Mr Lansing wished Mr Wilson to go upstairs and try to get some rest in Mr Lansing's room till the police had time to talk to him. Still with that blank, unseeing face poor Annie's husband permitted himself to be led away.

"The chief will never forgive himself for this," muttered Gloria Quackenberry, brushing at her eyes with her knuckles. "As if – as if..." She stared at me defiantly. "Maybe he has come a cropper this time. Nobody ever batted a thousand per cent, but-but-they don't come smarter than my boss."

"I don't doubt it," I said and then added cautiously, "You've been working for him a long time?"

"Five years! The happiest five years of my life..." She broke off, gave me a suspicious look, and then went on swiftly, "Yes, I'm in love with him, if that's what you're trying to smell out; but it isn't his fault, see? And it'll never come to anything, and that isn't my fault."

"I-er-"

"The boss has never been in love," she declared with obvious pride in this accomplishment. "All women fall for him, and lotsa times he has to play up to them. Business of finding out things, you know, since our sex just will talk themselves into jams. But he despises them, the poor fools! He-he's got ideals, and the woman who snares him will have to be right out of the top drawer."

"Yes?" I murmured, thinking of Kathleen.

"He doesn't despise me. He thinks I'm pretty regular, and that's something." She blinked hard. "That's a heck of a lot! But he'd no more think of falling in love with me than I would with Joe E. Brown."

"I-I'm sorry," I faltered.

She blew her nose violently and rose to her feet. "At least, I get to risk my life and worse for him every so often, and I wouldn't change jobs with anyone I ever heard of. Women are kittle cattle, aren't they?"

"Yes," I sighed.

"Heaven defend us!" She turned briskly toward the door. "Tell the boss," she said to the policeman on guard in the lobby, "if he needs me for anything, to hang out the window and holler, and I'll come running."

She swung off down the street, her large capable hands thrust into the pockets of her checked coat, her wide red lips puckered into a noiseless whistle, her small scarlet hat cockily tilted over one eye, and I do not mind confessing to a lump in my throat which had nothing to do with those ugly bruises beginning to throb and turn purple on my neck.

It was, I recall, about four o'clock when I went upstairs to my room, an hour earlier than I usually retire to dress for dinner, but I had a fervent desire to crawl into a tub of very hot water and stay there practically forever, or at least until some of my aches and pains subsided.

Before I left the elevator I heard Sophie Scott weeping in her room and calling Cyril's name over and over in a piteously broken voice that made my eyes sting. I hesitated a moment at her door, but, sorry as I felt for her, what could one say to comfort a woman whose husband has turned out to be that scum of all criminals, a white slaver, as well as a cowardly blackmailer and a thrice brutal murderer?

Shaking my head, I went slowly on down the hall, pursued by Sophie's wailing cry. "Cyril! Cyril! How could you?"

I had just finished my bath and was slipping into my black lace dress when the telephone rang. It was Stephen, speaking from the lobby booth – or so he said – and he wanted to run up and talk to me for a few minutes.

"You know, the inspector is going to interview you in a short while, Adelaide."

"No, I didn't know."

"He craves to ask you a question or two, just routine, I fancy, but I'd admire to speak with you first."

"All right," I said.

I was sitting by the window when he came in, looking tired and dejected. He attempted his old impudent smile, but it did not quite come off.

"How's the girl, Adelaide?" he asked. "Not too banged up, I hope." He grinned. "Sorry about that haymaker I handed you, dearie. It was just one of those things."

I motioned him to a chair opposite me. "I dare say I'll forgive you," I said. "It merely saved my life."

I, too, had attempted my former tartness, but it was anything except convincing. Indeed, there was a suspicious dampness in my eyes and, I suspect, considerable affection as Stephen Lansing and I exchanged a sheepish grin. After all, I had liked the young scamp from the first, though I fought against it, and I had reason to conclude that he entertained much the same regard for me.

"In that case, Adelaide," he said soberly, "maybe you'll forget the old conscience and do me a favour?"

"If you mean there isn't any point to be served now by telling the inspector about – about the Adairs, I thoroughly agree with you," I announced emphatically.

Stephen did not say anything, and I gave him an accusing glance. "It would be entirely unnecessary, now that the criminal is known. Simply a-a gratuitous stirring of nasty waters and, more undeserved heartaches for that poor child."

He sighed. "Her loyalty is one of the most touching things I ever saw."

"She's lovely in every way."

"Yes!" he cried.

So I had not been such an old fool, after all, when it came to matchmaking, I thought exultantly. Stephen Lansing may never have been in love before, I told myself, but he was in love now, head over heels in love with Kathleen.

"The bigger they come, the louder the splash," I observed with apparent irrelevance, though he caught the drift.

"Don't be silly!" he protested, then, avoiding my eye, laughed unsteadily. "Got my number, have you, Adelaide? Oh well!" He shrugged his shoulders. "Only she can't endure me, you know."

I had an entirely different idea, but I did not say so. Fond as I had grown of the dashing young Mr Lansing, I believed it would do the slightly too attractive gentleman no harm to occupy the uncertain seat for a change, if only briefly. It has been my experience that people, men especially, value most that which is most difficult to come by. And on one thing I had set my foolish and stubborn old heart. Not if I could prevent it would Kathleen's romance be aborted as had been her father's and mine. It was perfectly true that, but for circumstances, she might have been my own little girl. At any rate, that is how I felt about her, and still do, God bless her!

"Sophie is terribly broken up," I went on, more to change the subject than anything. "I don't suppose you and the police found Cyril Fancher in the basement, Stephen?"

He shook his head. "I didn't expect to, and the inspector was balmy even to look. He thought he had the basement bottled up. My eye! There are at least six skylights in the place through which a desperate man could crawl to the street."

"I never thought of that."

"Neither did the inspector till Sweeney discovered the one in the laundry chute hanging open. It leads onto the alley behind the hotel."

"So that's the way he went."

Stephen shrugged his shoulders.

I sighed. "Surely he can't have got far. Isn't-isn't there a very good chance of capturing him, Stephen?"

He shrugged his shoulders again. "We've sent out notices all over. Trains and buses and even airports are being patrolled, and we've got scout cars combing the town."

"Then he can't get away!"

He frowned. "The gang operating in and out of New Orleans, Adelaide, has a very thorough organization. We have been able to line up their connections at that end. We can arrest them any minute. The department has been waiting only till I grabbed my man here, for fear of giving the alarm and losing him, though I've muffed my part of the show, damn the luck! However, none of us has ever known for sure how the girls are taken to New Orleans. We think by a line of interstate trucks, most likely, supposedly carrying legitimate loads, probably belonging to some perfectly honest concern which does not dream that on certain nights their freight is human, bound for hell."

I shivered. "It's too terrible!"

"Not knowing more than we do about this end of the business, it is quite possible that, once safely out of the hotel, Cyril Fancher or anyone else could be carted away under the very nose of the police without our being able to do a thing about it."

"Oh dear!"

"It's certain arrangements had been made for a shipment tonight." He winced. "There was Gloriana and – and the Wilson girl."

"You think he killed her?"

"She has undoubtedly been wounded. Probably put up a desperate resistance when captured and had to be silenced, if only temporarily." He sighed. "Dead or alive, he took her with him."

"How-how do you know?" I faltered.

"She, also, isn't to be found."

"Oh!"

He scowled. "It's a strain on the imagination to believe he crawled through a skylight, carrying a severely injured girl with him, and got completely away in broad daylight unobserved."

"It sounds impossible!"

"Nevertheless, some man reported having seen a large covered truck near the alley entrance at two and later. Of course, it did not occur to the boob to take the number or investigate."

"People have so little foresight."

"Yes, including this boob," said Stephen ruefully, "or I shouldn't have made the mess I did of this."

"Ridiculous! As if you could help..."

However, at that minute Inspector Bunyan knocked on my door. He, too, looked tired and discouraged as he sank into the chair I offered him. There were dusty smudges on his dapper suit and a blob of soot astride his nose.

"Any luck?" inquired Stephen, plainly expecting none.

The inspector shook his head. "He stepped right through that skylight into the truck, sir, and dragged the girl in after him."

"Think so?"

"The truck was waiting for her and the Quack-Quackenberry girl?"

"Maybe."

"He wouldn't risk keeping them hidden in the basement a minute longer than absolutely necessary. I figure that's how he worked it all through. Once he nabbed his victim, he shipped her south as quickly as possible."

"But," I protested, "Annie's been missing since yesterday noon."

"He was going to make it a two-bagger," explained the inspector. "I mean, he held the Wilson girl over, probably tied up in another of those empty crates by the furnace, till he could get the other waitress to go along with her."

"Quite a risk, grabbing two at once," muttered Stephen.

"I think you guessed it, sir, when you said after he killed Reid, and then was forced to kill the others, he was preparing for a last big haul and a quick run out before it got too hot to handle."

"I simply can't picture Cyril Fancher as a murderer and b-blackmail... white slaver, I mean," I stammered. "He always struck me as such a spineless person."

"You're telling me," muttered Stephen.

"I never liked him," I admitted, "and I could imagine his being a petty criminal of some kind, the sort who's weak enough to get into trouble and too weak to get out again. I might even, by a stretch, imagine his being terrified enough to kill, to save himself, but never in ten thousand years would I have picked Cyril Fancher as the brains of anything, much less of such an elaborate and infernally clever scheme as this white slave horror."

"That's where I went wrong, Adelaide," murmured Stephen Lansing with a sigh. "I was so busy looking for the subtle and fiendishly clever brain with a taint of madness in it, which the inspector described to us, I never, worse luck, brought myself to take Cyril Fancher seriously."

The inspector flushed. "No matter how he impressed people, I think you'll admit, both of you, that I was right in my analysis of the criminal's psychology," he said stiffly and added with a touch of malice, "At least he was clever and subtle enough to walk right through my net, and yours, Mr Lansing."

"And is my face red!" groaned Stephen.

"I still can't see why he failed to take Gloria along," I said. "He must have known as soon as she was found his game was up."

"He didn't have time for everything in the minutes at his disposal," muttered Stephen, "and I dare say he didn't expect her to be found – not, at least, alive."

I shuddered, and the inspector pursed his lips. "The Wilson girl was bleeding. He couldn't hide her away, even in a trash heap, without a chance of somebody spotting the trail."

"I suppose," said Stephen thoughtfully, "you noted, Inspector, that an attempt had been made to wash away the stains in the dressing room. I think that is when he realized that Miss Adelaide was about to walk right in on him."

I remembered that I had heard the water running in the lavatory just before the light went out and shuddered again.

"That reminds me, Miss Adams," said the inspector, "I have to get a statement from you describing the attack upon your person, a mere formality for the record but..."

At that precise moment Ella Trotter knocked at the door and then with her usual impetuosity immediately opened it and entered.

"I beg your pardon," she said, stopping short at sight of my guests. "I didn't realize you were occupied, Adelaide."

She looked wistful, as though she hoped to be asked to stay. Ella always enjoys being in on everything. However, I can be extremely firm if necessary.

"I am occupied," I snapped. "I'll see you later, Ella."

"Don't put yourself out, pray," she remarked huffily. "I only came to bring the hose I got Lou to mend for you – as a special favour, Adelaide."

"Thanks," I said, feeling guilty as I accepted the package but determined not to weaken.

"Don't mention it," she said, starting to close the door behind her, and then, putting her head in again through the crack, "I forgot to say, Adelaide, that Lou found your green spectacle case in your knitted bag when she went to fix it."

"My green spectacle case?"

"I hope you haven't needed it," she said.

I simply stared at her in silence, and finally she shut the door with a bang, this time for good.

"Why so agitated, Adelaide?" drawled Stephen Lansing as I began to fumble in the drawer of the bedside table.

"The woman's crazy," I snorted, picking my green spectacle case up from where only that morning I had deposited it in the table drawer.

"Maybe not," said Stephen Lansing softly. "Look in the-er-knitted bag, Addie."

My hands trembled slightly as I opened the package which Ella had given me and examined the contents.

Lou Trotter is nearly a genius. It was impossible to detect where the threads had worn in two on the knitted bag, but in the bottom lay my green spectacle case, or one so like it I had to see the two together to know that the one which James Reid had handed me outside Ella Trotter's door, shortly before he was murdered, was shinier and newer and a brighter green.

19

And so it all came out, everything which Stephen Lansing and I, poor fools, had tried so desperately to conceal. For under the lining of the second green spectacle case Inspector Bunyan discovered a number of thin sheets of onion paper covered with minute handwriting, James Reid's handwriting – his record of the seven days which he spent under the roof of the Richelieu Hotel with his findings – and there was little about the private lives of its guests which he had not ferreted out and set down in fine indelible ink.

We knew then what the murderer had been searching for in my old suite and also in Room 511, without success, for after the crime the papers were not concealed under the carpet in 511, where until the day of his death Reid kept them, nor were they to be found in the suite where he died. Sensing that he was walking in danger of his life, he had, subsequent to returning my case to me that morning in the lobby, secreted his notes in his own spectacle case. Then late that same afternoon, feeling the peril closing in upon him, he palmed his case off on me as mine, for safekeeping as he thought.

Only not five minutes afterward I gave the knitted bag with its contents to Ella Trotter's sister-in-law, and so it passed out of the hotel, but not, alas, forever. For that slim roll of papers had a terrible tale to unfold, one that blanched my face and Stephen's and cost us the most terrible night of our lives. It was all there for the inspector to read aloud, as inescapable as death and the grave.

I had guessed correctly in one respect. It was Mary Lawson who employed the private detective, employed him to trap a blackmailer who was bleeding her dry. According to James Reid's record, Mary had received dozens of those lascivious notes, such as I received, attacking her dead husband's honour, claiming that there was a notorious woman of the town with him the night he died in an automobile wreck, claiming he had been intimate with the woman for months, even enclosing a snapshot of her, nude, in his arms, a snapshot which the blackmailer threatened to sell to the local scandal sheet unless Mary paid and paid.

" 'Of course,' " James Reid explained in his note, " 'the film is doctored, fixed up to look like what it ain't, but try and prove it to the average person who all he knows is what he sees in the papers. At least it'll comfort Mrs L when I tell her that her husband was never guilty of anything, except having one of his photographs superimposed on that damned woman's after he was dead.' "

"Oh, thank goodness!" I breathed, knowing the anguish which Mary must have lived through, believing anything so shameful of the husband she still loved enough to make every sacrifice to preserve his memory.

" 'But the only way to kill the thing,' " James Reid wrote on, " 'is to get the film, except to do that you got to catch your blackmailer first. _Note – This stunt smacks of Broadway, the kind of smart racket they pull off on the big stem._ Whoever he is, there are no hayseeds on this guy. That water pitcher is as clever a dodge as I ever run into for collecting the dough without leaving a trail to himself, to say nothing of the brown wrapping paper. But they don't come so smart, they don't stump their toe sometime, and sooner or later I'll set a little trap and he'll walk into it.' "

I shook my head. The blackmailer had not walked into James Reid's trap nor mine nor yet Stephen's. The inspector read on. Lottie Mosby's sordid history was there in black and white, but James Reid believed she had been deliberately enticed into gambling by the blackmailer. " 'He let her win at first, and then when she got in so deep she couldn't get out, he forced her to sell herself to men and took half her receipts not to tell the husband.' "

Nowhere, however, was there any mention of the threatening note which the distracted girl admitted she wrote and which she was supposed to have left in James Reid's box at the desk a few hours before he was murdered.

"Come to think of it," murmured the inspector with chagrin, "the note had no salutation. She started right out saying she couldn't pay any more. There is a chance it was not addressed to James Reid at all."

"So I noticed at the time," remarked Stephen dryly.

"If she didn't write it to him, then she wrote it to the blackmailer!" I exclaimed.

"Precisely," muttered Stephen.

"We found it torn up in James Reid's wastebasket," stammered the inspector. "Naturally we supposed-er-we supposed that –"

"I believe you've said all along, Inspector," interrupted Stephen, reciprocating malice for malice, "that our criminal is both clever and subtle."

"Er-yes," admitted the inspector.

James Reid next had something to say about Howard Warren. " 'He's in a bank, with access to plenty money. The B.M. [which abbreviation Reid had adopted for the blackmailer] would give his eyeteeth to get his hooks in the boy. Has tried it, as I found out by a secret peek at the Lawson girl's diary. Warren's in love with her, and it looked like a good bet to work him through the kid, but she reversed the tables on B.M. by deliberately disgusting Warren with herself. That's why she turned into a baby wampus-cat overnight, although from her diary she's nerts about the boy.' "

I felt like clapping my hands for gallant, plucky little Polly, who had preferred to break her own heart rather than serve as a stalking- horse to lead the man she loved to ruin.

" 'B.M. is trying to work the gambling racket on Warren now,' " James Reid wrote. " 'At least, somebody gave him a tip on a horse yesterday afternoon and he won. The idea being that he'll win a couple of times, and then he'll lose his shirt and, if possible, a large slice of the funds he's trusted with at the bank. Pretty clever of BM' "

"The dirty dog!" breathed Stephen.

The inspector nodded and read on: " 'I am sure now that the money bet in this hotel never actually leaves town. Blackmail isn't B.M.'s only source of revenue. Unless I'm all wet, he has an arrangement with the bookie down the street. They hand out tips, most of them punk, pay the winnings, if any, out of their own pockets and split the rest between them. That smells of Broadway too. *Note - Who around here is all that wised-up to the slick money?* Might be the Anthony dame. I wouldn't put anything past her, except risking her own hide.' "

Stephen scowled. "She worried me, too, from the first. I tried to take her to a mental cleaning, but she was too cagey for me. I couldn't get her to spill a thing."

"And when she was ready to spill, he killed her!" I cried bitterly.

The inspector nodded and sighed as he turned a page. " 'Got an answer to the wire I sent to New York police. Anthony woman never under arrest. Mixed up with all the people who run the rackets but thinks too much of herself to tackle anything she can't get by with by law. Specialty: legal gold digging, alias alimony. *Note - What's she doing off down here where there ain't no import-ant pickings?*' "

"And that's what worried me about her from the first," I said bitterly.

Without comment the inspector read on: " 'Wired Anthony woman's bank. She's mailed as high as a thousand dollars at a time to be deposited to her account since she landed at the Richelieu. She must be B.M.' "

"Good heavens!" I whispered.

The inspector frowned me into silence and continued: " 'Anthony's getting her share of the take all right, but can't believe she's B.M. Crooks stick to their own last. It's more likely she's working B.M. for her part of the booty. She may have thought up some of the stunts or copped them off her Broadway pals, but it's not her stripe to risk burning herself by pulling her own chestnuts

out of the fire. Not that dame! _Note - Who's doing her dirty work?'_
"

I think I should explain that each sentence after the key word 'note' was heavily underscored. Evidently they stood for points which the private detective considered important enough for immediate attention and investigation.

The next entry was in the same vein. " 'The Anthony dame's getting her rake-off and getting plenty, but she's not doing any of the rough stuff herself, and I'd bet on it. Can't figure what guy she's got on the string. Doesn't act sweet on any man here. I think she'd like to give that federal dick, Lansing, a run for his money, and they say he's got it all right. But she shies off him for some reason. _Note - Why's he here?_ Never heard of the G man being detailed on a blackmailing rap.' "

Stephen made a grimace. "He had me ticketed."

"Along with everybody else," I groaned.

The next day James Reid had received a report. " 'Wired Jones in Washington. He wires back it's the gossip that Lansing's working on a white-slave trick. What the hell! I haven't run onto anything like that here, barring a hint of it in the case of the Mosby trail. _Note - Is girl snatching another one of B.M.'s little rackets?_ He's beginning to sound like one of these here master crooks you read about. It's screwy to expect a guy of that calibre in this little two-by-four burg – or is it?' "

"He's beginning to suspect what he's up against," muttered the inspector.

"Yep," said Stephen grimly. "He's loaded his hook for a minnow and got caught on the wrong end of a shark."

James Reid continued to be plagued by Hilda Anthony. " 'Maybe it ain't a man who's sweet on her,' " he wrote. " 'Maybe it's someone she's got a club over. _Note - Find out what Cyril Fancher's doing in this rural hide-out, married to an old woman._ He's got Times Square wrote all over him. The kind of nice boy who used to hang out at Child's Forty-seventh Street Restaurant after 1 a.m. Maybe he and the Anthony woman are old side-kicks. Maybe she followed him off down here or he sent for her. Maybe the money she's mailing back is her drag from what he's lifting off his fat slob of a wife.' "

"This is getting on my nerves," I whispered. "It's like-like a séance."

"The voice from the dead," quoted Stephen and shook his head.

We were neither of us prepared for James Reid's abrupt switch in the next entry. " 'Run into something funny today, wasn't even looking for it. The Adair woman's a sneak thief.' "

I could not get my breath, and Stephen's fingers tightened on the pencil in his hand until his knuckles were a shiny white.

The inspector glanced from one to the other of us, whistled softly to himself, and then went on in a dry voice. " 'I caught her in the act today. She lifted a red glass clip off the buzzum of that stiff necked old maid, the Adams cat.' "

I gasped and then by main strength produced a grin. "He tick-eted me all right," I stammered ruefully.

Stephen did not raise his eyes, but the inspector smiled faintly before he resumed reading. " 'The old gal didn't even know the jewel was gone. Not till the Adair girl realized I was hep. At that she covered up like lightning. Old hand at it, I guess. "You dropped your clip, Miss Adams," she said as cool as a cowcumber. But it was lucky for yours truly that looks can't kill. _Note - What's the attraction in this place for a smart shoplifter and her cub?_ My God, is this the criminals' Grand Hotel or a crooks' convention or what? Anyway, those two court watching!' "

"Oh!" I gasped.

Stephen never looked up and to my relief James Reid's next entry tacked back to Cyril. " 'The Anthony woman's got something on Fancher all right. Heard her tell him yesterday that he'd better sit up and do his little trick cute or she'd mention him in her next letter to Spute Madigan. Fancher turned whiter than a toad's belly. _Note - Wire Bim in New York about who and what is Spute and_ _why is he poison to Fancher.'_ "

I sighed. "So Hilda Anthony was back of it all."

"She had a killing coming to her," muttered Stephen.

The inspector read on: " 'Madigan boss of mob, known as a killer. Fancher's real name is Roger Tuttle. Member of Madigan's mob for years. Did all the little routine jobs no one else would do. Sort of office boy for the gang. Tried to break away several times. Madigan thought it funny to yank him back. Shot at him three four times. Scared Fancher silly. He was a nervous wreck when he tipped the police off to Madigan.

" 'Fancher claimed it was his only chance to get free. Claimed he'd tried to go straight again and again, only couldn't for Madigan. Madigan sent up for twelve years on Fancher's testimony. Swore he'd kill the squealer if he ever got out. Madigan paroled last year through political pull. Fancher promptly took a run out powder. Madigan back on Broadway, says he'll kill Fancher if he ever catches up with him. Madigan and Anthony woman old cronies.' "

"So that's why," I cried huskily. "She devilled Cyril into it!"

"She furnished the brains while he did the work," said the inspector, "and she got most of the profits."

"And finally she was ready to turn on the poor louse, so he killed her. Is that the theory, Inspector?" asked Stephen.

The inspector nodded. "It fits," he said and read on: " 'Adair woman snitched a green blouse out of the Lawson girl's room today. Stood on a chair and hooked the thing over the transom with the handle of an umbrella, like she was fishing.' "

"Oh God!" I groaned to myself.

" 'B.M. has overlooked one bet,' " went on James Reid. " 'Guess he figures the Adairs haven't got it. He doesn't know what I know. The old maid is rolling in coin, and the Adair girl is the daughter of Adams' old beau. I heard the Adair woman say so tonight while I was listening outside their door. They come down here to chisel off the Adams' bankroll. _Note - Might pick up something on the side for myself._ The Adairs ought to pay all they got to keep me from spoiling their play with Adams.' "

"Oh!" I cried.

The inspector looked at me sharply, frowned and then glanced at Stephen's bowed head.

Keeping his eyes down, Stephen murmured wearily, "You said Reid wasn't above a little left-handed blackmailing of his own, Inspector."

The inspector did not answer, but his expression darkened as he continued with the notes. " 'Approached Adair girl this morning,' " said Reid. " 'Claimed to know all, and she broke down and blew the works. Mother's been in the pen for theft. Out now on parole. Broke it and come down here to work on Adams. Girl flew at me like a crazy woman when I threatened to turn them up to the cops. Said she'd see me dead before she'd let her mother go back to jail.' "

"Oh God," I whispered to myself again, and in Stephen's hands the pencil snapped in two.

" 'I was dumbfounded at her strength. Her fingers went into me like steel bits,' " wrote James Reid. " 'I told her to put up or else. She said they haven't any money. Said her mother wasn't going to live long, said she wouldn't last a month back in the pen, begged me to be merciful. I laughed in her face.' "

"The cad!" I cried.

"The bastard!" groaned Stephen.

The inspector cleared his throat. "We come now to James Reid's last day on earth," he announced solemnly.

I shuddered, and Stephen muttered fiercely, "For God's sake, get it over."

James Reid began his final entry in high glee. " 'The rat's asked for the bait at last,' " he wrote. " 'And I've got what I've been waiting for. Mary Lawson has received another note, the first since I've been here. She's to place five hundred dollars in her water pitcher and leave it on the fourth-floor landing of the fire escape tonight at 7:45. Oh boy, and when B.M. collects I'll be there! In the Adams suite next door where I can get one good look at the gentleman.

That's all I want. Just one glimpse of his face and he's my meat. Mrs L is going to keep the old maid out of the way, but I'll have to use the skeleton key again to get in.' "

"Oh dear," I whispered.

However, the next entry, written about noon the same day, had changed in tenor. " 'Must be getting jittery in my old age,' " Reid wrote. " 'Ought to be feeling set up over the juicy little melon I'm going to cut myself, thanks to the Adairs. Ain't like me to get steamed up over a hot headed little filly with a mother who's more than half batty. But the way the girl stared at me after I called the Adams' attention to her spectacle case this morning wasn't healthy. The expression on the old maid's face was funny though. She can't figure how it got downstairs. If she had eyes, she'd have seen it fall out of the Adair woman's handbag when she dropped it. Someday it will dawn on Adams to wonder how I knew it was hers. It's a good thing for me she doesn't know I've been through her suite with a spy glass, along with everybody else's.' "

"The sneak!" I gasped.

The inspector read on: " 'If I scared easy I'd lay off the Adairs; that gal is plenty desperate. I think she meant it when she said she'd see me dead before she'd let me turn in the mother. It is to laugh. After the wild Arabs I've handled in my day I can protect myself from a chit of a girl.' "

I could not get my breath and, like Stephen, I did not dare lift my eyes, but I could feel the inspector's grim scrutiny before, clearing his throat, he went on to the last entry in James Reid's sordid case history.

" 'Well, the fireworks went off this afternoon, and I don't mean perhaps. The Adair gal asked me up to her room and told me straight out that she'd get me if I didn't let her mother alone. She put the federal dick onto me, too, for he called me up later and warned me to stop snooping on the Adair women or he'd knock my block off. Anybody can see at a glance he's sweet on the girl.' "

Stephen's face turned perfectly white under the inspector's

prolonged regard.

"So," said Inspector Bunyan softly, "that's why neither you nor Miss Adams has played fair with me, Lansing. Each had your reasons for doing everything in your power to prevent my uncovering a lead to the Adair girl."

Stephen made no reply, but I could not be silent. "The mother is a kleptomaniac, Inspector. She – it's a disease. She's not responsible."

"A taint of madness," murmured the inspector softly.

I bit my lip. "She only takes things, pretty, colourful things, for the girl whom she adores. Kathleen invariably returns them."

"Yes?" murmured the inspector sceptically.

"She wouldn't steal if Kathleen had everything she could possibly want," I said desperately, "and from now on she shall have; I'll see to that. There was no point in our telling you this tragic story about the Adairs. I am going to take care of them. I'll see to it personally that the mother never has either the temptation or the opportunity to steal again. She can't live long, Inspector. It's an unnecessary piece of cruelty to send her back to the penitentiary. Naturally" – my voice faltered – "had they been connected with the murders, both Stephen and I should have felt compelled to tell you everything. But their unhappy problem has no part in the – in the crimes here."

"I wonder," said the inspector in so silky a tone I shivered.

"Is that all of the notes?" asked Stephen hoarsely.

"No, Mr Lansing," said the inspector, looking very grim, "there is more to come."

I remember I instinctively clenched my teeth as he began those last damning lines. " 'I put a crimp in the Adair girl all right,' " Reid wrote, " 'when I informed her that it would do her no good to rub me out, because I've got it all down in black and white. She looked like she could kill me when I warned her that, if anything happened to me, my notes would land her on the gallows. Come to think of it, I'd better find somewhere else to hide them. Beneath the carpet ain't so hot when you're dealing with big-time crooks, and that dotty mother of hers is entirely too smooth about lifting things out of people's rooms. If I stick them under the lining in my spectacle case I can always, if necessary, palm it off on the Adams snoop-cat. She'd never know the difference unless she saw the two together. And, anyway, I'll be in her rooms for quite a spell tonight. I can pick it up then unless I still have this damned weird feeling that eyes are following me about, boring into my back; only when I turn around, there's nothing there.' "

"Then B. M. had seen through him!" I cried. "Cyril Fancher knew what Reid was up to and had him marked for death even then."

"It doesn't sound like it," said the inspector dryly and read on: " 'Of all people in the house I'd never have picked the guy who is actually doing the rough stuff. It's hard to believe even after the Anthony dame spilled the dope.' "

I gasped and so did Stephen, but the inspector went impassively on with James Reid's confession of his own abominable treachery. " 'Her room is next door to the Adairs. She heard me talking to them and laid for me when I came out. "Didn't know you went in for a little fancy blackmailing," says she, "but maybe we could use a wise guy like you." Then she took me into her own room and opened up. Good Lord, what a brain that woman's got! Even with the lame duck she's been working with, she's a wow! What could she and a bird like me do together! It's a rank trick to pull on Mrs L, but every dog has to scratch his own fleas.

" 'Guess I'll have to go through the trick tonight though. Can't back out without arousing her suspicions. Won't be any trouble to tell her I kept a faithful watch for B.M. but he failed to show. Lucky I haven't told her her man was on the square. That's why I always demand a week on the job before I hand in a report. You never know what'll turn up. But, for that matter, as long as we've got the film she don't dare squeal, whatever she suspects. And that five hundred dollar retainer she paid me looks sick now when I'm due to get half of everything she coughs up. Did I say I'd laid a juicy melon for myself? And how!' "

"Oh!" I cried. "Of all the unprincipled scoundrels!"

Stephen stared defiantly at the inspector. "The Anthony woman was going to team up with Reid, so B.M. killed him," he muttered.

"Doesn't sound like it," repeated the inspector as he continued.

" 'I had my doubts about how B.M. would take my homing in,' " was almost the last thing Reid wrote. " 'But the Anthony skirt said he'd never had the guts for the raw stuff, and when she arranged for me to talk to him he all but fell on my neck, the poor fish! Now all I got to do is clip the Adair girl's claws, and I'm set.' "

I was shuddering again, and Stephen's face was ghastly.

"These are the last lines the dead man wrote," said the inspector impressively. " 'Slipped the spectacle case to the Adams hen, feel safer, though I think the Mosby woman saw me, but she's as harmless as new milk. If only I could shake off the feeling that crazy eyes are following me everywhere I go!' "

The inspector slowly refolded the thin sheets of paper amid a deathly silence, and then Stephen cried, "They fooled him, B.M. and Hilda Anthony! They just pretended to let him in on their rotten business. Soon as they got him on the spot in Miss Adams' room, one or the other of them polished him off."

"You think so?" drawled the inspector.

"Probably he opened the door to them himself," I cried excitedly, "or let them in at the window. He wouldn't look for danger from them till it was too late."

"They didn't know about the spectacle case," the inspector pointed out.

"Lottie Mosby knew!" I cried. "I saw her peeping out of a room down the hall just after Reid handed it to me. She could have told them."

"She knew all right," said the inspector. "That's what she was after in your suite when she was killed."

"How did she get in?" demanded Stephen sharply.

"We didn't mention it, but we found a skeleton key on her dead body. I suppose B.M. gave it to her. It suited his purposes to make it convenient for her to slip in and out of various men's rooms."

"Oh!" I cried with a foul taste in my mouth.

The inspector looked from one to the other of us. "There's no use evading the issue. Painful as it is, it must be faced," he said at last.

"What-what do you mean?" I gasped.

"I have said before that criminals do not change their habits any more than the rest of us do. It's still true. Hilda Anthony was a bad egg but not a killer. Neither was Cyril Fancher, as both of you felt instinctively. He played the B.M. role because the Anthony woman forced him to, but he didn't kill Reid; just as Fancher could never bring himself to kill Madigan, his tormentor back East."

My lips were terribly stiff. "But he attacked Glory and me in the basement this afternoon. He would have strangled me to death – except for Stephen."

"In my opinion," said the inspector, "Fancher with the Wilson girl was gone before you ever entered the basement, Miss Adams, or very soon afterward, fleeing for his life in the truck. I agree, however, that it was he who knocked the Quackenberry girl out, though by her own statement she never saw the face of her assailant. Right, Mr Lansing?"

With a face like death Stephen nodded.

"Fancher probably intended to go back for Miss Quackenberry after he put the other one in the truck, but your scream frightened him off, Miss Adams. Running away from danger is his style of self-defence, not murder, and it was not he who killed James Reid or Lottie Mosby or Hilda Anthony, nor was it he who attempted to strangle you today."

I could not speak and apparently neither could Stephen, and finally the inspector went softly on, "You did a very foolish thing yesterday afternoon, Miss Adams, when you changed your will."

I was trembling. "With so many tragic occurrences, I-I thought it a good idea."

"Nevertheless," said the inspector sternly, "you very nearly signed your own death warrant when you had your lawyer come here after Lottie Mosby's death and draw you up a new will, leaving everything of which you die possessed to Kathleen Adair."

Stephen was on his feet, his face convulsed with rage. "If you think you can pin these murders on-on..." He choked and could not go on.

The inspector tapped the green spectacle case in his hand.

"James Reid warned Kathleen Adair that his notes would land her on the gallows," he said.

"Oh," I cried wildly, "it isn't true!"

"She killed Mosby to keep the notes out of her hands, then failed to find them herself, as she had previously failed to locate them when she searched the room which James Reid occupied and the ones where he died."

"It isn't true!" I wailed again.

"Kathleen Adair's mother is off mentally, but in her case, also, murder is not her forte. However, she bequeathed the girl a tainted brain which, under the threat of exposure, took a homicidal turn."

"No, no!" I cried. "They aren't even kin. I swear it! Mrs Adair is only Kathleen's foster mother."

"Nonetheless, the girl is thrice a murderess," said the inspector grimly. "She and the woman came here to worm their way into your good graces and so into your fortune, Miss Adams. When James Reid endangered the success of their plans, Kathleen Adair killed him."

"I don't believe it!" I wailed.

"Just as she killed the Anthony woman when, in fear of her own life, she was about to tell me that she overheard the Adair girl threatening Reid."

"It isn't true!"

"Kathleen Adair was seen on the stairs with your afghan, Miss Adams, not ten minutes before you discovered it wrapped about Hilda Anthony's dead body."

"Oh! Oh! Oh!" I cried, beginning to sob wildly.

Stephen put his hand on my shoulder. "This is all a tissue of circumstantial evidence, Adelaide. It doesn't mean a thing." He glared at the inspector. "And, by God, I'll prove it!"

The inspector smiled pleasantly. He was again smug and wonderfully hepped up over having stolen a march upon the federal man and covered himself with glory by breaking the case against all odds.

"There's one test we can make," he said softly, "the infallibility of which neither of you can deny, if you'll come with me."

Silently we followed him down to the fourth floor. Kathleen herself opened the door when the inspector knocked. She stared at us as if she did not see us. Her eyes, though perfectly dry, were heart breaking.

"She's dead," she said dully. "Died a minute ago, just as the doctor said she would, as though she were falling asleep. I was holding her hand. She smiled at me so tenderly, and then her fingers loosened and and she was gone."

"My poor child!" I cried.

I would have drawn her into my arms, but the inspector stepped between us.

"Roll up your sleeves, Miss Adair," he said brusquely.

She stared at him blankly. "My-my sleeves?"

He caught her wrist and swiftly pushed up the sleeves of her frilly white blouse. Behind me Stephen Lansing gasped – it was almost a sob – but I could only go on staring at that half-moon of tiny red wounds on Kathleen's exquisite arm just above her slender wrist.

"Your teeth branded the murderess, Miss Adams," said the inspector, "and James Reid's notes will hang her."

"Oh!" gasped the girl. "I – I –"

"You are under arrest for murder," snapped the inspector.

20

In spite of Stephen's furious protests and my impassioned pleas on her behalf, the inspector took Kathleen Adair away from the hotel in a police car within fifteen minutes of her sensational arrest.

"But he can't keep you in jail!" Stephen told her as they were leaving. "I'll hire the best lawyers in the world. I'll-I'll..."

The inspector shrugged his shoulders. "Come on, miss," he interrupted and took her arm.

The girl, with one piteous glance at Stephen, went. She had not spoken a word. She acted dazed, as if the series of tragic blows which she had suffered had numbed her senses – as I have no doubt they had.

"I can't bear it!" I sobbed.

Stephen had his arm about me. "At any rate," he said huskily, staring at the silent figure on the bed, "that poor soul is out of it all."

I gulped and nodded. "I'll have her put away beautifully for Kathleen's sake."

He tried to smile at me. "You're such an old trump, Adelaide. God knows what I'd do without you."

"You mean," I said tremulously, "what would I do without you?"

I was leaning on his arm as we walked to the elevator, and morally I was relying on him in every way. Stephen was going to police headquarters. He was going to see Kathleen. He was going to set every possible wheel in motion to secure her release.

"Because she isn't guilty, she couldn't be, Adelaide."

"Of course not," I said, though neither of us could meet the other's eyes, and I knew he was seeing, as I was, that terrible ring of angry red dents on my darling's arm with which, God help me, I had placed the brand of Cain upon her.

It was after seven, and Clarence had already taken over the elevator for the night. He was, plainly to be seen, bursting with the astounding news which, with Kathleen's departure under heavy police guard, had swept through the hotel like a prairie fire.

"Law," he said, "I never would have thought that nice young lady was a murderer."

"She isn't," snapped Stephen, "and keep your big mouth shut about her."

"Yas suh," quavered Clarence. "I never meant no harm."

"You are an inveterate gossip, Clarence," I said severely, scowling at a dark rusty spot which I had acquired by brushing up against the wall of the elevator with my shoulder. "It's a pity," I went on tartly, "that you wouldn't put in a little time keeping this old rattletrap clean, instead of busying yourself with matters which do not concern you."

"Yas 'm, Miss Adelaide," stammered Clarence.

As a rule I am indulgent of Clarence's well-known tendency to shift a good many of his tasks off upon someone else, but on this occasion I felt if I did not snap at somebody I should explode of sheer internal combustion.

"It is nothing less than a disgrace when the guests in this hotel cannot ride in the elevator without ruining their clothes," I continued, rubbing at that dingy spot on my shoulder which appeared to be composed of equal parts of rust and oil and grime.

I glanced at Stephen and made a grimace. "Looks almost like, like-"

"Blood?" he finished for me. "So it does."

I shuddered. "I suppose, one will never get over feeling that the past three days have left their gory stain on all of us, beyond recall."

"I suppose not," he murmured, his thoughts obviously elsewhere.

He left me in the lobby. "I'll call you, Adelaide, as soon as I've talked to the police," he promised. "In the meanwhile, don't worry. Everything will come out all right."

He smiled reassuringly and squeezed my hand, but I did not think he believed what he said, any more than I did. People stared at me with morbid curiosity that night. From every indication my poor thwarted romance had been dragged from its grave and thoroughly worked over. However, my expression must have been sufficiently intimidating, for not even Ella Trotter dared broach me upon the subject.

I had no appetite, but neither was I in the humour to face down the battery of curious eyes trained upon me in the lobby, so I went on into the Coffee Shop, which at that late hour I had to myself until Sophie Scott crept in through the kitchen, looking like the wraith of herself, her plump cheeks haggard and flabby, shadows like bruises under her reddened eyes.

She paused for a minute at my table, although there was no one I was less anxious to talk to. "I know you never liked Cyril, Adelaide," she said heavily, "and I admit the way it's all turned out, you were right about everything except that he loves me. Old and fat as I am, he loves me. He has had such a hard time, and I've been kind to him, Adelaide. Perhaps he looks upon me more as he might a mother, but he-he isn't bad. If he did wicked things, that woman is to blame. He hated her. He tried to keep away from her. He used to shiver and moan in his sleep at night. Nothing would quiet him but for me to hold him in my arms as if he were a child."

I remembered then that Sophie had always wanted a baby. It had been the regret of her life that she and Tom Scott had been unable to have children.

I put out my hand and awkwardly patted her arm. "I didn't understand, Sophie; I'm sorry," I faltered.

She began to weep again, softly and wearily, as though she had no strength left for violent tears, and finally she moved slowly away, back through the kitchen, while I drearily cut up the food on my plate, without being able to eat a mouthful.

Stephen had promised to telephone, but I had no desire to receive his message in the presence of an audience, even if I had had the effrontery to sit there, self-conscious and distressed, the cynosure of every speculative glance in the lobby. So right after eight, holding my head very high, I went up to my room. Once there it was a relief to let down and give way to my intense dejection. It was nine when Stephen called, and he still had been unable to get in touch with Kathleen at police headquarters.

"They're keeping both her and the inspector incommunicado," he said savagely, "God knows why. But I'll crash through their smoke screen if I have to get the authority from Washington."

He promised to call me again as soon as there was news, but time dragged on, and it was eleven and then half past and no word from Stephen. I was horribly tired, both physically and emotionally.

Wearily I got into my bedroom slippers, removed my false curls, and scrubbed my face. I slipped off my dress. I thought it possible that if Stephen had nothing good to report he might come by my room instead of telephoning. It was my intention to replace my bridge if he knocked at my door. I took it out only because in that fracas in the basement it had been pressed into my upper jaw so hard by my assailant as to cut a small place in the gum.

"The idea of their accusing that child of attacking me!" I fumed, beginning to pace the floor because I was too nervous to keep still.

I thought nothing at first of that faint knocking sound above my head. Being an old building, the Richelieu Hotel is alive with queer snappings late at night. I do not know just how long I had subconsciously been aware of this particular noise or when I first noticed that it was different from any other I had heard the old floors and walls give out.

"It reminds me of when we used to have a branch telegraph office in the lobby," I remember thinking with a small part of my wits, the rest of my brain frantically engaged, as it had been all evening, with the plight of the girl who was the daughter of my heart if not of my body.

"It sounds just like the click of a telegraph key," I muttered absently and then stopped dead-still in my tracks, my face stinging as if I had broken out with prickly heat.

After a while I tottered over to the telephone and called the desk. My voice was hoarse with excitement, and I had totally forgotten my bridge, the absence of which causes me to lisp unintelligibly. However, I finally made Pinky Dodge understand.

"No," he said, "Mr Lansing hasn't come in, Miss Adelaide. I'm certain, because I've been watching for him myself, to-to offer my sympathy."

He hesitated. "Miss Adair seemed such a sweet young lady."

"Pinkthy," I stuttered, "get Mr Lansing on the phoneth for me at onceth. You'll find him at policeth headquarters. It's terribly importanth."

"Yes, Miss Adelaide."

However, he called me back in a few minutes to say he had been unable to locate Stephen Lansing anywhere. My hand trembled on the receiver.

"I musth see him as soon as he cometh, Pinkthy. You won't forgeth?"

"No, Miss Adelaide."

"No matterth how late?"

"Yes, Miss Adelaide."

"And-and, Pinkthy," I went on, my voice quivering uncontrollably, "could you possibly get me a copy of the Morse codeth?"

"The Morse code, Miss Adelaide?" repeated Pinky as if not sure he had heard aright.

"Yes, Pinkthy, and I musth have it at onceth. It's a question of life and death."

"Yes, Miss Adelaide, I'll bring it right up," said Pinky wearily.

I suppose there are few objects, however improbable, which in his twenty years as night clerk Pinkney Dodge had not been required to produce at a moment's notice for some impatient guest.

Nevertheless, he seldom failed to supply a demand, and I had no uneasiness on the delivery of the Morse code.

"Pinkthy will locate one somewhere," I told myself comfortably.

It was the last comfortable moment I was to know for some time. I heard the elevator stop on my floor, and then somebody kicked at the door.

"Who is it?" I called out, popping my bridge into my mouth.

"It's Pinky, Miss Adelaide."

I was fastening my dressing gown and having trouble with the snaps. "Just a minute, Pinky," I spluttered, "till I hook this dratted thing. Women's clothes always fasten in the most ungodly places." Later I was to thank God the snaps were particularly stubborn that night!

"Yes, Miss Adelaide."

Still muttering under my breath as I struggled with the last recalcitrant snap, I moved toward the door. At that moment the window on the fire escape slid noiselessly up before my very eyes.

I had until then imagined that the expression 'frozen in one's tracks' was a literary figure of speech. I was mistaken. As that window eased silently upward I literally turned to ice. I could not have taken a step or uttered a sound to save my life. I had room for only one thought. What in God's name was lurking on the fire escape and how soon would it pounce?

"Pull yourself together, Adelaide," whispered Stephen Lansing. "Act, if you've never acted before. I'm not here, understand?"

I stared at him, unable to believe my eyes. He was crouched down upon the landing of the fire escape, and in his hand he clutched a stubby blue-black revolver.

"Don't you dare faint, Addie," he added.

"Young man," I snapped, "I never faint."

"Oh yeah?" murmured a hoarse voice.

For the first time I realized that the bulky shadow below

Stephen was Officer Sweeney. I had involuntarily kept my voice down to match theirs, but I had forgotten Pinkney Dodge until Stephen motioned toward the door.

"Let him in," he said and added in a grim voice, "Everything now depends on you."

"I haven't the slightest idea what you're talking about," I muttered crossly.

"You will have," said Stephen and again motioned to the door. "Remember, I'm not here."

My knees were trembling when I opened the door. I was still fumbling with the snap on my dressing gown. Thank heaven, the light was behind me. Pinky was standing there, gazing at me in his vague way, and he had a paper in his hand.

"Is that the code, Pinky?" I asked and reached for it.

Pinkney continued to gaze at me without speaking. It was then I became aware that there was something wrong with his eyes. It occurred to me that I had never met Pinky's direct glance before. Usually his eyelids drooped, but they were wide open now and his pupils were unnaturally dilated.

"You've brought it on yourself," he said as he stepped forward. "I'd rather not have hurt you."

I was having trouble getting my breath because of the knife which he was holding against my ribs, a common butcher knife from the Richelieu kitchen.

"You're the only person in this house who ever treated me as if I might be human," Pinkney went on, his voice dull and lifeless yet somehow dreadful.

I made a slight movement, and the knife pricked me even through my heavy robe. "Keep still," said Pinkney Dodge. "I'm desperate, you know. I have been for a week."

The inspector and even Stephen Lansing had believed that back of the Richelieu murders there was a diseased brain which had gone off the track. They were wrong. There was only poor frustrated Pinkney Dodge, terrified for his life, killing as a cornered rat might kill in a frantic effort to save itself.

He gazed at me with dumb entreaty. "Life has cheated me for years," he said. "I never had anything other men have – friends or fun or sweethearts." A spasm twisted his face. "Not until I met Hilda Anthony."

So it was Pinky whom the Anthony creature had used to pull her chestnuts out of the fire, I thought with a shudder. It seemed incredible until I recalled that it had taken all Pinkney made to keep his mother. No other woman had ever looked at him, and Hilda Anthony was beautiful. She had also been clever, clever enough to realize that a clerk in a residential hotel, especially a night clerk, has every opportunity for blackmail and other sordid rackets.

"She cared nothing for me," whispered Pinkney as if he had read my thoughts, "nothing except what she could get out of me. But I wanted her, wanted her as I'd never wanted anything on earth."

My voice trembled. "It was you who-who ..."

He nodded. "To all of you I was that poor worm, Pinky Dodge, whom nobody ever noticed. Just a robot with a voice who waited on you at the desk and took your orders over the telephone. I could pass right through the lobby in front of everybody without any of you seeing me."

It was true. No one ever paid any attention to Pinkney Dodge. He was merely part of the landscape at the Richelieu, like the drinking fountain behind the elevator or the coat rack by the door.

"What about Cyril?" I stammered.

Pinkney's long upper lip curled. "She tried Fancher first. He was horrified at her ideas, but she had a hold on him. She made him help me."

"And you fell for her!" I cried in an outraged voice. "How could you?"

"I told you," he said. "I wanted her. Enough to risk anything! Nothing seemed to matter except that at last I was to get something out of life."

I have said that if frustration had a body it would look precisely like Pinkney Dodge, poor weak fool who had fallen prey to an unscrupulous and conniving woman.

"Then," said Pinky, his face ghastly, "James Reid came and he got onto us. He was going to turn us up if we didn't give him half our takings. I was in a panic, but Hilda was unwilling to split with anybody, and I can't afford to get caught, Miss Adelaide. You know I can't. There's my mother. I had to get Reid; I had to. Surely you understand that."

Again he stared at me entreatingly. I think it was a relief for him to talk to someone, anything to unbosom his soul of its dreadful burden. But the knife in his hand did not waver nor did the stark purpose in his red-rimmed eyes.

"So I killed him," he said, sucking in his breath with a gasp. "Hilda put him on the spot for me and I killed him. Cut his throat and then hung him to the chandelier. You see, I had to be sure. I couldn't risk his coming alive again, could I?"

I shuddered. That was why each of his victims had been murdered twice. He had been afraid, scared out of his wits. It was no subtle brain behind the crimes. It was only panic-stricken Pinkney Dodge, berserk with terror, striking blindly again and again to make sure his victims were dead.

He licked his lips as if they were very dry. "But the danger didn't die with Reid. He left some notes. Hilda heard him tell the Adair girl so. Only I couldn't find them. I looked everywhere – in your old suite, in the room he occupied. I couldn't find them. But Lottie Mosby knew where Reid hid the notes. That was what she was after when she ran away from the police. She meant to give them the notes and let me hang for it. So I had to kill her too."

He gave me a pathetic look. "After that, everyone's hand was against me, even Hilda's. She thought she could betray me to the police without my knowing. But I am going deaf and I can't afford to on my job, so I've studied lip reading. I read every word Hilda said to you this morning. It's funny she was afraid of me when I loved her so. She would have betrayed me. I had to kill her. There was nothing else to do. But the Adair girl will hang for it."

"You fiend!" I gasped.

"I have to save myself! I have to!" he cried hysterically. "I couldn't stand to die on the gallows! I tell you, I couldn't stand it! I've seen nothing else for a week except the black hood settling over my face."

He was trembling and drops of sweat stood out on his long upper lip, but he gave me a reproachful look. "I didn't want to kill you, Miss Adelaide. Only you will meddle in things which don't concern you; first this afternoon and now tonight. I can't have you babbling to Stephen Lansing about Morse codes."

"The waitress Annie," I faltered, "she's somewhere above me?"

"In the attic," he said.

I had known but forgotten that there is an attic of sorts at the Richelieu, no higher than the head of the average child and unfinished. Unlike more modern buildings, the hotel does not have a penthouse. The elevator swings from the roof. If it gets out of adjustment, the mechanics have only two choices. They can get at the machinery through an open space behind the shaft in the basement or work on it from above in the attic. More significant still, I recollected that the only entrance to the attic is by a trap door in the tiny room on the fifth floor which Pinkney Dodge had occupied for years. The trap door was kept locked, but that was no protection against Pinkney, who as night clerk possessed a pass-key to every lock in the house. No wonder bolts had come to mean nothing at the Richelieu.

"She's in the attic!" I gasped.

"I've arranged to ship her to New Orleans late tonight by truck," he said. "Along with Cyril's body."

"His body!" I quavered.

He nodded. "Cyril lost his head this afternoon and attacked me. He believed I was planning to kill Sophie. I had to cut his throat.

It was his bloodstains I was washing up when you all but walked into me in the basement."

Poor Sophie, I thought. But she was right and I had been wrong about Cyril Fancher. He *had* loved her. He had loved her enough to give his life for her.

"Where is he now?" I faltered.

"Tied to the top of the elevator."

I knew then what I had got on my sleeve that night which resembled rust. It was not rust; it was Cyril's life blood. But not till later did I know it was that which first set Stephen Lansing on Pinkney's trail, that and Stephen's stubborn refusal to believe in Kathleen's guilt. He warned the police that Pinkney Dodge was back of everything. They laughed in his face. They said the idea was preposterous. Fortunately for me, Stephen did not think the idea preposterous.

He and Officer Sweeney were watching Pinkney from the darkened Coffee Shop when I telephoned for the Morse code. Pinkney said he would send it up by Clarence, but he sent Clarence off on an errand down the street and prepared to take the code up to me himself. One glimpse of his face off guard was enough for Stephen. He beat it to the fire escape along with Sweeney, who thought he had lost his senses. But Stephen had not lost his senses. Even now I shudder at what would have happened if Stephen had failed to be outside my window when I opened my door to Pinkney Dodge.

"You cut his throat and left him to die on top of the elevator!" I cried, staring with horrified eyes at Pinkney. "But how did you get him out of the basement?"

Pinkney smiled faintly, a terrible smile. "It is possible to get at the roof of the elevator from the basement, you know. It is also possible to ride on top of it. I have seen the mechanics do it many times, but I never dreamed I'd dare till the police hemmed me in this afternoon."

He looked at me, and I began to edge away from his dreadful stare, but he came on, his hand curling at his side. I could not draw a full breath for the pounding of my heart. Inch by inch he forced me backward. Still he came on. Then suddenly I could retreat no farther. My shoulders were against the window frame. I felt the cold air on my neck.

"You're going out the window," he said. "They'll think you couldn't live and face Kathleen Adair's guilt. They've got to believe you committed suicide. I can't afford another murder with Kathleen Adair framed to hang in my place."

My knees buckled beneath me, and the knife drew blood as I collapsed on the window ledge.

It was then Stephen shouted. "Drop, Adelaide! For God's sake, let go and drop! Sweeney will catch you!"

To this day I do not know if I obeyed him or if Pinkney Dodge pushed me through the window, but there can be no doubt about his own action. He had said he could not stand to be hanged. He had a horror of the black cap; and so while Sweeney and I sprawled upon our faces on the fourth-floor landing of the fire escape, Pinkney, with a shrill animal-like scream, plunged past us, his body writhing and twisting until it thudded horribly against the paved court far below.

21

I have never denied that I am a substantially built woman and I do not doubt that in my descent from the roof on that occasion I resembled a zeppelin in full flight. Nevertheless, I did not, as Ella Trotter insists, straddle Policeman Sweeney's neck and ride him to the floor of the landing, nor did I, while scrambling to my feet, plant my stout military heel in his face and walk on it.

However, it is true that the next day Sweeney had a very black eye and a number of assorted aches and bruises which he called Charley Horses, but which Stephen Lansing with a grin suggested might more fittingly be described as Adelaide Mares, whatever he meant by that. It is also true that to this very moment Policeman Sweeney regards me with intense antipathy and never, if humanly possible, does he allow me to come within striking, much less biting, distance of his person.

I myself stayed in bed till noon the following day. My physician said there was nothing wrong with me except undue fatigue and too many acrobatics for a woman whose arteries have hardened a bit. Just the same, I should probably have defied him and got up, except that I still continued to occupy the centre of the stage in the Richelieu that morning. Practically everybody connected with the case called upon me to make sure that I had emerged unscathed from the fracas of the night before. After having looked upon myself for years as a thoroughly disagreeable and unpopular old woman, it was a pleasant shock to lie there and discover how many people seemed genuinely concerned about my welfare.

The inspector was my first visitor, looking as dapper as ever and extremely well pleased with himself – as he had every reason to be. Since Stephen was an undercover man, it was deemed essential by the powers that be to conceal from the general public his share in the solution of the crimes, so in the end Inspector Bunyan reaped all the glory in the Richelieu case.

"Though of course," he conceded in a deprecating voice, "the entire credit belongs to Mr Lansing. As you know, I was convinced of the Adair girl's guilt."

"Some people are like that," I remarked with a sniff.

The inspector preferred to ignore this interpolation.

"It is easy now to see why I went wrong so consistently," he said. "From the beginning Pinkney Dodge was my chief source of information about the people in the house. Naturally, to clear himself he drew first one red herring and then another across my path."

"Like my poor Kathleen," I sighed.

The inspector nodded. "After I got her down to police head-quarters last night she tried to explain about how she came to be in possession of the afghan which figured in Hilda Anthony's murder. It appears the Adair woman filched it off you in the lobby, Miss Adams, right from under your eyes, so to speak."

"Yes?" I murmured, my cheeks feeling very hot.

"The girl said she had started down the stairs to return it to you when she met Pinkney Dodge on the second floor and he offered to deliver it into your own hands. However, when I questioned him later, he flatly denied her story."

"And you were fool enough to believe him," I said dryly.

"Yes," admitted the inspector with a rueful smile. "Just as I believed him when he said that Kathleen Adair lied about the bracelet."

"Bracelet?"

"You know the heavy bracelet which she always wears? A gift from her father, so I understand." I winced and nodded. "If you've noticed," said Inspector Bunyan, "it has a large crescent-shaped ornament on top set with brilliants, an unwieldy thing."

I nodded again.

"That," explained the inspector, "is where Kathleen Adair acquired the ring of red dents on her arm. Pinkney Dodge passed her in the hall on her floor right after the excitement in the basement. He pretended to trip and seized her wrist. He must have pressed the stones into her arm with considerable violence, for they cut the skin."

I shuddered, and the Inspector gave me an apologetic glance.

"Naturally, when I questioned Dodge, he denied the whole incident. Thank heaven, Stephen Lansing refused to accept the Adair girl's statement as pure fabrication. Acting on the assumption she had told the solemn truth, he arrived at the inevitable conclusion that Pinkney Dodge was the criminal. I regret to state that I scoffed at the idea."

"You would," I remarked with acidity.

"However, I did agree to lend Mr Lansing a man to shadow Dodge. And so, fortunately, fortunately for you at least Sweeney was on the fire escape to break your fall."

"This should be a lesson to you, Inspector," I pointed out with some malice.

"Don't think it hasn't been," he said earnestly. "Of course you know why Mr Lansing allowed you to play out that scene with Pinky at - ah - quite a risk to yourself."

"No," I said shortly. "I've wondered, seeing that I might very well have broken my neck."

"Although convinced of Dodge's guilt, Mr Lansing had no proof. None, that is, which I-er-which the police could accept. He counted on your wringing a confession from the murderer at the crucial moment." He smiled faintly. "He says he staked everything on your well-known goading qualities."

"Did he indeed?" I inquired in a nettled voice.

The inspector gave me a distinctly admiring glance. "You're a remarkable woman, Miss Adams," he said so cordially I blushed.

"Oh yes?" I asked, adopting Officer Sweeney's favourite retort, though I was both pleased and touched.

"Thank God, your bite's worse than your bark," the inspector paraphrased and added grimly, "Did you know we found the prints of your teeth on Dodge's forearm?"

I shook my head and I must have turned pretty white, for the inspector hastily apologized for tiring me and left. Almost at once Conrad Wilson and his Annie came in to see me. She looked pale and shaky from having been tied up hand and foot in that small stuffy attic for over thirty-six hours. Pinky had even gagged her.

But, praise to her resourcefulness, she had managed to telegraph an SOS with the heel of her shoe on the attic floor. And, thank God, I finally recognized its significance.

"We want to thank you for what you did for us," they said with one voice.

"Didn't do a thing," I protested gruffly.

"Except nearly get yourself killed twice trying to rescue my Annie," said the telegraph lineman, beaming at me.

I finally got rid of them by pressing a check upon them.

"But, Miss Adams," stammered Annie, "we can't take all this money from you!"

"Pay your house out," I said, "so I won't have to bother about the likes of you again."

I am afraid they were not deceived when I tried to act as if their demonstration bored me. I was, in fact, crying a little to myself, because they had succeeded in getting so far under my crusty surface, when Mary Lawson came in, followed by Polly Lawson and Howard Warren. Their shining faces were proof enough that for them, at least, all was lovely in this muddled old world where we so often manage completely to miss our heart's desires.

"You've been a real friend all during this nightmare, Adelaide," said Mary, holding my hand tightly. "I don't suppose you need to be told how I feel about it."

Polly, however, could not let it go at that. "You're an old peach, Miss Adelaide!" she exclaimed.

"Isn't she!" cried Howard emphatically.

I smiled at them, rather mistily, I confess. "A girl who would deliberately wreck her reputation to save the man she loves is pretty much of a peach herself," I said.

"She's wonderful!" said Howard unsteadily and kissed Polly before us all until she was perfectly rosy and quite breathless.

Mary lingered after they took themselves off.

"I'm sorry, Adelaide," she faltered, "about the use to which I put your rooms and the way it dragged you head-first into this dreadful and sordid affair."

"Why didn't you expose Pinkney Dodge when they arrested you, Mary?" I asked curiously.

She shivered. "They wrote me a note, one of those awful slimy things. It said if I gave anything away I'd never see Polly again."

My hands tightened over hers. "Of course you know now, Mary that John was true to you, as true as you believed him to be."

She nodded and went on painfully to explain, "When Stephen Lansing arranged for my release from jail this morning, he showed me James Reid's notes and he had made it his personal business to go through Pinky's hiding places in the attic and recover that horrible film. He let me burn it with my own hands, so it will not appear as evidence in the records of the case."

"Dear Stephen," I whispered.

"He's splendid," she cried tremulously. "They also found the rod in the attic, Adelaide. The one with which Pinky fished up the aluminium pitchers off the fire escape. It was made of several hinged pieces and could be made as long or as short as desired and taken completely apart when not in use."

"And Pinkney seemed such a perfectly futile person," I sighed.

"He was," said Mary, "until a thoroughly bad woman got hold of him. There is no doubt she worked out the details of all their criminal activities."

"And so sealed her own doom," I muttered.

"Yes," said Mary bitterly, "but for Hilda Anthony none of this would ever have happened."

It was just noon when Stephen thrust his handsome head in at my door. "Want to see somebody very special?" he asked gaily and ushered in Kathleen.

I held out my arms and she came into them. Stephen turned away to the window, leaving us alone together, and for the first time since that faraway June night when I drove Kathleen's father from me my heart ceased its bitter repining.

After a while Stephen came over and sat down on the edge of the bed beside us. "Feeling all right, Adelaide, light of my eyes?" he asked in a tone intended for raillery, though it was more affectionate than playful.

"Young man," I snapped, trying to achieve my former severity but sounding, I fear, like the doting old fool which Ella Trotter calls me nowadays, "how do you suppose I feel after all I've been through?"

Stephen grinned. "Nonsense!" he exclaimed. "You know you've had the time of your life, you old Hessian, hanging out windows by your knees and leaping off the eaves into space like the circus lady on her flying trapeze!"

"I'm afraid you're partly right," I confessed sheepishly.

"Right!" cried Stephen Lansing, slipping one arm about Kathleen and the other about me. "Sure I'm right. Everything's right. As-as right as rain after a drought!"

She was looking up into his eyes, and their faces were so radiant that I pranced with joy. That may sound like an impossibility lying flat in bed, but Ella Trotter has always said I am the only person she ever saw who could strut sitting down. And the fact remains that I had every cause to rejoice. After all, I had for years wanted not only a daughter like Kathleen but also a young scamp of a son to bully and tease and adore me exactly as Stephen does, bless his heart!

1

It was not, as my foster son Stephen Lansing likes to intimate, that I had developed a taste for wild adventure which drew me into that macabre and sinister tangle at Mount Lebeau. Nor is it true, as Ella Trotter insists, that I rushed in where even angels feared to tread because I could not bear for her to steal my thunder. As I pointed out, to no avail, when the body of the third disembowelled cat was discovered in my bed, had I foreseen the train of horrible events which settled over that isolated mountain inn like a miasma of death upon the afternoon of my arrival, I should have left Ella to lay her own ghosts.

As a matter of fact, but for Ella Trotter's fantastic letter I should never have gone near the place at all. Ella has been my close friend for years, although we long ago agreed to disagree on practically everything. We are both, to put it mildly, what is commonly alluded to as strong-minded women. That is why the moment I had Ella's letter I knew something was up, in spite of the pains which she took to put me off the scent.

Ella likes to be in the centre of any excitement and she has never forgiven me for having, as she said, deliberately shoved her off the stage at every opportunity during that sequence of trage-dies which the police referred to as the Hotel Richelieu Murders. Heaven knows why she should have envied me my role in the affair, seeing that I was all but throttled in my bed upon one occasion and next door to murdered in a couple of other unseemly places. Nevertheless Ella did resent what she described as the persistent manner in which I had hogged the spotlight at that time.

She was distinctly cool to me for the next three months and for the first time in years she did not suggest that we take our summer trip together. Instead she barged off without a word, to me at least.

July and August are torrid months in our little Southern city and well-nigh unbearable cooped up in the small residential hotel where I live. Moreover, with my adopted children, Stephen and Kathleen, indulging in a belated honeymoon to the West Indies, I was left stranded and decidedly lonely, as Ella knew perfectly well.

Nevertheless, although we had been in the habit of picking a convenient resort every summer, not, I admit, without considerable wrangling, and escaping to it till cooler weather, upon the last day of June Ella put her nose in the air and departed. Under the circumstances I did not expect to hear from her, except the customary "Wish you were here" postcard which, as Ella is aware, always infuriates me. However, after exactly two weeks I had the letter which was responsible for everything.

There was nothing extraordinary about the body of the letter, and that alone excited my suspicions. It is unlike Ella Trotter to be noncommittal, but she had taken a great deal of trouble to give me a completely colourless account of herself and Mount Lebeau Inn, where she was staying. There were no crossed out words, such as usually clutter up her communications, Ella being the kind to blurt out whatever pops into her head and think it over afterward. The letter was painstakingly neat, if not prim, and more legible than anything which I had ever seen her write. I was positive she had recopied it, perhaps several times, and that in itself was enough to put me on my guard. Why should Ella Trotter, of all people, have gone to so much pains to give me an expurgated account of her activities, I asked myself with, I am afraid, a snort.

I did not at once notice the postscript. It was on the reverse side of the inner page. Ella had made an effort to treat it as an afterthought, but as soon as I read it I knew it was the motive for the entire letter. I have not played bridge with Ella for years for nothing, and she should have realized that I am not the sort of person who can be utilized to pull other people's chestnuts out of the fire without my knowledge. If she had surrounded the postscript with huge exclamation points in red ink I could not have been more certain that Ella was up to something and determined to keep me out of it.

"By the way, Adelaide," she wrote, "I wish you would send me that book on spiritualism or séances or swamis or whatever it is that you have on your book shelf. I want to prove to a woman that it is all tommyrot, just as you always said, about the dead coming back to consort with the living, and the like of that."

Now Ella will argue with the Angel Gabriel when her turn comes, so there was nothing unusual in her wishing to prove somebody wrong. Nor was there anything particularly startling about the book for which she asked. I had bought it some years before immediately after the war, I think - when a wave of pseudo-spiritualism swept the country. I do not believe in tampering with matters which do not concern this world, granting it is possible to do so, which I had never granted until I stubbed my toe and literally nearly broke my neck over those weird and incredible manifestations at Mount Lebeau Inn.

The book in question was an obscure but clever exposé of the tricks and wiles of the gentry who prey on a gullible public with fake messages from the dead. I was surprised that Ella even recalled the book. I had been quite worked up over the subject at one time, but Ella had pooh-poohed the whole business, her argument being that only a fool would bother to expose what only a fool would be taken in by. Nevertheless she wanted the book enough to forget her pique and write for it and she spoiled her elaborate pretence of its being of no special importance by adding a sentence to the postscript.

"Send it by air mail, special delivery, Adelaide," she wrote and here for the first time she crossed out a line. In fact she blacked it out with conspicuous thoroughness, but I was able after some time to make out the words "before it is too late."

Like many well-to-do women, Ella Trotter has a phobia about being unduly careless with money. Nevertheless, although the time saved could not be great, she had enclosed more than enough postage to send the book by air mail and special delivery, and where she had blacked out the last line there was a large blot, as if her hand had trembled. I cannot explain how I knew that Ella was terribly excited when she wrote that postscript, but I did know it, just as I knew she would rather have died than have me suspect it.

I anticipated her reaction when I wired her that I was bringing the book by hand, arriving late the following day. I was prepared for her telegram in reply which insisted that there was no need for my doing any such thing. I simply paid no attention to the telegram.

As Stephen says — and I am in no position to deny it — I had no one except myself to blame for walking into that dreadful business, myself and my hunch that Ella was trying to put something over on me.

My only defence is that my hunch did not go far enough. But I have never pretended to be clairvoyant and I still maintain that there was no way on earth in which I could have foreseen that malignant spirit which had apparently returned from the grave to take up its abode in another's body; nor do I yet understand how I could have been expected to know anything about Dora Canby's horror of can openers or the chipped place in Judy Oliver's ear.

Lebeau Inn is in the extreme northwest and most inaccessible corner of our state, located on Mount Lebeau, the highest spot between the Cumberlands and the Rockies, or so the prospectus reads. About twenty years ago the place had considerable reputation as a summer resort. I myself went there once with my father, who was an invalid. The cool mountain air was highly recommended for elderly people and teething babies. The inn was new then, a huge rambling place with enormous porches and large, high-ceilinged rooms. As I remember, the place was filled that year, although it never made any pretence at being fashionable.

From what I had heard, it had gone steadily to seed of recent years. For one thing it was inconvenient to get to. For another a newer and more modern hotel had been put up, closer to the rail-road and blessed with the same salubrious air. I had been surprised when I heard that Ella had gone to Lebeau for July and August.

Then I learned from somebody or other that the bank in which she is a major stockholder had been forced to take over the place and was making a mordant effort to turn the old white elephant into something resembling a paying proposition.

It was exactly like Ella to further her pocketbook, even at the cost of some inconvenience to herself. I did not doubt that she had demanded and received a special rate because of her bank stock, any more than I doubted that she was doing everything in her power to drum up business for the inn. But I did not delude myself into believing that she would receive me with any enthu-siasm. To tell the truth, the nearer I came to my destination the more I regretted the impulse which had taken me there.

It was an unseasonably hot day, one of those days which people call weather breeders. It did not matter so much until I was com-pelled to leave the air-cooled parlour car at Egger's Junction in favour of a small, dirty, local train which stopped at every wide place in the road as it worked its tortuous way up into the moun-tains. I have said that Mount Lebeau is in the most inaccessible corner of the state. It not only is not on the main line of the rail-road; it is off the principal paved highways.

"And in this machine age one might as well be dead," I remem-ber thinking crossly, perspiring and covered with cinders, as I stared morosely out the window at the rutted dirt road beside the tracks.

Carrolton, where one leaves the train for Lebeau, is a sleepy country town located at the foot of the mountain and separated from it by a short tricky river. The town, so far as I could judge, had changed for the worse in the twenty years since I last saw it. It did not improve my temper to observe the vehicle by which I was to make the last lap of my journey. It was a disreputable-looking bus with a homemade body composed of four long narrow seats mounted upon what had once been the chassis of a Ford sedan. The driver was a snub-nosed, gangling mountaineer in blue jeans, distinguished by a huge cud of chewing tobacco in one leathery cheek.

"Is one expected to risk one's bones in this outlandish contraption in order to reach Lebeau Inn?" I asked him indignantly.

He shifted the cud to the other cheek before he condescended to answer. "Well, lady," he drawled, "it'd be quite a climb for your build."

Somebody chuckled, and for the first time I realized that I was not the only passenger bound for Mount Lebeau. Standing just behind me was a rangy, broad-shouldered young man with extraordinarily blue eyes. It was the impudence in Chet Keith's eyes which prejudiced me against him in the beginning, that and the too natty cut of his light grey suit. He was wearing a lavender tie which exactly matched his equally expensive shirt, and his dark hair looked as if it had been applied to his jaunty head with a brush. The glance I gave him should have withered him, only, as I was to learn, he was not the withering kind.

"My build," I remarked tartly, ostensibly addressing the driver but making certain that my voice carried, "may be a source of cheap levity to others, but it is my own concern, or rather it has ceased to be any concern to me for a number of years."

The young man with the lacquered hair grinned. "Don't look daggers at me," he said. "I can't help it if we're headed for the jumping-off place in the lineal descendant of the famous one-hoss shay."

I made no reply. It is not my habit to scrape acquaintance with strangers, especially slangy young upstarts who act as well pleased with themselves as this one did. My manner was intended to put him in his place once for all as I turned away with no inconsiderable hauteur to enter the bus. Unfortunately the desired effect was marred by the fact that, the space between the seats being extremely narrow, I had to insinuate myself inside by degrees and, becoming slightly flustered in the process, succeeded in hanging the placket of my skirt upon the handle of the ramshackle door. As a result I found myself in the embarrassing position of being able to go neither forward nor backward without an ominous ripping sound.

"Hold everything!" exclaimed the young man behind me.

As it happened there was nothing else I could do until he had unhoisted me by the simple process of prodding me from the rear while he lifted up on the door. To do him justice he accomplished this feat with the minimum of effort, even with a certain éclat, for which I might have been grateful if he had not spoiled it by another chuckle in which the bus driver joined. I gave him a look that wiped the grin off his face in a hurry.

"Have we taken root here?" I demanded.

The bus promptly started up with a jerk that knocked my hat down over one eye. By the time I had restored it to its position, along with the row of false curls which it is my custom to wear across my forehead, we were leaving the town behind. The driver was carrying on a desultory conversation with the other passenger, but I was in no humour for talk. It was still extremely sultry and I have never seen a more lurid sunset. Toward the west an ominous bank of clouds was sluggishly gathering. I remember thinking to myself that I should hate to be caught on that lonely road in a storm.

Two miles out of Carrolton it is necessary to cross the Carol River. "So this is the famous pontoon bridge," murmured the young man beside the driver. "No wonder they advertise it as the longest pontoon bridge in the world." He glanced back at me with a chuckle.

"I don't suppose they'd tolerate one anywhere outside this state."

I bristled. His accent, as well as his self-assurance, stamped him as an Easterner; from New York, I thought. It has always nettled me, the way New Yorkers have of looking down their noses at everything west of the Hudson. The pontoon bridge over the Carol River is a ridiculous piece of work and maddeningly inadequate, as I was to realize, heaven knows, before we were through with that ghastly affair at Lebeau Inn, but I had no intention of admitting as much at this stage.

"If you are pointing your remark at me," I said icily, "I am not responsible for this bridge or any other, but I believe it has served for a number of years and will probably continue to do so, no matter what you may think on the subject."

"Pleasant old girl," he murmured sotto voce to the driver, "if one likes snapping turtles."

The driver shook his head. "This here pontoon is all right," he said cautiously, "provided it don't get beside itself."

"Beside itself?" I repeated with some sharpness.

"Course a pontoon bridge is just a floating raft tied to each bank," he explained, "and the Carol's like all mountain streams. If it goes on a rampage, can't nothing hold it. Three-four times it's done up and scattered this here pontoon bridge high, wide and handsome."

"Isn't that something to look forward to!" exclaimed Chet Keith with a sardonic smile. "I can think of several thousand places where I'd prefer to be marooned."

I studied him with some curiosity and I thought he changed colour when he met my eye. It occurred to me that he was an odd type to be going to Lebeau. It had never attracted bright young people, and I was increasingly of the opinion that he was more at home in Times Square than anywhere else. I should have expected to find his prototype at Atlantic City or Jones Beach, entirely surrounded by pretty girls in very brief bathing suits, but not at a down-at-the-heel summer resort which catered to elderly invalids and teething babies.

It seemed to me that he changed the subject with suspicious haste.

"What did they lay this road out with? A corkscrew?" he asked, wincing a little as the ancient bus jounced alarmingly on a hairpin curve.

"You would think that, with a gasoline tax of seven cents on the gallon, we might at least have decent roads," I muttered, holding on to the sides of the vehicle for dear life while we wheezed up the incline.

At this moment, with a warning blast upon its twin sirens, a long sleek machine passed us, throwing a flurry of fine pebbles and stifling dust into our faces.

"Let somebody run that can run, eh?" murmured Chet Keith.

The driver shook his head. "We'll overtake him," he said with what I considered unjustifiable confidence.

However, on the second hairpin turn we did indeed overtake the other car. It was having difficulty negotiating the narrow curve.

The chauffeur was backing and filling, close enough to the edge of the precipice to make me shiver. I caught a glimpse of a tall thin man in the rear seat. He was fuming over the delay and he gave us a black glance as we went by. I heard Chet Keith whistle softly.

"Thomas Canby!" he exclaimed.

I don't say I should have recognized the power magnate if I had not heard the name, although I had met both Thomas Canby and his wife twenty years before, met them by a coincidence at Lebeau Inn the summer I was there with my father. Naturally that was before Canby developed into the millionaire he was to become.

He was, in fact, at that time merely a lineman for the local light company, one of the companies which he later organized into his tremendous utility group.

As I have had occasion to recall, he and his wife had a very difficult time finding the money to keep her and their baby at Lebeau that summer. The child was quite ill and the doctors had prescribed mountain air. I had not thought of it in years, but I distinctly remembered now how terrified little Mrs Canby had been and how she had hung over the baby day and night until it was better. She was a pathetic, colourless little woman, one of the timidest women I ever knew. I had not thought of it before, but I wondered what effect her husband's tremendous fortune and national reputation had had upon her.

"It's queer for Canby to be going to Lebeau," I remarked without realizing that I was speaking aloud. "I thought they were supposed to have a summer home at Southampton."

"They have a duplex on Park Avenue, a lodge at Asheville and a tepee of forty rooms down on Long Island. So what?" demanded Chet Keith.

I knitted my brows at him. "The daughter must be about twenty-two now," I murmured, still thinking aloud.

He gave me an odd glance. "Didn't you know that Gloria Canby died last fall?" he asked.

I got the feeling that he was watching me closely.

"Died!" I exclaimed. "And so young. What a pity!"

"Perhaps," he said with an ugly twist to his voice.

I gave him a scathing glance. "Are you one of those bolshevists who envy a capitalist everything, even his innocent children?" I demanded.

He shrugged his shoulders. "Thank God I've outgrown that rash," he said, "and God knows nobody envied Thomas Canby his daughter."

At this moment the power magnate's long maroon car passed us again with another indignant flirt of loose gravel. "Apparently Mr Thomas Canby is in a hurry," I remarked dryly.

Chet Keith nodded, then smothered a sharp exclamation. The machine ahead had stopped so abruptly, it was all our driver could do not to pitch directly into it. For a moment both cars hung sickeningly on the edge of the bluff, and I felt as if my stomach had turned a somersault.

"What the hell!" exclaimed Chet Keith. "Sorry," he muttered with a perfunctory glance at me as he swung out of the bus.

The Canby chauffeur, a wiry, muscular-looking man in livery, had also leaped to the ground. They were joined by the bus driver. All seemed to be staring intently at something just around the short curve in front of us. I could see Thomas Canby craning his long thin neck from the back seat of the limousine. I suppose they expected me to have no natural curiosity. At any rate Chet Keith gave me an impatient glance when I crawled out of the bus and walked toward them.

"You might as well go back," he said curtly. "It's just a rock in the road."

"I can see that for myself," I retorted in a tart voice.

There was a large boulder lying on the inside of the curve. It seemed to have fallen from the side of the mountain just above, where there was a gaping hole of loosened earth and gravel.

"We'll have it out of the way in a jiffy," murmured the chauffeur, "if you'll lend me a hand, brother."

He glanced at the bus driver, who was scratching his head.

"Funny what made that rock fall," he muttered.

Chet Keith again shrugged his shoulders. "Wouldn't have been so funny if either of us had hit it going round that curve," he said.

I shuddered and glanced away from the sheer drop at the edge of the precipice to our left.

"You'd think on such a road they'd take precautions against things like this," I remarked.

The bus driver was still scratching his head. "That's what makes it funny," he said. "They do."

The utility magnate spoke for the first time. "Can't you clear that rock away, Jay?" he asked in a testy voice.

The chauffeur touched his cap. "Watch me," he said.

He and the driver fell to and with considerable heaving and panting shifted the boulder off to the side of the road. Chet Keith did not lend a hand. Instead he climbed up the side of the mountain and stood looking down with a frown at the hole from which the rock had fallen. He was still there when the maroon car went on its way. The bus driver had gone back to his own machine, where he tooted his horn several times to attract our attention. I had not returned to the bus either. I was watching Chet Keith. He gave a start when he saw me staring up at him.

"Wind must have blown it over," he said, giving me what I regarded as a distinctly shifty glance.

"Except that there has been no wind all afternoon," I replied.

He frowned and tried to slip something into his pocket which he had picked up from a clump of withered grass at his feet.

"Accidents will happen," he murmured.

"I wouldn't call it an accident if a cold chisel had been employed to dig a rock loose," I said with a sniff.

He looked at me as if he would have enjoyed wringing my neck, but he produced the object which he had attempted to secrete in his pocket without my seeing it. It was a cold chisel. Bits of gravel and clay still clung to its side.

"It's probably been lying here for weeks," he observed in a defiant manner.

"That's why it's all rusty," I commented with elaborate sarcasm.

The cold chisel was not rusted. It looked bright and new.

"You don't miss much, do you?" inquired Chet Keith.

This time it was I who reached up and plucked something from a clump of withered grass clinging to the side of the mountain.

"Not a great deal," I said and would have pocketed my discovery without another word, but he caught my wrist and held it.

"A woman!" he exclaimed.

I nodded. "Looks as if."

The object which I was holding was a hairpin, an amber-coloured hairpin made of cheap celluloid.

"Jees," he said softly and then grinned. "Any reason why somebody at Lebeau Inn should crave to see you reach a sudden end?"

I thought of Ella and shook my head. "If I should have been taken down with a mild case of poison ivy it might not have been unwelcome, but" – I took another shuddering glance at the bluff on our other side – "nothing like this."

"I wasn't expecting to be met with a brass band either," he admitted with his cocksure grin. "However, as you say, murder is a cat of another odour."

I caught my breath. "Murder!"

He gave me a sharp glance. "The real question before the house is: Who tried to send Thomas Canby to kingdom come?"

I gasped, but he was already walking toward the bus and, feeling suddenly infirm in the region of my knees, I followed.

THE
AMERICAN
QUEENS OF
CRIME
SERIES

Made in the USA
Monee, IL
03 November 2021

81376560R00156